# THE DEATH OF A SMILE

# THE DEATH OF A SMILE

## PETER BRIGHTON

**POCKET BOOKS**

LONDON · SYDNEY · NEW YORK · TOKYO · SINGAPORE · TORONTO

First published in Germany by Econ Verlag in 1998
First published in Great Britain by Pocket in 1999
An imprint of Simon & Schuster UK Ltd
A Viacom Company

1 3 5 7 9 10 8 6 4 2

Simon & Schuster UK Ltd
Africa House
64–78 Kingsway
London WC2B 6AH

Simon & Schuster Australia
Sydney

A CIP catalogue record for this book is available
from the British Library

ISBN 0-671-02275-X

Typeset by Palimpsest Book Production Limited,
Polmont, Stirlingshire
Printed and bound in Great Britain by
Caledonian International Book Manufacturing, Glasgow

My thanks go to those who assisted in researching this book, B.J., U.St. and M.B.

# 1

Every time the jeep hit a pothole, the engine let out a loud screech and the driver glanced quickly into the rear-view mirror. For a few seconds a broad grin spread over his face. He wore his colourful shirt unbuttoned over a pair of beige shorts. On his smooth, tanned chest hung a lucky charm made of some metal or other, dangling from a long, thin leather strap around his neck.

This is how it had been for the last half-hour, on a late August afternoon in 1997. He drove the vehicle up the narrow mountain path, his foot hard down on the accelerator. He was of Indian origin. Left and right, broken branches smashed against the vehicle.

Edward sat in the back, without batting an eyelid or making any movement that might betray his inner thoughts. He was tall and scrawny, in his mid-forties; his face was pale and narrow. His black hair was cropped short. His eyes were alert and active, but he had the look of someone who would not easily be ruffled. Edward had taken off his jacket before getting inside, hanging it carefully over the back of the passenger seat, and opened his top two shirt buttons. At every pothole the small brown suitcase at his side jumped up and down. Edward looked neither to the left nor to the right but simply stared straight ahead through the windscreen, in mental and physical anticipation of the next bump. The driver gave him no such chance. Time and time again, he wrenched the steering wheel round for no apparent reason and drove into the nearest pothole. The man with the aquiline nose and the clear-cut profile took immense pleasure in torturing Edward along this route for as long as possible.

'Is this the only way to get to Mr Red's?' asked Edward in immaculate Queen's English, without taking his attention off the inevitable potholes.

'This is not really a road, Sir. It's the old river bed,' answered the Indian. 'The proper route is twice as long and not much better, Sir.'

Suddenly, something banged against the floor of the jeep. The Indian had driven over a pile of rocks, some of which had knocked against the undercarriage.

'How much further is it?'

'Not far, Sir. If you lean out you can see the house.'

Edward looked quickly at his watch. He stared once again at the rocky river bed and resigned himself to fate.

After a while the Indian swiftly changed direction to the right, drove out of the river bed and landed in the under-growth, the wheels of the four-by-four labouring through the thicket.

The driver turned round to his passenger for the very first time on this journey.

'We're nearly there, I promise you,' he exclaimed with a grin and put his foot down on the accelerator again. The jeep had now hit the right road but it was no wider than the river bed. As far as potholes were concerned, what the Indian had said was true. They were not so deep but there were more of them here than in the river bed.

'Shall I wait for you once we're there?' the Indian called out towards the back of the vehicle.

Edward thought for a while. 'Just for a few minutes, perhaps, until I have located Mr Red. I don't even know if he's at home.'

'Mr Red is often away for some time, Sir, but I think you'll be in luck today.'

The driver wrenched the wheel around again, this time to the left. In front of the jeep a sort of driveway came into view, at the end of which was a barbed wire fence, a good six feet high. The driver brought the vehicle to a halt and turned round to Edward again with a grin.

'If I drive up any further, Mr Red will be mad at me, Sir. He likes being on his own and does not like to be disturbed. I hope you understand.'

Edward gave a quick nod. He opened the door and got out. He realized that his back had been put out by the journey with the Indian. After stretching carefully, he bent down inside the jeep and removed his jacket and the small suitcase.

'Wait here for me, please,' he said curtly and slammed the door behind him. He threw his jacket loosely over his shoulders and made off in the direction of the fence.

There was no sign of a house anywhere. His eyes scoured the dense vegetation behind the fence. Suddenly, he became aware of a gentle chirping sound. Obviously Red's property was protected by an electric device. Instinctively, Edward kept his distance and walked along the perimeter, following a narrow, untrodden path down a slope that led towards the south.

The air was humid, but fortunately not so hot as it had been down in the valley. Fanned by a gentle breeze, the leaves rustled, almost drowning the quiet noise of the electric wire fence.

'Are you looking for someone?'

Edward froze and looked in the direction of the voice. He caught sight of a ledge in the wall, on which a man was standing, legs apart and arms folded. He was of medium height, wide-shouldered and stockily built; his rotund face was deeply sun-tanned and his thick, dark hair visibly greying.

Edward held up his hand to shield his eyes from the blinding sun.

'Are you Mr Red?'

'Red? I don't know anyone called Mr Red. Who's he?' came the answer from above.

'Well, I enquired after Mr Red down in the village below and they sent me here by car.'

A sort of grunting sound came from above.

'Just because they send you here does not mean that a *Mr* Red lives here,' he said sarcastically, emphasising the word 'Mr'.

'Pity,' replied Edward, pulling his jacket straight on his shoulders. 'I had news for . . . Red.'

'News is what you hear on the radio, or on TV, or what you read in the newspapers. Go back the way you came. There's no Mr Red out here,' came the languid reply. The man looked as though he was about to turn back.

'You can't get news about Uncle Sam from the media,' retorted Edward placidly, knowing that the man up there must be Red. As if by way of confirmation the man turned around towards Edward again.

'What sort of news does Uncle Sam have for this infamous Mr Red?'

'I am supposed to invite Red to Uncle Sam's birthday party!'

'OK! And how old is this Uncle?'

'Sixty-seven.' Edward tried to detect some reaction on the man's face but he was too far away.

'When is this Uncle's birthday?' came the response from above.

Edward was prepared for the question. He replied quickly and clearly. 'Uncle Sam was born on November 14th, 1930, in Kingston, New York State. That is exactly 74 degrees latitude.'

The man looked him over for a minute or two, critically. He then gazed pensively in the direction of the valley from which Edward had come.

'Did you come with the Indian?' he asked, this time in a more friendly manner.

'Yes.'

'Send him off and then take the opposite route along the fence. You'll find a gate there.'

With this, the man disappeared. Edward picked up his small suitcase from where he had put it during their exchange and turned back. There was a sudden silence. The chirping noise from the fence had stopped. A smile spread over Edward's face. Red seemed to be quite sure about him.

The outline of the jeep slowly appeared from within the undergrowth. The driver had got out and was leaning against the side of the vehicle. He had lit a cigarette and was grinning at Edward.

'Mr Red is at home, Sir? I was right then.'

Edward gave a quick nod and thought for a moment or two. 'How can I get hold of you if I want to be picked up again?'

'Mr Red knows where to find me. You just need to tell him when you want to leave.'

Edward nodded again. Turning round, he briefly paused. 'What's your name?'

The man shrugged his shoulders.

'I've forgotten. Everybody calls me "The Indian".'

Without further comment he swung back into the driver's seat and revved up the engine. With a lurch the jeep moved off, leaving behind a stinking cloud of exhaust fumes.

## 2

Edward returned slowly to the property, this time skirting
the path to the left of the fence. On this side, also, it showed
few signs of use. After a good twenty yards, the path began to
rise gently. Then, after a sharp bend to the right, a high wall
loomed into view with a vast iron door, the top of which
was jagged and covered with barbed wire, like the wall itself.
The gate was slightly ajar. Edward cautiously opened it wider.
Neither Red nor the house were visible. Edward entered the
property and, just as he was about to shut the door, he felt
a hard object, presumably the muzzle of a gun, between his
shoulder blades. A firm hand gripped his free arm and, before
he could even react, pinned down his body with his face
against the door. It swung to with a loud clang and locked.
His case slipped out of his grasp as he tried to suppress a cry
of pain. Quick as lightning, a second hand frisked his body
and groped for his case. The muzzle of the gun was slowly
withdrawn from his back.

'You can turn round again.'

The man stepped back. He replaced his 38mm in the
holster; asking no questions, he opened the case. As rapidly
as he had frisked Edward's body, he now rummaged through
his luggage. Obviously satisfied, he closed the case and held
it out to Edward.

'Welcome! The name's Red.'

'My name's Edward.'

Edward stretched again and this time felt the pain in his
back and also in his left arm which Red had twisted against
his spine.

'I hope you're not angry with me. I can't take the risk of uninvited guests. That's a business risk!' Red gave a loud, hearty laugh and looked encouragingly at Edward. 'You're not a front man – an office clerk, I'd say.'

Edward gave an embarrassed nod, attempting a friendly smile.

'But you're not with the CIA?'

Slowly Edward regained his composure.

'No.'

'Or anybody else?'

'No.'

'Aha! But you talked to Uncle Sam?' Red had now turned along a narrow path. Edward followed him.

'The CIA only hinted that you could be our man and just gave us your name and address out here.'

Red turned round and gave a short laugh. 'That's usually enough for my bosses. But you said "we". I'd like to know who "we" are.'

'Sorry!'

'Aha!' Red turned round again and walked on. A small white house now emerged from within the undergrowth, a little too pretty for this wild setting. It looked very neat and clean, almost twee. The windows were furnished with some rather dainty curtains. Left and right of the entrance door stood two white statues, symbolizing, presumably, spring and summer, and on the roof a silver weather vane shone in the sunshine. All this fitted into the local surroundings, Edward thought, about as naturally as they fitted into the life of the character who lived there.

Red had taken in Edward's look of surprise. He stood still and gazed in the direction of the house.

'Yes, that is my private domain. You collect these things over the years – souvenirs, gifts and a little junk for old time's sake – an antidote to my work.'

He walked up to the front door and opened it. Edward followed him and soon realized that the Persian carpets scattered in the hall were the genuine thing. An oil painting on the wall concealed the door to a switchbox, which Red now opened. He pulled at one of the numerous switches; Edward assumed that the chirping sound of the perimeter fence had started up again.

'We don't want to be disturbed, do we, Edward?'

Edward shook his head. 'We most certainly don't!'

'Then I'll take you to my guest room. You'll need to freshen up, I am sure, after that journey.'

'Splendid! I wonder if you know how much you go through when you drive with that Indian.'

Red grinned. 'No, I haven't had the pleasure, but I think I can do without that experience!' He removed the holster with the 38mm and slung it over a bulky hall stand as he went past. He beckoned towards the staircase and let Edward go up ahead of him. On the first floor, his host opened the first door on the right and entered the room. Edward followed and cast a quick glance around the room. It was extremely spacious and luxuriously furnished, the sort of room that might be found in one of the five-star hotels in New York, London or Paris. One small corner, however, next to the patio door, distinguished it from the standard luxury hotel suite. A computer, telephone, fax machine, photocopier and a radio had been fitted inside, closely stacked together on top of each other.

'Feel free to use anything you see here. It's guaranteed bug-free and operates via high-security satellite transmission. You'll find the user manual in the drawer to your right, if you have any trouble,' explained Red.

'I don't think I'll be needing the workstation. But you'll have had a number of guests who . . .'

Red interrupted him. 'A large number of guests! Often very serious decisions are made here. Are you authorized to take decisions?'

'To a limited extent,' answered Edward with some hesitation. 'But we shall certainly be talking this over soon. I am not here on a pleasure trip, you realize.'

Red looked at his guest — almost half a head taller than he was — with an engaging smile. 'Why don't you take a quick shower right now? I'll be waiting for you downstairs on the patio below.'

He turned round as if to leave but looked back again from the door. 'Oh, by the way, do you have any special requests for dinner tonight? You will have to put up with my culinary skills. It's not worth going down into the village; the food's not much better there than it is here!'

Edward shook his head. 'No, I have no special wishes, so long as you don't serve up snakes, grilled spiders, or whatever.'

'Don't worry! I haven't enjoyed anything so exotic for quite some time!'

Red left the room and Edward placed his case on the table and opened it. Its orderliness had been thrown into violent upheaval by Red's search for weapons. He painstakingly trans-ferred his clothes into a highly-polished mahogany wardrobe. Around him, the room was decorated in marble, with mirrors and gilded bronze fittings. He undressed, got into the shower and played with the thermostatic controls until he found the right water temperature.

Meanwhile, Red had eased himself again into a large wicker chair, in which he had spent half the afternoon awaiting the arrival of his guest. To the left and the right were piles of newspapers and magazines — those he had read on one side and those he had not read on the other. When both stacks had reached the same height, Red usually lost all interest; apart from the odd details, they all repeated the same news.

He squinted at the sky, reflecting whether the arrival of his guest was due to an event or a person he had read about in these newspapers or magazines recently. Edward, quite clearly, was not an American. Red hesitated whether he might be either an Englishman or a European who had studied or lived in England. Deep in thought, Red stood up and picked up his glass from the window-ledge. Two or three flies had meanwhile drowned themselves in the liquid. Red poured the contents over the stone parapet of the patio and went back into the living room. He took out a fresh glass from the cabinet, placed both glasses in turn under the crushed ice dispenser on the left-hand refrigerator door and filled them more or less half-full with ice. He then opened the right-hand door and poured orange juice from a container over the ice.

As he made his way back to the patio, Edward appeared.

'Follow me and make sure you're not seen,' said Red. 'I assume you'd rather sit on the patio than sweat it out inside. Besides, I thought I should pour you an orange juice. I take it you like the stuff?'

Edward nodded. His host lowered himself into a chair and indicated to Edward that he should also sit down. Edward, however, walked over to the balustrade and gazed into the dense greenery in front of him.

'Marvellous place, Red! How long have you been here?' he asked, without turning towards his host.

'Sometimes it feels as if I have been here since birth. But it must be close on thirty years now. In those days the trees back there were not so high; you could look right down into the valley.'

Edward now turned round and sat himself on the balustrade.

'Did you have this house built?'

Red grinned. 'Originally the land and the house were, so to speak, conveyed to me. As I had to disappear for a while, I spent the time making alterations, extensions and renovations. Since then, I have invested more and more in luxuries from my contract work, so that I can enjoy them in this lonely private life I have created for myself up here – a sort of compensation for the lost freedom that my job entails.'

Red pointed towards the orange juice in the glass he had put on the small side table. 'Please help yourself.'

Edward picked up the glass and sank into the chair next to Red. He took a sip and placed the glass down again on the table.

'How did you get into the CIA?' he asked, spontaneously.

Red closed his eyes and folded his hands on his stomach. The wind gently ruffled his greying hair. He took his time before answering. Edward also shut his eyes, leant back in the chair and made himself comfortable.

'I don't know how you came to the conclusion that I was with the CIA. They only hired me out or engaged me for short-term contracts. I never was with the CIA, or any other secret service. I work for them all, dammit! And over the years I've got used to earning my keep by doing a few days' work each year, and I enjoy my creature comforts as well.' He paused briefly, then asked, 'Are you from the UK?'

'Correct. I'm from London but I was born in Liverpool and went to school there. After that I was commissioned into the armed forces.'

'Which branch?'

'The Royal Marines.'

'Aha! The Falklands War?'

Edward gave a nod, his eyes still closed. A quick smile spread over his face. 'Were you ever called up by Uncle Sam?'

Red shook his head. 'No way! But a certain kind of guy always has the same career. In my case it was Vietnam, in yours the Falklands. For the next generation it's the Gulf War and Bosnia, or whatever.'

'And you've been doing this type of work since Vietnam?'

Red shook his head again. 'No. That's when they first discovered my talent and made use of it. Since then my profession has taken hold of my life.'

They both sat in silence for a while. Then Edward straightened up and reached for his glass.

'Do you get used to this sort of work?'

Red opened his eyes and looked at his guest reflectively. He sat up slowly and shrugged his shoulders. 'Get used to it?

At the beginning I used to suffer for days, weeks even. But then I said to myself – if people like that exist, there's got to be others; and that's where *you* fit in!'

He paused again and stroked his hair with his right hand.

'When I realized as a young soldier that I could not improve the world by fighting battles but could only change it, it was as if all the ideals my parents had passed down to me had fallen apart. I can still see them now, as they saw me off, full of pride. I had been chosen to fight for America! I was the one to set a nation free! I was the guy who was to become a hero! All bullshit! I've been to Hell and back! That was a lesson I learnt overnight.'

Red paused yet again and leaned back in his chair. He glanced over towards Edward, who had closed his eyes again and seemed to have taken everything in calmly.

'You asked about my job. Well, I took to it as naturally as a duck to water. At that time I had been about two years in Vietnam. My troop was stationed in the region of Que Nhou. As Battalion Commandant and Machine-gun Mechanic, my duty was to ensure that all mobile equipment was ready for combat. Everything, that is, that had not been shot or burnt to bits. After Pleiku and Que Nhou came under siege from the Viet Cong, the field staff moved their rendezvous area to our camp. This was a little out of the way and pretty well unknown. Then one day a meeting took place. To this day I can't recall exactly what it was supposed to be all about. I can only remember that I was stretched out on the tailboard of a lorry one evening, gazing at the night sky after a tiring day's work, when suddenly two characters loomed up out of the darkness. They were whispering, but loud enough for me to overhear them up there on my lorry. I could make out in the moonlight that these guys were both high-ranking and highly-decorated officers. Now, one of the officers who had called the meeting had made himself "dispensable", as you would elegantly put it. So he had become a security risk. The two men were discussing how they could get rid of this guy without trace. They were thinking of planting explosives in his vehicle. I don't know why, but there was a sudden squeaking noise next to me, up there on the tailboard. They grabbed hold of me and pulled me down. I thought my final hour had come. But one of them recognized me and they dragged me to a location outside the camp. So, from that moment on things went speedily. As soon as they had seen who I was, they hit on the idea of an accident. They knew I was handy with vehicles. I refused point-blank, as I or someone else in my troop would have been suspected. But from what I had overheard from my hiding place, I said I was happy to help solve their problem. And then, suddenly, I hit upon this idea of the rear lights.'

Edward leaned forward, absorbed. 'I always thought that accidents were arranged by fixing the brakes or the steering wheel. But rear lights!'

Red ignored his guest's sudden sign of curiosity. He stood up, took his empty glass and disappeared through the French windows. Edward could hear the sound of the glass being filled with ice. Red soon reappeared on the patio and sat down again in the wicker chair.

'Where was I? Oh yes, the business about the rear lights. I knew that, for safety reasons, the vehicles always moved off in single file after a commanders' meeting and at irregular intervals in case the Viet Cong located us and had us all in their sights. I say for safety reasons, because this route led along a steep slope that could not easily be spotted. For a short bit of the journey, though, all the vehicles had to take the same route. It came to an end about five hundred yards after a sharp bend to the right. From that point there were any number of alternative routes back. Most of the guys were picked up from here and flown back to base. Just above this right-hand bend was a huge tree with wide branches. My plan was to fix two rear lights on to a wooden board that I could leave dangling directly above the steep cliff-edge behind the curve, so as to create the illusion that they were real rear lights on a genuine track. Certain death for anyone who followed close behind!'

Edward laughed out loud. 'Are you trying to kid me that this really worked?'

Red swung his glass with a grin on his face. 'And how! Simple and stupid as my idea was. You should also know that the commanders were always escorted by a second vehicle in front. And, for safety reasons, the officers' vehicles moved at night without lights. But the escort jeeps drove with dimmed lights, the point of the exercise being that the guerillas would only pick out those vehicles in an ambush. My only problem was that the officers' meeting was due to last only two days, so I had little time to get my act together. And also nobody but my two accomplices and myself were to know about the plan.'

Red took a large gulp from his glass and stood up. He strode slowly along the balustrade and put his glass down on it. Then he turned round towards Edward, who was silently staring at him.

'The next day, I made a short trial run with one of the jeeps, under the pretext that I was making a recce in the area. I inspected the sharp right-hand bend and made a crude sketch of the local features. After nightfall, I set to work. I fixed the board with rear lights with the precise spacing, got hold of a rope, some wiring and a car battery, then climbed with all this gear along the mountain path till I reached the big tree. Step by step – it was pitch-dark that night – I groped my way along the branches until I hung directly above the drop near the sharp right-hand bend. Then I attached the battery to the tree and lowered the board by trial and error to what I judged to be the level of the rear bumpers of a moving vehicle. All damned amateurish, but the next morning I could report ready for action!'

Red ran his hands through his hair again.

'To this day, I have no idea how I survived the next twenty-four hours. My brain was throbbing like hell and in my mind I went over each step and rehearsed each action that I had to execute that night. The only thing that pricked my conscience was the thought that the driver had to be written-off as well.' He paused and suddenly stared at Edward extremely seriously. 'I should also make it clear that if anything went wrong I was expected to fall over the edge of the cliff. So my life was in danger as from my very first assignment.'

Suddenly the gentle noise of a vehicle could be heard in the distance. Red started and looked at his watch. 'I apologize! I forgot that today was Wednesday. That's when Lucy generally drops by.'

He saw Edward's anxious expression and immediately added, 'Don't worry! Lucy is only interested in me, not my job and not any of my guests. I'll introduce you as the son of one of my old Vietnam pals, OK?'

Edward nodded his agreement, although the situation made him feel uneasy. What were the chances, he wondered, of avoiding Lucy?

'It will be a while before Lucy finds her way up here. Let me finish the story.' Red took his glass and slumped into his wicker chair. It creaked under his weight.

'At my request, one of the two commanders allowed the escort vehicles on this occasion to move at a greater distance from the officers' vehicle. After nightfall, I climbed into the tree again. I knew that the targeted person would be picked up by chopper and would therefore be carrying a small radio set. So I could make out when his arrival time was notified. Only then would both vehicles start off from the camp. It was a long time before the chopper eventually gave the signal. I lowered the board into the yawning hole below and waited. Then along came the escort vehicle. The driver couldn't see the concealed board since the dipped front lights only illuminated a little bit of the path immediately in front of his vehicle. No sooner had the jeep turned round the sharp bend to the right than the officer's vehicle came into view.

Quick as lightning, I connected the second piece of wiring to the battery and saw the rear lights flashing on my board. It seemed to last for ever until I could hear the noise of the engine. The wheels of the vehicle started to whizz round – they were no longer in contact with the ground. For weeks afterwards I could hear the crashing and clattering of the battered vehicle in my ears. As quickly as I could, I ripped the wiring from the battery, pulled up the board and hid the instruments in the dense foliage. Then I drew the branch back and climbed down. The soldiers from the escort vehicle had noticed the missing officer's vehicle and returned on foot. It was only after daybreak that they located the debris and the two dead bodies. The next night I crept back to the same place to remove my equipment.'

Red looked expectantly at Edward. But he appeared to be less interested in the rest of the story than the impending arrival of this girl called Lucy. Red went up to Edward and squatted in front of him, so that they could look each other in the eyes.

'That's the only story I tell my clients,' grinned Red. 'It has all the seeds of my success. The key thing is not how to turn some screw or other but the ability to recognize local data and to make use of them and arrange them in such a way that accidents can be made to happen very simply. Nothing else is quite as reliable.'

With a jolt, Red pulled himself up.

'OK, now let's enjoy Lucy's cooking. By the way, you needn't worry about your cover. Lucy doesn't want to hear about Vietnam, the War and all that bullshit. Please excuse me for a moment.'

Red hurried back into the house. Edward guessed that his host was on his way to the control panel, to admit Lucy safely into the house.

# 3

Some minutes later, Red reappeared with Lucy on his arm.

Lucy was younger than Red, whom Edward judged to be in his late fifties. With her blonde hair and curvaceous figure she gave the impression of a slimmer Marilyn Monroe. She wore a coloured T-shirt over a tight-fitting pair of jeans.

Edward stood up and greeted her with a slight bow. She stretched out her hand with a friendly smile.

'Have we met before?'

'I don't think so. This is the first time I've visited Red here,' answered Edward, still a little unsure of himself.

'Oh, then I guess you haven't seen him for a long time.'

'Not for a very long time, darling.' Red kissed Lucy on the brow.

'Should I prepare something for us three tonight?' asked Lucy.

'Right. Edward is a polite guest and won't complain about your cooking.'

'Lucky I bought enough food. Red didn't mention he was expecting a guest.'

'I simply came unannounced,' apologized Edward.

'That doesn't matter. I'm always happy when Red has someone along to talk over old times. I just can't listen to these stories myself. I believe a man is better suited for the bed than for war.'

Red grinned. That was typically Lucy. He liked her manner, which was frivolous, sometimes cheeky and often downright shameless. He wondered how this stiff young

Englishman had reacted to her comment, but Edward looked quite relaxed, not at all surprised.

Interestingly enough, Edward was thinking about Red at the same time. The man he had killed in Vietnam must have been an important person if the CIA had later taken note of Red and had obviously engaged him for big money. And yet it seemed that Red had not turned into the usual contract killer.

From the kitchen came the clatter of pans. Evidently, Lucy was already in full swing.

'How do you spend your time when you have no assignments?' asked Edward.

Red spread out his arms and stretched back in his wicker chair. 'I read a lot. Mostly technical books on automobiles, general mechanics or the latest electronics. Now and then a good novel. Lucy brings me the books, so that I don't degenerate mentally, as she puts it. And she has very good taste where literature is concerned. And of course I'm a great DIY enthusiast. Not that I can always put my ideas or plans into effect immediately,' Red continued. 'Most of my ideas can usually be put into practice in my assignments.'

Lucy began to lay the table at the other end of the patio.

'How about sharing a bottle of Californian red with us?' Lucy called to Edward.

'That's fine by me.'

'Then we can eat in five minutes.'

'I do hope you haven't put yourself out on my behalf,' Edward replied.

'You won't believe this,' laughed Lucy, 'but we would have had supper even if you hadn't come!' She then laid out a place for each of them and hurried back into the kitchen. Edward had imagined his visit to Red differently – rather more businesslike, in a cool, clinical environment. It had turned out to be the exact opposite.

Lucy shortly returned to the patio with a bottle of red wine and three glasses. Then she brought in the meal on a large tray – Indian corn and kidney beans, fried potatoes and huge T-bone steaks, garnished with onions.

'This looks quite delicious,' Edward observed. Lucy thanked him for his compliment by throwing him a kiss.

'Your guest is most charming,' she said to Red. 'I think you'll have to keep an eye on me!'

By now it was dark and cold on the patio. Red had lent Edward a knitted jacket and he himself had put on a coarsely-knitted pullover. Both men remained seated outside whilst Lucy cleared up in the kitchen.

'I think we should continue our conversation once Lucy has gone upstairs. If she had known you were coming she would not have bothered to call today.' Red briefly dipped a cigar into the bourbon Lucy had brought him as a chaser.

Edward was still on the red wine; it tasted excellent. 'I have time,' he replied. He waited till Red lit up his cigar and blew the first puff of smoke into the night.

'Lucy is your . . .'

Red interrupted him at once. 'We sleep together. She calls by every weekend and once during the week. It's been like that for a number of years. As to marriage or whatever, we've never even thought about it. I believe she's still married. We never talk about that subject because we never speak about myself. And that's fine by me. She respects the fact that from time to time I go away for a few days, or even longer. She never asks where I am going, how long I'll be away or what I'm up to. But when I'm back she's always there and everything is the same as before.'

He paused again for a moment and glanced at Edward. 'Are you married?'

'No, probably for the same reasons as you. I live with my mother about an hour away from London. My father was one of the 265 soldiers killed in the Falklands. That was a terrible blow for her. She's happy I'm not in the armed forces.' He smiled. 'My mother thinks I'm in the diplomatic service. It's enough for her that she can feel proud of me. She's led rather a sheltered life since my father was killed, and I have simply adapted to that sort of existence.'

'Are you in Her Majesty's Service?' asked Red.

Edward's face took on a stark and serious expression. His answer came quick and clear. 'I serve my country!' He took hold of his glass, draining it to the last drop.

Red, who had observed Edward's reaction closely, refilled his glass. 'As a rule, I never take much interest in who gives the orders. But I took a liking to you right from the start. Please excuse my curiosity!'

'I never knew anyone could afford to have feelings in our sort of work,' Edward stated, now a little more relaxed.

'I have experienced so much and known so many people that I can sum up a situation or a personality very quickly. Besides . . .' Red broke off as Lucy appeared on the patio.

'Hi, you two! I suppose you'll want to carry on talking, won't you?'

Red stood up and took hold of Lucy's arm. 'Darling, you're psychic! Edward and I wanted to stroll a little longer down memory lane.'

Lucy gave Red a kiss and slipped out of his grasp.

'Please excuse me then. I'm going to bed now. Perhaps you'd kindly wake me up, if you feel the urge!' She winked at Red and held out her hand to Edward, who jumped up awkwardly.

'Oh, there's no need to be so formal!' she laughed. She drew Edward close and gave him a kiss on the cheek.

'I'll take Lucy upstairs.' Red put his arm round his girl-friend's narrow waist and vanished with her into the house.

Edward could hear them both laughing as they went upstairs and leant back in his chair. He did not quite know how to place Red. This warned him to be cautious. But he was quite clearly his man. At least, Red had given him that impression. Tell-tale sounds could be heard from above. Were they sounds of happy laughter or gentle passion? Considering the amount of time that slipped by, he decided the latter. He was not surprised when Red came down again almost twenty minutes later. He had changed into blue jeans and a dark blue T-shirt.

# 4

'Come on inside!' said Red and took his whisky glass. Edward stood up, taking his own glass, and followed him into the house. In the middle of the entrance hall Red suddenly stood still. Edward only heard a quiet click, then everything around him was pitch-black. He could feel Red's strong, firm grip on his left wrist. 'Don't panic, just hold on tight,' said Red. Edward could feel Red's other hand on his right shoulder, as he guided him through the darkness. They took a few steps into the darkness. Something or other moved in front of them; a breath of cool air blew into their faces. He's probably opened a door, thought Edward. 'Down the steps – take care!' said Red quietly. 'It gets a little narrow here. Feel your way along the wall to your right.'

Edward reached out with his right hand and touched the wall. Red guided him down the steps. The wall was rough and cold to the touch. 'Twenty-two steps,' said Red. Edward started to count. There was a stench of oil and the air was cooler. A gentle, continuous hum could be heard; it became louder as they made their way forward. What was Red up to, where was he taking him?

'Duck!' Red called out. The thought briefly ran through Edward's mind that he had fallen into a trap but, just as quickly, he suppressed the idea. In the darkness ahead of him he could distinguish a couple of small lights, one red and one green – nothing else. It was impossible for his eyes to adjust so quickly to the dark. Red's hands gave Edward the message to halt. There was a crackling sound and the main light suddenly came on.

They were now in a big room. The red and green lights were evidently computer control lights, about four or five yards away from Edward, situated on a large desk.

'Please excuse me!' said Red in a friendly tone, drawing Edward towards a swivel chair. 'Sit down, and relax from your frightening experience. But this is the only way that anyone can get to my work room. Only with me and via this route.'

Edward looked around the room to which he had been led – a strange combination of office, workshop, storeroom and laboratory. Massive bookshelves lined one wall, crammed with files, books and magazines. Nearby was a writing table, on which stood a computer, printer, telephone, fax and radio. To the rear of the room was a large work bench, above which a pulley mounted on a track was fixed to the ceiling. Near the work bench was a sizeable shelf with machine parts of every description, none of which Edward could identify with any machine he was familiar with. And finally, opposite the work bench on a laboratory table stood test-tubes and Bunsen burners and more than a dozen large and any number of small glasses, similar to those that can be found in any chemist's shop or chemical laboratory. In the very far corner Edward detected a welding torch on a trolley and next to it a kind of vacuum cleaner, but much bigger, and a huge metal box with fine chicken wire over the large, black opening. From inside this box came the humming sound that Edward had heard earlier, in the dark – evidently an air-exhaust or air-conditioning unit.

'This is the heart of my kingdom,' laughed Red, delighted with his guest's surprised, inquisitive look. 'Here I generate new ideas and those ideas result in new projects.'

'You're not just an expert on motor cars, then?' asked Edward, looking round, still captivated. He then singled out a few more objects, which puzzled and fascinated him.

'No. By profession I'm an expert in mechanics. I like investigating everything in detail, but my real passion is automobiles. I am interested only of course in the ones I might perhaps have to work with some time, mainly luxury limousines. On the shelf over there you'll find everything on the vehicles those people drive – trade literature, construction manuals, service booklets . . . Rolls Royce, Mercedes or the big Toyotas. I know all there is to know about the type of automobile used by statesmen, captains of industry, Mafia bosses or VIPs, including special models and customized fittings. So, over the years my job has also become a hobby. You wouldn't believe the amount of enquiries I get, not only from the official sources that usually engage me but big businesses as well, or rich private individuals who come to me through certain channels. Many people have not the slightest idea of their real exposure to risk, so attempts are made on their lives and methods are devised to eliminate them "naturally". The motives are usually political but I have also worked on espionage cases where some traitor or other has had to be removed accidentally before he could do further damage.'

Red pulled out a thick file from the shelf at random and held it up. 'Inside you'll find all the technical data on the famous Pope-mobile. No, no!' he added defensively, 'I have no plans to kill the Pope tomorrow. But it is well-known that such plans exist. Or do you happen to believe, like some other people, that the predecessor of the present Pope died without "assistance"?' He paused briefly and stared at Edward expectantly. 'Don't worry, it wasn't me. But the facts point to that conclusion. As soon as they realized they had chosen the wrong guy – bingo, he was dead! Natural death is something normal, practical. Assassination is simply messy. You just raise the dust. Suspicion, rumour and conjecture are not good.'

He placed the file back on the shelf and pulled out another. 'This is the car Mubarak currently drives. His predecessor, Sadat, was brutally eliminated. The murder raised hell, the whole country was in tumult. Don't assume I have an assignment to remove Mubarak. But that could be one of my future assignments. That guy has enemies. So I am prepared.'

He grinned at Edward, who was listening in amazement. 'How many people make a living from love, affection or loyalty? Starting with the Church, through florists and souvenir shops, down to brothels and whores. Our profession, on the other hand, which is admittedly much smaller, makes its money from the opposite. Does that mean we are worse? We create a kind of equilibrium; we allow the rest to enjoy a clear conscience.'

Red shoved the file back on to the shelf and pointed to the lower shelves. 'These contain all the data on King Juan Carlos, industrial moguls, arms salesmen and drug dealers. And if I see there is something missing, I'll find it.' He paused. 'I have often asked myself what the hell I am playing at. I have not made things easy for myself. But why should it be a criminal act to get rid of some crazy dictator who mindlessly sacrifices human lives in pursuit of his own political ambitions? And is it really unethical to get rid of some big businessman who has piled up a fortune for himself but whose workers face social extinction when his firm goes bankrupt, or someone who has polluted the environment to make even bigger profits? And what about those arms and drug dealers who don't give a damn about human lives? Ruthless men justify ruthless methods. I now have no inhibitions left about such people. Today I just laugh when I think how I started off in my career. That business with the wooden board and the rear lights was just child's play compared with what I do today. The basic principles have not changed, only the techniques. In each case I control the given circumstances, the natural reactions of the participants and any special factors; those have to be convincing.'

Red emptied his glass in one gulp and put it on the desk.

'I have only failed once. I was supposed to bring down a small aircraft. That must now be almost ten years ago. The objective was to eliminate a German politician; he either knew too much about illegal arms dealings or had possibly become too closely involved. I can't recall the precise details. Once my job's over, the data up there inside my brain are wiped out. In that job the preparation time was extremely short and I underestimated the gliding speed of the aircraft. Maybe the pilot was also more skilled than I had been told. It just went wrong. The guy survived with fractures and a few bruises. It was acutely embarrassing for me, but I could do nothing about it.

My boss, understandably, no longer had any confidence in me. My competitors later put my error right. Anyway, it wasn't a clean job. There were rumours and speculation that could simply have been avoided. But in the end, the objective was achieved. The guy was removed from the scene and could talk no more.'

Red shrugged his shoulders. 'After that, I didn't dare take on any aircraft jobs for some time. But my interest was revived quite recently. Particularly in the types of machine that firms buy or charter or acquire for so-called business transfers – the Falcon 10 or the Cessna Citation. Or helicopters. Most politicians fly by chopper. You've got to adapt, according to the circumstances.'

Red was leaning against the shelf and silently contemplated his guest for some time. Edward, still absorbed with his surroundings, did not at first react to the silence; in his mind, Red's stories were running like a film show. He then took in the fact that Red had stopped; the film had snapped.

'Is it my turn now?' Edward asked soberly.

Red gave a nod and looked into his whisky tumbler, disappointed. He put it to one side.

'Down here I can only offer alcohol-free drink – Coke, orange juice, mineral water. What will you have?'

Edward refused. He waited till Red turned towards him again.

'Who "we" are is not relevant in your case. I think the recommendation from Uncle Sam should be sufficient.'

Red nodded, attempting, however, to interrupt. Edward refused to be put off, and briskly carried on. 'We can see a problem on the horizon. The engagement we should like you to carry out is highly dangerous. The orders come from right at the top but are linked, so far as can be ascertained, to various other factors on which I have not been briefed. The action will commence very shortly and has to be executed rapidly. Where, when and how are, at this stage, open questions. Here we need your advice and experience. Not that we lack experts, or are unable to carry the job through to the end, as you will realize, but the fact is that in this case we wish, for a number of reasons, to engage an outsider. So far as our target is concerned, we are speaking of a high-profile person who is also highly popular with certain sectors of the public, which will not make your job any easier. The fact that this person is almost always followed by a large section of the media makes the problem of elimination more complicated than usual.'

Edward paused briefly. 'I can't give you details as to the identity of the target figure at this stage. As I mentioned, no final decision has yet been taken. The timing of that decision is still a matter of conjecture.'

The corners of Red's mouth twitched. Edward took no notice. 'If there's agreement on both sides, your first task would be to come over to see us in the UK and then to stand by. The logistics of the engagement would be agreed with you in person but the technical details would be entirely up to you. Bring over what you need, or else we'll provide it on the spot. Once we've agreed, you'll fly initially to New York as Red. There you'll be given new papers and will travel quite officially to the UK. Your only contacts there for the time being will be my colleague, Walter, and myself. Walter will give you all you require. I can't give you any further information at this stage; I can't tell you any more about when the assignment starts.'

He waited for a reaction from Red, who was still leaning

against the shelf, standing in silence and gazing reflectively into space.

'I know this does not amount to very much, but I suspect that you're not necessarily interested in the details at present. The financial aspect will certainly be of more interest to you than the background details of the engagement.'

'You Brits are really rather arrogant!' grinned Red.

'I've heard rumours to the effect that in pecuniary matters you're not usually very formal,' said Edward quietly.

'Which brings us to the key issue. What is this accident worth to you?' asked Red.

'Name a figure and I'll tell you if we can accept it or not.'

Red pulled himself up and walked along the shelves, returning to the work-bench. He took a large screwdriver into his hand, tossed it in the air and caught it playfully.

'I expect the risks are rather high.'

'Lower, perhaps, than the degree of precision and the one hundred per cent success rate we expect of you – with no ifs and buts.'

Red squinted at Edward.

'I'm not entirely sure yet if I'll accept the commission,' he said slowly. 'I'll need to sleep on it tonight. How much time do you have?'

'I don't have an unlimited amount of time, but enough to allow you to think matters through calmly.'

'In that case we ought to talk over our problem again tomorrow. Lucy can then take you back to the village, or else we can discuss things together quietly once again, without being disturbed.' Red walked up close to Edward, who automatically jumped up from the chair he was sitting in.

'You'll understand that we'll have to play that little game once more. There's no other way back to civilisation.' Red took hold of Edward's wrist and purposefully led him back through the room. Edward felt a slight draught and warmer air from above. Then came the twenty-two steps, which he counted to himself so as not to stumble. A few more paces, a lowering of the head, then the hall light switched on. Edward turned round but could not see any secret door or tell-tale entrance.

'Don't try to find it,' said Red with a grin. 'I wish you good night! I won't wake you tomorrow. Just come downstairs whenever you like.'

Red turned round and disappeared into the living room. Edward looked around once more, inquisitively, towards the position where he thought the secret door could be. But there was nothing to be seen – no wiring, no cover-up slats, no conclusions could be drawn. He made his way up the stairs, disappointed but determined to solve the mystery the following morning.

Red had walked from the living room into the kitchen and filled his glass with crushed ice. He grabbed a small bottle of Veuve Cliquot from the icebox, turned off the lights, reached for a champagne glass as he passed by the living room cupboard, and poured a generous portion of bourbon over the ice. He turned off the lights and crossed the hall. Gently, he climbed up the stairs to the first floor and cocked his ear to the right, towards the guest room. No suspicious noises were to be heard. He quietly opened the door of his own bedroom. The indirect light from outside cast a soft glow within the room. He undressed without making any noise. Carefully, he opened the small bottle of champagne and emptied half its contents into the glass. He let a few drops fall on to Lucy's skin. She woke up with a start. Before she could even let out a cry, Red pressed his mouth to her lips and gave her a gentle kiss. Lucy took the champagne glass out of his hand, sipping tentatively at its contents. Then she nestled down again, put the glass on the floor near the bed and pulled Red towards her body. She kicked the bedspread off and wrapped her legs round Red's thighs.

# 5

Red and Lucy were both at the breakfast table on the patio when Edward came downstairs the next morning. Edward gave a slight bow. 'Good morning!'

Lucy was wearing a checked blouse with her jeans. Red still wore his bathrobe.

'Please sit down; the coffee is still warm,' Lucy called. 'Do you like eggs and bacon?'

Edward nodded and sat down in the same chair he had sat on the previous day.

'I can't offer a real English breakfast, with toast and marmalade. Red likes heartier fare in the mornings.' She pointed to a plate laid out with various cheeses, hams and fried chickens' legs.

'No problem,' said Edward, 'I shan't die of hunger.'

'I am curious to know what sort of job you have, Edward,' said Lucy.

To Edward's relief, Red came to his assistance. 'Our guest is a loss adjuster for an insurance firm. He investigates accident claims, rather like a detective. You realize how many so-called accidents these days are simply insurance frauds. And Edward's a specialist in that field. Have I got it right?'

Edward just gave a nod and reached out for a slice of brown bread, which he hadn't expected to find out here.

'Help yourself. It's been baked by a neighbour of ours. Her husband was a baker and emigrated here from Germany some years ago. His wife does the baking now and follows his recipes. This has a strong flavour of malt. Give it a try.'

Edward sampled the bread and agreed that it was extremely tasty. 'Are you staying here today?' he asked cautiously.

Lucy shook her head. 'No, I would normally have left by now but I just wanted to say goodbye to you.'

'Pity,' said Edward. He did not know whether he had made his spontaneous remark out of politeness or whether he had really meant it. He wanted to continue his talks with Red as soon as possible.

As if she could read his thoughts, Lucy got up and stretched out her hand. Edward stood up briskly.

'I didn't mean to scare you off with my question . . .'

Lucy laughed. 'You would not have had much chance! But I really have to go now. I enjoyed meeting you. Perhaps we shall meet again some time.'

'Maybe.'

Edward waited till Red and Lucy walked off the patio. Then he sat down and got on with his breakfast. He was pleased to be with Red on his own, but admitted to himself that he found Lucy extremely attractive. He leaned back in his chair, his eyes blinking at the morning sun. It then occurred to him that he had to find the entrance to Red's workroom. Surely it could not be so well disguised as to be completely invisible. Edward reflected how a foreign colleague would have been handled under similar circumstances in the UK. There had been a case in London some years ago, when a fellow who would later give evidence for the Crown against the Mafia had introduced himself to them. In the days of Margaret Thatcher, discussions were held in an icy atmosphere. The comparison now was clearly in Red's favour. He had to admit that he found him extremely charming. According to the CIA, Red was top-rate and very much in demand. Unlike his London colleagues, however, Edward was slightly uneasy that Red was working for a number of different bosses.

He could hear Lucy's far-off laughter. She must have distracted Red, since he did not reappear at the French windows for another half-hour.

'Please wait for a moment or two; I need to put some clothes on.'

Dressing took less than five minutes. Edward hardly had time to gnaw at a chicken leg.

Lucy's car engine could be heard in the valley below, but soon faded way. Red cleared the breakfast table. He then sat down by Edward and looked at him pensively. Edward returned his gaze, waiting to hear whether Red had reached any conclusion overnight. Stroking his hair, Red finally looked away into the far distance.

'Edward?' he said slowly, 'To be frank, I have not made any decision yet. This is the first time anyone has approached me to carry out an assignment without mentioning the name of the target person.' He paused and folded his hands. 'OK, you have your reasons. Perhaps you can think up some way you can convince me, that might influence my decision. You know that I don't have to take on any job that comes along. For me, there's always quite a bit at stake. That's why I'm pleased I can still pick and choose my jobs. Of course, Uncle Sam is a letter of recommendation to some extent, but it's no guarantee. I hope you understand.'

Edward fully understood but he had no specific instructions. 'Perhaps money might put your mind at rest. Just name a figure.' He tried to get away from the awkward question of their target. It could be that money – big money – was not a convincing enough argument.

Red did not answer and looked as if he wanted to change the subject. He glanced towards Edward and grinned. 'I apologize for the fun and games last night. But they mean I can feel secure, and so can you.'

Instinctively Red felt that Edward was mentally feeling his way around the walls in the hall and the cellar, groping for the entrance or exit.

'Forget it,' said Red. 'Other people have tried and failed.' He stood up and walked along the patio, his head bowed, placing one foot slowly in front of the other. When he returned, he came right up to Edward.

'What's so very special about the target that you've got to be so cagey? Is it someone from your side?'

'No,' said Edward.

'Then I don't get it.' Red turned round again, paced up and down the patio once more, then sat down in a wicker chair. He appeared to be struggling with himself and his decision. Every so often he shook his head. The problem, Edward thought, could not just be money. Red only needed to quote an amount, any amount. And he certainly did not seem to be the sort of person who had reservations about demanding large sums. Edward was secretly reckoning with a demand of one million dollars. In principle, that had already been agreed by London.

Suddenly, Red stood up. 'I'll have to leave you on your own for a moment.' A few seconds later Edward heard the click of the lock in the main door. Had Red gone off and left him all alone? Or did Red simply want to find out if he would grope around the house for the secret door? Edward looked around on the ceilings and walls for hidden cameras, without success. He decided to behave as naturally as possible; and for him it was natural, he decided, to return to the hall and look around once again for the secret door.

He stood up and slowly trod across the living room. At the entrance to the hall he could see that Red was no longer there. He searched the spot where he thought the door must be. The wall itself betrayed no obvious signs – no wiring, no hidden panel, no cupboard fronting an entrance door. Edward tapped along the entire wall, inch by inch, then the adjoining wall, and finally the opposite wall. Red had been right; there was no chance of finding anything. Steps could be heard outside. The main door opened and Red entered the hall.

'Well, did you find anything?' he asked in a friendly tone. Edward shook his head.

'I already told you that you'd find nothing. Why didn't you want to believe me?' Red took great pleasure in Edward's lack of success.

'Will you show me the trick some time?'

Red laughed. 'Never!' He then beckoned Edward on to the patio. When he had sat down, he came out with the key words, 'One million!'

'Dollars?'

Red shook his head, smiling broadly. 'The job is to be done in the UK. So it's sterling!'

Edward took in a deep breath and stared Red in the eyes.

'Very well, once I have financial approval. Here's to a successful joint venture!' He gave him his hand. Red shook it firmly.

# 6

The room was discreetly and appropriately furnished. A large, round oak table stood in the middle, surrounded by eight black leather chairs with high backs. Above the table hung an imposing chandelier, shedding its artificial light over the gloomy atmosphere. Set in one of the long walls, opposite the window grilles, was a huge padded swing-door. On one of the short walls hung a portrait of Her Majesty, Queen Elizabeth II, set in a simple wooden frame and, underneath, a table with glasses, cups, jugs of milk and fruit juice, and several Thermos flasks.

Opposite, hung smaller portraits of the Royal Family, set in simple frames – the Queen Mother, Prince Philip and the children, Princes Charles, Andrew, Edward and Princess Anne. Near the portraits of Prince Charles and Prince Andrew, two lighter areas were visible, where other portraits must originally have hung. Below, on a sort of sofa table, lay some English newspapers and magazines.

Two men in dark suits were already sitting at the round table, studying the *Sun* and *The Times*. The door opened quietly. Both men stood up. Bowing slightly, they greeted a lean, white-haired gentleman in his mid-sixties; he returned the compliment, pulled back a chair and sat down. He placed a folder of assorted files a few inches in front of him, on the table.

'May I bring you a cup of tea, Sir?' asked the man who had been reading *The Times*, folding the newspaper. The white-haired gentleman nodded appreciatively.

'Certainly, Arthur.'

He drew a pair of gold-rimmed spectacles from a case and started to pore over a file. On the lapel of his dark jacket shone a gold decoration, inset with a small diamond. Arthur carefully moved the teacup towards him. He looked up briefly.

'Thank you. When do the others arrive?'

Arthur looked at his wrist-watch.

'They should already be here by now, Sir,' he replied and returned to his seat.

'George, would you kindly enquire in the waiting-room whether they are inside the building yet?'

Silently, George got up and left the room.

'Quite disgraceful, this lack of punctuality,' murmured the white-haired gentleman, burying himself in the file.

'Have you read the latest reports?' he asked Arthur, without raising his head.

'Yes, Sir.'

'What is your opinion?'

'One can only hope that Edward will be able to provide some convincing answers. Time is running out . . .'

'. . . and the situation is getting more precarious every day,' added the white-haired gentleman.

Arthur got up, pointing towards a filing cupboard near the door.

'Excuse me, Sir, perhaps I should . . . ?'

He went to the cupboard and opened it. Next to some files were two trigger switches. Arthur turned them both on. A light shone behind a round, frosted-glass panel above the folding door. He then shut the cupboard.

'Yes, Arthur. We live in bad times. I never thought I would have to carry out such an unfortunate assignment just before my retirement.'

Silently, Arthur nodded in agreement.

'Over the years, this country has seen dirty business, to a greater or lesser degree, in which we have sometimes been obliged – I repeat, *obliged* – to participate. But now . . . ?' He closed the file pensively. 'I can see no other alternative. It is inconceivable that the Royal Family is finally about to bow out. Where impotence, homosexuality and war have failed, these little . . .'

The door opened slowly and he turned round. Edward and his colleague Walter entered the room, followed by George. The white-haired gentleman got up from his chair.

Walter was about thirty years old, visibly younger than Edward. He looked very Irish, with light-reddish hair and freckles all over his face.

'I hope you are pleased with my report, Sir David?' asked Edward and shook his boss's hand.

'Your report, Edward, is, as usual, excellent. Clearly, the details we are interested in most are better dealt with person-to-person.'

Edward checked the frosted-glass panel over the folding door before sitting down. Sir David took it in.

'Arthur has already switched on the debugging device; we can start straightaway. Kindly fill us in, briefly, on the details that you omitted to mention, for obvious reasons.'

Edward glanced at the report summary he had submitted to Sir David the previous day and expanded on what he considered to be the most relevant data.

'I now suggest we examine this chap Red's offer,' he said, concluding his introduction.

'What would happen,' George enquired, 'if it all blows up in our face at the last minute?'

'We have spoken about that as well,' Edward quickly explained. 'We pay all his costs, plus ten per cent.'

'One hundred thousand plus for damn all!' said Arthur with a groan. 'How on earth do we justify that?'

'The cash comes from the slush fund,' Sir David assured him. 'That is none of our business.'

Walter stood up and looked inquiringly at Edward, who merely nodded; whereupon he walked over to the drinks table and returned with two cups of tea.

'During your absence I talked to the CIA on two occasions.

Apparently this chap, Red, has been working with them for years. No complaints. He is absolutely discreet. Otherwise he would have been dead long ago. Hartmann, from the German BND, who have also used him once, said that to his knowledge Red had done a job for the IRA. He couldn't recall the exact details and I've not found anything in the files that bears his trademark.' Sir David cast his eyes around the circle expectantly. 'Have you come up with any disturbing facts in your investigations?'

The question was generally answered in the negative. Sir David continued. 'I had an extensive and highly confidential discussion this morning. They have decided that the little game should be brought to a halt. Princess Diana has earned sympathy everywhere, which raises considerable problems for the Royal Family. Furthermore, her behaviour and the whole of her private life has become one large scandal; this affects not only the Palace but also the United Kingdom. Also, she has inevitably dragged her own sons, William and Harry, as well as the Heir to the Throne, into the scandal. Highly irresponsible!'

'What thought has been given in the upper echelons, for the time being, as to the consequences of her elimination?' asked Arthur.

Sir David raised his eyebrows; he voiced his own opinion, loud and clear. 'Better a shocking end than endless shock and high-level risk!' He laid down his gold-rimmed spectacles and folded his elegant hands.

'I am absolutely sure that not all of us here present understand and appreciate, with the same degree of conviction, the action that is expected, not to mention demanded, from us. But that is not – nor should it be – a problem.'

Edward asked to speak. 'I have told Red that only Walter and myself are to be his contacts as soon as he sets foot in the UK. Is this to be the final scenario?'

Sir David sat back in his chair.

'I have received no instructions to the contrary. Why do you ask?'

'Only for my own information, Sir. Up till now, I have the feeling that Red and I . . . let us say, get along well together, without being too friendly.'

'How far is Princess Diana's official engagement calendar booked ahead?' asked Walter, looking in George's direction.

'Short-term, till the end of the year, and some bookings already for 1998 and 1999.'

'I doubt we can keep our baby alive for as long as that,' said Arthur sarcastically.

Sir David fidgeted impatiently.

'None of that, please, Arthur! May we get back to the agenda? What do you think, Edward?'

'Well, at present we are too far removed from the point of no return to make concrete plans. But my view is that if Princess Diana has to disappear and that if Red is our man, then we should send for him as soon as possible, here in London. Walter and I will go over the various scenarios with him and aim for zero-hour, however and whenever that may be.'

Sir David cleared his throat. 'Let us now move on to item number two. You will all have read the newspaper articles about Prince Charles. If one understands the background message, the fundamental question is how the public sees the relationship between Prince Charles and his children.' He made a strategic pause and glanced around his circle of colleagues.

Arthur was the first to grasp the point. 'We'll need to refurbish the Prince's image as a father figure.'

Sir David nodded in agreement. 'Quite right, gentlemen. If you scrutinize the articles carefully, you will read between the lines that Prince Charles is really awkward when it comes to his own sons – too remote, and too little human contact. Compared with their mother, he appears cold and unnatural. We need to work on this. What do you suggest?'

'Am I correct in assuming that the children spend most of

their school holidays at Balmoral, or has the pattern changed?' asked George.

'No', replied Edward. 'I have just checked on the computer. No change as yet.'

'Good, then we should arrange a Press engagement with Prince Charles and the boys. Obviously not in the Castle, but in a pleasant, natural environment somewhere. Father and sons together on their own, but far away from Princess Diana and the other Royals.'

'I find George's idea simply brilliant.' Edward looked towards Sir David. 'How soon can this be arranged?'

'What is the latest on Princess Diana's scheduled trip Arthur referred to yesterday?' asked Walter.

Walter shrugged his shoulders. 'I've read the minutes of a phone call between Princess Diana and Andrew Roberts of the *Sunday Times*. Unfortunately there was a great deal of background noise, since Diana was phoning on her mobile from some restaurant or café. Some bits of the conversation couldn't be fully understood. But she informed Roberts about a long journey, apparently towards the end of the month. I haven't been able to trace this on the computer yet, so presumably it's some trip with Al Fayed that no one knows anything about, apart from him and her. Beyond that, there's a weekend planned at Martha's Vineyard on the New England coast, where she'll be joining the Clintons.'

Sir David looked at his watch. 'I think this Press meeting seems to be the most urgent point. I shall attend to it immediately.'

'But please leave Camilla Parker-Bowles out of it,' Arthur giggled. A rather pinched smile spread over Sir David's face. He clasped his file under his arm.

'Thank you, gentlemen! I shall prepare my confidential report tomorrow morning and ask if we can hire this fellow, Red. Please stand by tomorrow afternoon.'

The others, meanwhile, stood up and bowed slightly as Sir David disappeared.

## 7

'Shit!' muttered George. 'Who gave these instructions? The CIA, Tony Blair, the Tory Party or our own people? Or is this a mission request from another service?'

'George, old chap, people who ask too many questions don't usually live long,' scoffed Arthur. 'Basic training – Lesson One'.

'None of your little jokes, please! This matter's far too serious.'

George was not to be put off. 'The rule used to be that the enemy had to be eliminated; but who is the enemy in this case?'

Edward gave George a look of pity. 'You've got a lot to learn, George. Perhaps you should apply for a transfer to another department for a while.'

George blushed suddenly; he took a deep breath. 'Where else would I be able to throw up, apart from here? Since I've been around in this department I've always served my country and loyally carried out all instructions. But that doesn't mean I have to take it all lying down.'

'Then you must draw your own conclusions, George, but please be quick about it,' replied Edward. 'You should have met this fellow, Red – an absolute professional. A cool, calculating businessman when it comes to his job. But when you get to know him, an extremely nice chap. He can pick them off, you understand, just pick them off! And that's the only way to survive in this business. Red's a killer, a routine killer, in fact an artist in his chosen field. We need people like him. In wartime and in peace. And if there was no Red, we'd have to find a Ted, a Pat, or an Ed.'

George looked at him sideways on and nodded vigorously. 'That's right, Ed . . . That's right, Edward. If we do our job properly, that makes us *all* murderers. If we have to act in the name of national security or in the national interest, then it's obvious why. But what's the point of removing Princess Diana from the scene? What's the point?'

Edward walked up to George, putting his left hand on his shoulder. 'George, until I know the answer to that question, I won't take the job on, I can assure you.'

Arthur and Walter had taken in this discussion without comment. Arthur now stood up and walked towards the cupboard. 'I think I can turn off the switch now.'

Edward gave a brief nod and signalled to Walter. He stood up and followed him to the door. Edward turned round again, briskly.

'If anyone wishes to drop out, I won't call him a coward. But do so quickly and without making a fuss.' He left the room, with Walter. The light behind the little round frosted-glass panel went out.

# 8

Edward was seated in his office at the computer, searching an index. Meanwhile, Walter, who shared the same room, was thumbing through the *Daily Mirror*.

'Have you seen the latest photos of Princess Diana on the Al Fayed yacht?' Walter folded the paper and passed it to Edward, who glanced at the page and dived back into his screen.

'I would be fascinated to know how they'll fill all this space when Princess Diana has gone,' he mumbled. 'Is there nothing but those two? Why is she already back?'

He changed the file and searched for her calendar. 'Is that so? The cruise is scheduled for five days.' He continued his search.

'Have you read the report about a certain Kelly Fisher? According to the agencies, Al Fayed was leading a double life over there. She's an insignificant, third-rate model. Dodi was apparently engaged to her, or perhaps just given her an expensive ring which the stupid tart took for an engagement ring.' He turned to Walter. 'We'll observe Diana's reaction tomorrow. Perhaps she'll dump the playboy because of this Fisher girl.'

'Wait and see how the Fisher story develops. She'll certainly try to make herself appear interesting. Al Fayed would never dream of swapping a goldfish for a jellyfish!'

Edward reached for the phone and dialled a short number. 'Edward here. Gentlemen, please follow up the Kelly Fisher story. I'd also like to have some of Diana's phone calls on my desk as soon as possible, never mind to whom. And then

I'll need as many of her appointments as you can dig out, private or official. I can't find out anything relevant on the computer, apart from a few trivial bits of information. Please make an effort!'

He hung up and turned to Walter. 'How about shadowing her for a few days so as to give me an idea of how she spends her time, day-to-day matters such as the doctor, hairdresser, gym sessions and so on?'

'Do you think that'll lead to anything?' queried Walter sceptically.

'You never know. I have the feeling this sort of sleuth work might be helpful for us when zero-hour comes along.'

# 9

The room was decorated in light-blue wallpaper and dominated by imposing bronze candelabras and a gigantic portrait of Queen Elizabeth II in an ornate gilt frame. At a massive writing table sat a small, white-haired man with a pale face and a pointed nose. He was elegantly dressed; his exquisitely polished shoes gleamed. The desk was empty, apart from a telephone, a gilt writing set and a dark-brown leather folder lying open in front of him. He flipped through one letter after another, scribbling his signature at the foot of each with a gold fountain pen. There was a gentle knock at the door. He looked up. A lady in an elegant blue suit entered, with some hesitation, shut the door carefully behind her and waited for the hand gesture that signalled that she was permitted to speak.

'Sir David is here, Sir.'

She turned round and opened the door again. Sir David entered the room with a short bow; the lady retired behind him. Quietly, he sat down in one of the brown leather armchairs in front of the desk; the little white-haired man at the desk carried on working. Two or three minutes slipped by in silence. Finally, he closed the folder and replaced the gold fountain pen into a gilt holder belonging to the writing set. He then leaned back in his chair and looked at Sir David expectantly.

In a high-pitched voice he enquired, 'What is the reason for your visit, David?'

'There are two reasons why I am here. Firstly, I'd like to arrange for a meeting with the Press to be called as soon as possible, where Prince Charles can be photographed, in the company of his children, as a family figure, ideally in a natural, relaxed setting.'

'What is the background?'

'In view of forthcoming events, it would seem advisable to strengthen the image of His Royal Highness as a father figure in the public eye. My department has already identified a considerable public relations gap between him and her in this respect . . .'

'When is this meeting due to take place?'

'As soon as possible.'

'We'll fix that. And the next point?'

'The US Secret Service has put us in contact with a highly experienced expert in . . .' He paused for a moment and then continued. 'You had considered that Princess Diana should be eliminated quickly . . .'

'Considered?' The voice of the white-haired gentleman said scornfully. 'There is no need for consideration after her affairs with those characters James Gilbey, Oliver Hoare, James Hewitt and all the others, and now this . . . Al Fayed. This person must go, and as soon as possible. I hope you and your people realize what's at stake for the whole of Great Britain and the Royal Family?'

Sir David nodded and, lowering his voice, continued. 'We have found someone who would take this job on. His demands, however, are a little on the high side.'

'What is he asking?'

'A million pounds, Sir.'

If Sir David had been concerned that the gentleman opposite might be shocked at the figure, he was soon put right. The reaction to the price came swiftly.

'A ridiculously low figure when you consider what damage she has already done and might still do. It is vital that this man is quick, reliable and that nobody can suspect anyone. There must be no hint of suspicion. You understand what I am driving at?'

'The CIA gave our man the very best references.' Sir David waited for a further reaction. There was none. So he resumed, 'Are those your final instructions, Sir? Should we invite our man over?'

'Yes, let him come. Arrange the financial details with your customary discretion and, apart from yourself, take great care to involve only a reliable and preferably small circle of people on the job. The fewer the better.' The white-haired gentleman's hand groped for a button underneath the desk. 'Thank you for calling.'

At that moment the door opened and the lady in the blue suit reappeared.

'Take Sir David outside and phone through to Prince Charles. In case he's unavailable, find out when he can be contacted.' Then he turned to Sir David, who had meanwhile got up from his chair. 'Thank you very much, Sir David.'

Sir David made a slight bow again and followed the lady out of the room. Both doors closed behind them.

# 10

That afternoon, Sir David summoned his team of four – Edward, Walter, Arthur and George – to the scheduled meeting. 'I assume you all know Princess Diana is now back in England. You have found out everything about the Kelly affair from internal memos and the Press. In case any of you still need some basic details . . .' He looked round the circle and paused at Edward, who gave him a nod. 'Edward will fill you in.' Also, it has been arranged that Prince Charles' private secretary will invite the Press. The idea has been warmly welcomed by the whole Royal Family, so I am informed, and the invitations go out today. Charles has decided on the scenario – the banks of the Dee where he was once photographed with Diana after their wedding. We shall just have to wait and see how far the media take up the theme and how they interpret it. Are there any questions so far?'

Arthur butted in. 'You did not mention William and Harry. Can we take it that . . .'

Sir David intervened. 'Of course, the boys will be there. That's the whole object of the exercise.'

'Thank you, Sir.'

'If there are no further questions,' Sir David continued, 'I ought to inform you that I have had a further discussion in order to confirm that our commission concerning Princess Diana is still on. We are authorized to hire this American hit man. His financial demands will be met.'

There was a pregnant silence all round. George's eyes were shut; he was shaking his head. Edward and Walter stared at the table; Arthur nervously twiddled his fingers.

'Gentlemen, I am aware how you feel,' he eventually concluded. 'I know that you all have reservations about this whole matter. That is a good thing. I am pleased Edward has located someone who can help us with this assignment.'

Sir David stood up without saying anything and left the room. They all remained seated, as if frozen to their chairs. It was Arthur who finally broke the silence.

'Well, chaps, that's where we stand. Let's call up Red. I am quite excited about him. He sounds like a first-rate chap.'

'Arthur, please!' whispered George across the table. Everyone could see that the youngest member in their team was battling with his emotions.

Edward stood up and knocked on the table. 'Gentlemen, I suggest we adjourn for today and sleep on it overnight. Unless Sir David pulls rank on me, I ask you all kindly to be here at 10 o'clock tomorrow for a further meeting. By then I'll have spoken to Red and fixed a date.'

Edward, Walter and Arthur left the room. George stayed behind for a while sitting in his chair. Tears poured down his face. His hands trembled as he gathered the files together. He then stood up, switched off the debugging device in the cupboard and closed the door behind him.

# 11

Scarcely ten days had elapsed since Edward first rode with the Indian, by jeep, up to Red's house. He vividly recalled his back pains. He was now seated in the rear of the vehicle again. The driver had recognized him immediately when he knocked at his door.

'Are you now one of Mr Red's regular visitors?' he asked, his face beaming. 'Then Mr Red won't be so lonely. It is good for a man if he has many friends. Mr Red has many, many friends. I drive nearly all his friends.' He looked into the rear-view mirror, the same cheerful smile on his face. 'Some days ago I drove very rich people. Two men with much jewellery.' He pointed to his neck, wrists and at the areas of his fingers where rings are worn. 'Much, much jewellery, Sir. They did not speak our language. I did not understand one word. But when I see them I know at once where to take them. Who else do such rich people want to see?'

Edward was only half listening to the driver's chatter. He could not help feeling that the number of potholes had doubled since the last visit. This time he had taken a black attaché case with him, which he clung to tightly on his lap, as well as the small brown leather suitcase. He would dearly liked to know if Lucy also took this route along the river bed. At last the driver pulled the wheel over to the right, the jeep climbed up the hill and made off towards Red's property.

This time, having left the driver, Edward took the correct path. Red had already noticed that he had arrived, since halfway to the gate the chirping noise from the fence stopped.

As Edward turned the corner, Red was already standing at the entrance, with a smile on his face.

'Welcome, Edward. When we said goodbye, I never thought we'd meet again so soon.' He stretched out his hand towards his visitor and shook it vigorously. Red seemed to be genuinely pleased to see him again. He closed the gate and they both walked along the narrow path towards the house.

'Can I take a guess at what's inside the black attaché case?' asked Red, rather over-eagerly.

'You may,' answered Edward and handed it over without further comment.

'You won't be asking me for a receipt, I take it?'

Edward stood still and turned round towards Red. 'Correct. Do you want me to count?'

Red did not react.

'Then you count it!' Edward bowed ironically, turned round and continued walking.

'When you talk like that I get the impression that I haven't really got your support in London.' Red's cocky smile had disappeared. 'And I hope your rather tense mood is no reflection on me personally.'

They had arrived at the house. Red opened the door and let his guest go in first. 'You should know your way around by now. The guest room's at your disposal. Make yourself comfortable.' He turned on the security system for the perimeter fence and moved the oil painting back against the wall so that the switchbox behind was no longer visible.

'You freshen up, and meanwhile I'll count the cash.'

Edward looked thoughtfully at the black case Red held in his hand. He then turned round and went upstairs.

Red took the case into the living room, placed it on a sideboard and tried to open it. The attempt failed because of the security lock. Red thought it best not to force it and laid the case down. He prepared two drinks in the kitchen, with orange juice and ice, and brought them out on to the patio. Outside, it was warm and muggy. The surrounding countryside lay under light cloud cover.

It was not long before Edward reappeared. Red pointed to the glass filled with orange juice. 'I thought I'd fix you a drink.' He then pointed to the case. 'Please help me score the final hit of the day. I wouldn't want to damage the locks.'

Edward went to the balustrade and took a swig at the drink. Then he picked up the case and handed it back to Red.

'171961,' he said, with deliberation. Red turned the little wheels and the locks sprang open. He opened the lid. In front of him were stacks of used English pound notes. Red picked up a bundle and counted. He nodded.

'I hope you haven't miscounted,' he said and put the money back into the case. 'If you'll kindly excuse me for a moment.' He disappeared inside with the back case.

Edward was sure this time that Red would not leave him on his own for long, since Lucy was obviously not there. He sat down in a wicker chair. In a flashback he recalled the events that had taken place since his first visit to Red's. Clearly, by handing over the attaché case to Red, he had sealed Princess Diana's fate. He felt how his hand had begun to tremble, holding the glass with the orange drink; he tried to focus his mind on other things. He gazed up into the clouds. Suddenly he had a vision of Lucy standing in front of him; his thoughts collected round her, her tousled blonde hair and her narrow waist. He remembered the kiss she had given him at the dinner on the patio and wondered how good she was in bed. He saw her blouse and how she tied it around her breasts, he could hear her clear laughter. Diana was also a blonde, she also liked to laugh. Her laugh! Soon she would not . . .

'All correct.'

Edward jumped. Red stood behind him, grinning.

'I assume the case was some sort of gift-wrapping – or do you want it back?'

'No, of course not,' Edward said in a nervous voice.

Red looked at him, surprised. 'Does jet lag affect you?' he

asked, with some concern. Edward shrugged off the question but Red did not let go. 'You look pale.' He grinned. 'I hope they didn't deduct the money from your salary.' When he realized that this kind of remark did not cheer Edward up, his tone became more serious. He sat down on the balustrade and stared at Edward, slumped in the wicker chair. 'Problems?'

Edward said nothing and gazed into the greenery beyond. He tried to breathe silently and deeply. As if from afar, he could hear Red speaking.

'Edward, what's up? Edward!' Red leaned over his guest; with his fingers on his wrist, he felt Edward's pulse. It was racing. Red went back into the kitchen, grabbed a napkin from a cupboard and packed it with ice. He hurried back to Edward, still slumped in the wicker chair, opened a few of his shirt buttons and pressed the ice pack to his forehead.

'It's jet lag, I'm sure,' groaned Edward slowly and tried to pull himself up.

'Stay there quietly. It'll pass soon. It's unusually sultry today, even up here. And also the journey,' said Red, trying to calm him. 'Try to relax. Drink some liquid.' Carefully, he drew the glass up to Edward's mouth. He took two sips and opened his eyes again. With trembling hands he reached for the ice pack.

'Thanks,' he gasped.

'You gave me a nasty shock. I am just not prepared for incidents like this up here. The nearest doctor is at least two hours away. I don't normally think of using him so long as there are no problems.' Red drew up his wicker chair close to Edward, who slowly began to revive. 'Maybe we should go to my workroom; it's cooler and more pleasant down there.'

Edward gave a nod. He sat up and tried to support himself, both hands on the arms of the chair. Red hurried over and propped him up. 'Let's move . . . but take it easy.' Carefully, Edward made his way into the house, supported by Red. They paused at the clothes stand in the hall. 'Hold on tight and wait there for a moment,' Red insisted. He grabbed a

coat from the stand and hastily threw it over Edward's head.
'It's necessary, I'm afraid.' For Edward it made no difference.
He could sense that Red was standing close before him.
Taking Edward's hands, he placed them from behind on to
his shoulders, just as Edward used to do as a child when he
played railways with other kids.

'Come along,' said Red. And, taking the first step forward,
he called out, 'Twenty-two steps.' Edward felt a cold draught
around his legs. Step by step, they walked down.

'Now lower your head.'

They reached the bottom of the stairs at last. Red pulled the
coat off Edward's head and held on to his arm. Edward indeed
felt much better down below. The light came on again with a
gentle click. Red led Edward to one of the office chairs, into
which he slumped. Gradually, he came to.

'I'm OK now.'

'I can't say,' replied Red. 'Nothing like this has ever happened
to me before.'

'Nor to me,' came the reply.

Silently, Red went over to his desk, piled high with files,
books and documents. He closed everything that was lying
open, so that no one could guess what he was working on.

'Preliminary work for another job,' said Red casually and
sat down in one of the chairs in front of the desk.

'Everything OK?'

Edward nodded, pulling a handkerchief from his trouser
pocket and wiped his face, neck and throat. 'None of us is
getting any younger.' Nervously, he attempted a smile but
could not manage it.

'In my opinion, you ought to stay here for a couple of days
at least, so that there's not a repeat of this in London . . .'

'I can't, the job . . .'

'When are we supposed to start?' asked Red. 'As a matter
of fact, I've just been offered another job. Not uninteresting
and quite straightforward, so it would seem.' He grinned. 'It
should cause quite a stir in Great Britain,' he added.

'Your business appears to be doing very well,' Edward cut in. 'You'll soon be able to retire.'

Red laughed out loud. 'Retire? Me? What would I do all day in this goddam country? Work on theory? No, Edward. If a guy meddles around with ideas, he's got to put them into practice and see the results. Did you know, for instance, that you can manoeuvre a Chrysler from eight yards by using the remote control mechanism of a toy vehicle? I found this out by pure chance. And did you realize that by means of a telephone decoder and a little ingenuity you can outsmart the ignition safety system of the entire BMW 700 series? No, if you know the tricks of the trade, you can't give up; you've got to find a use for them. Technical tricks with remote controls, decoders or radio pilot systems for model aeroplanes; they have been quite a hit on TV comedy programmes but they often have their tragic aspect as well. Mostly, they just need slight adaptation or simple adjustment to the technical specification and they are ready for use.'

'You make me worried,' said Edward with a sigh and pulled himself upright in his chair.

'That was not my intention. Particularly in your present condition. How do you feel now?'

'I think I'll be OK.'

'Then maybe we should go through my assignment contract. You've made the first move.' He turned round and pointed behind, to where the black attaché case lay. 'How do we proceed from here?'

'I already mentioned that when we first met. You will fly to London next Monday via New York. Our contact man will give you an impeccable set of papers and a new profile; this will get you into the UK. I shall pick you up at the airport. Then we wait until we know how, when and where the accident will take place. We have no clear picture of that at this moment. And at the appropriate moment . . . you strike. Immediately after that you fly back to the USA and return the papers in New York. And I shall then pay you a visit, like today.'

'That'll please the Indian.' Red rubbed his hands.

'I can imagine,' Edward replied drily.

'Can you now tell me a little more about our target?'

The question, as before, was answered by a curt, 'No'.

# 12

Red was standing on the patio, listening to the early morning sounds. The noise of the jeep's engine got quieter and finally faded away. He returned to the house and began to clear the breakfast table. Edward had got up very early in order to be sure of catching the midday flight to New York, where he had to change aircraft. Red brought the tray into the kitchen and rang Lucy. From her sleepy voice, it was obvious he had woken her up. They arranged to meet at midday.

Red went into the hall and, by force of habit, strapped on the shoulder holster with his 38mm. He never left the house unarmed, whether he was on a job or was simply travelling as a tourist or on business. Any period he happened to be without a weapon went under the heading of professional risk. His route took him along the house, then through a narrow path between some tall bushes on the slope. He paused in the middle of a clearing and looked round with surprise. The bushes had grown considerably in the last few weeks. He continued in the direction of the perimeter fence. The Indian, true to his word, had left all the most recent newspapers in a plastic bag, at Red's request. Or else Lucy would bring the papers. He picked up the bag and returned along the same route to the house.

On the patio he laid out the newspapers on the floor to his left, as usual, and began to read. He flipped through the politics and world news sections, then read the New York stock market report and the business pages.

Finally, he opened the supplement. According to rumour there was a quarrel amongst the Kennedys and yet another revealing book on JFK was in preparation. Then he suddenly came across the name Al Fayed. At first he assumed the reference referred to Mohammed but then realized it was all about a certain Kelly Fisher, photographed on the page together with her mother and lawyer, who had started a lawsuit against Dodi, Mohammed's son, claiming damages for desertion. It was also casually mentioned that Dodi was rumoured for some while to be having an affair with the ex-wife of the heir to the English throne, Prince Charles. When he came to the amount of damages claimed, he laughed out loud. She almost had his own price tag. He felt sure this matter would be settled some other way.

He picked up the next newspaper. Once again, he flicked through the pages in the usual sequence: politics, world news, stock market, business and the supplement. He then turned to the third and final paper. Skimming through the text, he alighted on a photo of Prince Charles with both sons in Scotland on the banks of the River Dee. The Prince was leaning on a shepherd's crook, dressed in a kilt, which Red had always considered a degenerate form of dress. The article accompanying the photo explained that the heir to the throne was spending his holidays in Scotland with his children and took a very close interest in their education and well-being. The Prince of Wales, it continued, placed his children first. The overwhelming majority of his subjects silently cherished the hope that her Majesty, Queen Elizabeth II, would abdicate in his favour, bringing a breath of fresh air into Buckingham Palace. The article finally raised the question whether Elizabeth should not have stepped down earlier, because her son was far less interested in his royal duties than in botany, ecology and environmental questions. Red lowered the paper, his brain in turmoil. Had he possibly been engaged, in the last forty-eight hours, to eliminate Prince Charles or even the Queen? The hints that Edward had dropped concerning his target applied equally to both. The job was explosive headline material, he had mentioned;

the target person always enjoyed media attention, and for MI5 or MI6, in so far as Edward belonged to either – he had not yet been able to find out which – it was a highly sensitive matter indeed. It dawned on him why the author of this assignment had selected an external partner for the contract. Nobody in the UK wished to dirty their own hands. It was inconceivable that the English secret service should be suspected, or any proof of their involvement should be traced in this affair!

It suddenly became clear to Red that he could have demanded a much higher price. It was also quite apparent why Edward had been under such emotional strain. It was highly likely that his guest's sudden nervous collapse had nothing to do with jet lag. It was absolutely certain, in his mind, that either Elizabeth or Charles must be the key person of the assignment.

He started to reflect which of the two candidates would bring more advantages to the British public if the one or the other were eliminated. The death of an elderly, undemonstrative Queen? Or the death of the awkward, moody Heir to the Throne, who had forfeited his rights of succession in public opinion because of his attachment to an old flame from his youth, with whom he had committed adultery.

But it did not matter much to him whether mother or son had been put on the hit list. He had been hired and had already been paid five hundred thousand pounds sterling, which he would be taking to the city bank in the next few days and either place it in the bank deposit box or else invest it immediately in blue chips. He recalled Edward's comment that he, Red, could complete this assignment and then quietly retire. He had shrugged off the question in Edward's presence but had to admit to himself that he had been toying with the idea, off and on, during the last few days. He had no family and no heirs. But there was Lucy. She would obviously inherit everything one day, but what would she do with so much money? It was far too much to spend on himself, and Lucy also had no children. Perhaps he should in fact look around at last for that old castle in the South of France which he had been dreaming about ever since he had got to know the area years ago. A beautiful castle, a moat, a long driveway and a vineyard in the background! Of course, Lucy had to join him. He had only to make up his mind whether he preferred the Atlantic or the Mediterranean side.

Red decided to mention this matter when Lucy came today. He shut his eyes and listened to the sound of the wind rustling in the trees and the bushes.

# 13

He woke up to the noise of the car's horn. He came to quickly and glanced at his watch. Had he really fallen asleep and not heard Lucy's car? He jumped up, turned off the electricity and, grabbing the key ring and his holster, opened the gate. Two large bags laden with provisions had been deposited there. It was some while before he heard footsteps on the narrow path to the fence. Then he caught sight of her. She waved to him, quite out of breath.

'Darling, I'm sorry. I was sitting on the patio and actually fell asleep,' he said, by way of greeting.

'Yes. And I had to go all the way back to the car to wake you up. You'll have to pay for that!' She laughed, shook her blonde curls and embraced him. 'How could you possibly fall sleep, anyway? What did you do all night without me?'

'I missed you,' answered Red. 'That was probably it. And I simply could not get to sleep. So I got up early this morning and read.' He picked up one of the bags and walked on ahead of Lucy, who took hold of the other bag and shut the gate.

'Right, the Indian didn't come by my place with the papers. Why was he up here?'

'I believe he went to old Jimmy's and dropped by here on his way back. It was pure chance. I heard his jeep, went down to the fence and found the papers there. I should have phoned you immediately and let you know. My apologies!'

'You can make up for it in a minute,' said Lucy temptingly. 'But first, let me get rid of this stupid bag.'

In the kitchen, Red took Lucy in his arms and kissed her.

'Was that all?' asked Lucy, as he let her go. She began to undo his shirt buttons but Red held on to her hands.

'Please, let's wait a little. I need to talk to you.'

'Oh!' she said, pretending to be anxious, 'I hope it's nothing serious!'

'Yes,' replied Red and walked out on to the patio. Lucy took an apple out of one of the bags and followed him. 'OK, you shoot first! I have had breakfast, so I'm armed.'

'She sat down in a wicker chair and stretched her legs out wide. Red leant over her and kissed her on the brow. 'What would you say if we packed our things and moved to the South of France?'

Lucy gazed at him incredulously. 'You mean you'd leave Fort Knox here for good? Are you serious?'

'I'm dead serious,' answered Red. 'I just need to wind up a couple of jobs and then we could both move to the South of France. Maybe we should buy some old castle or farmhouse, who knows? Somewhere in Aude, Hérault, Roussillon or Gascony?'

Lucy listened, speechless. What had happened? Was he panicking? Why the South of France? Sure, she knew how much he loved the place, but why now, all of a sudden?

'If you say yes, we'll leave next year,' he challenged her. He leant over her again and gave her a kiss. 'Or would you rather stay here?'

'No, no! But I can't make up my mind so quickly . . .'

Lucy could not figure out what lay behind his decision. Was he planning in fact to set up a new life, a different life? And for her, this raised a further question: was she really prepared to leave her country and join him? She would rather have set off for the village and sorted out these questions on her own. Would he build an electric fence around his French castle? Would he still need to have his 38mm handy whenever he left the house and walked round the grounds?

'That's a whole new prospect,' she answered, with some deliberation. 'This all comes as a complete surprise, do you understand? Out here, you live up the hill and I live down below. We've seen a lot of each other, spent time with each other and made love. Moving away would mean we live together, twenty-four hours a day. Have you really considered what that would mean?'

'To be quite frank,' Red smiled at the suggestion, 'I haven't thought through all the implications. But the idea has its attractions, so far as I'm concerned . . .'

'And when will you finish off these jobs?'

Red went up to Lucy and took her in his arms. 'Since when have you been interested in my business? I don't know . . . perhaps sooner than you think. I shall be flying off to London for a few days to meet some colleagues. If you're bored here you could fly later. And then I shall be standing by for a phone call from France, where you could join me, since I have only planned a couple of short meetings there. Meanwhile, you might look around some suitable real estate, if you wish.'

'When do you fly to France?' asked Lucy.

'The timetable for France has not yet been agreed, but I'll be flying to England the day after tomorrow, if everything goes according to plan.' He stroked her blonde hair. She closed her eyes and started to undo his shirt buttons again. This time he offered no resistance.

# 14

The aircraft engines on the New York–London Flight BA112 purred gently. All the passengers had settled down comfortably into their seats; some were already asleep. From time to time a stewardess walked along the aisle to check if they had any special requests.

For over an hour Edward had also been trying to fall asleep. He did not succeed, although he was exhausted. The events of the last days and weeks revolved round and round in his mind's eye like a film. One of the recurring images was of Sir David's features as he explained the instructions now passed down to him and his department. Edward searched for a suitable description to match Sir David's facial expression. He had conveyed the information coldly and soberly, without the slightest hint of regret in his voice. His eyes had been fixed on the centre of the round table; he had remained stony-faced, his hands folded. Edward wondered what thoughts had been in the man's mind at that time. Who had commissioned the assignment on which they had been briefed?

Having spent almost ten years in his department, Edward was familiar with Sir David's opinion of Princess Diana. Outwardly extremely conservative, he had an open mind so far as progress was concerned, provided he saw it made sense. He welcomed Diana's natural, easygoing manner as a positive development for the Royal Family and the monarchy. Andrew Morton's biography, however, had made him very sceptical, and also the later details of telephone communications between Diana and this James Gilbey. Edward was not quite sure, himself, what had unsettled Sir David most, the contents of the revelations or the fact that they had been leaked to the public.

When Anna Pasternak's book, *Princess in Love*, was published two years later, Sir David was beside himself with indignation. The news of Diana's interview with the BBC, Edward now worked out, must have been the final straw for Sir David. At the time he had been extremely tight-lipped about the programme, but the very next day he was unambiguous. 'One can understand why she should wish to take on the Establishment or petition for divorce. But I am at a complete loss to understand why she chooses to do so in this manner!'

That interview had converted Sir David into an outspoken advocate for a Royal divorce. When the Princess eventually announced that she was basically in agreement with the divorce solution, some two months later, he broke the news to them with obvious relish. He even seemed to approve of the fact that a joint custody settlement had been agreed, which was previously unthinkable. From that moment on, the Diana problem had been solved for Sir David and his team; no one thought that a new Diana problem was to follow so soon.

Just a few weeks after the divorce, rumours were spreading about some of Diana's new affairs. Confidential minutes were circulated but were largely ignored, although the name of Imameddin Fayed, whose father Mohamed was a red rag for the Royal Family and every loyal Briton, had already cropped up. The bomb finally detonated at the beginning of the previous month, when it was announced that Diana planned to spend a few days in St Tropez with her children, at the villa of Fayed's father. Sir David had instructed Arthur to fly there and keep watch on Diana and the children. What he put together from Arthur's reports and comments from St Tropez about the yacht *Jonikal* shook Edward rigid, even though by then he felt the Princess was entitled to a fairly free-wheeling, uninhibited lifestyle. But in the company of her lover and in front of the children – that was just too

much for anyone to take! He had a few nagging doubts as
to whether Arthur might not have exaggerated certain facts
here and there, since he could not abide her. Besides, he had
the feeling for some time now that Arthur had an eye on his
own job, if ever he should succeed Sir David. It was quite
conceivable that Arthur had embroidered the details a little in
his reports.

As the stewardess came down the aisle, Edward waved
to her. 'Could I have a mineral water, please?' She nodded
and went away. He looked at his wrist-watch and adjusted
it carefully to London time.

# 15

Flight BA002 was due in shortly before 18.00 hours but was half an hour late. Edward was sitting, waiting patiently in the Terminal 4 lounge at Heathrow Airport. As usual at this time of day, there was a lot of hustle and bustle. Queues were forming at the car-hire counters.

Edward gathered from the arrival board that Red, now travelling under the identity of a businessman called Avraham Rosenzweig, would have just landed. Edward kept an eye open for him but could not pick him out from the crowd of passengers filing out of the exit gates. Tall as he was, Edward stood on tiptoe to get a better view over the heads of the crowd. Red was nowhere to be seen. Edward glanced furtively over his shoulder at a man in motor-cyclists' gear complete with helmet, shrugged his shoulders, and looked over again in the direction of the automatic doors.

After a further ten minutes the crowd had dispersed. The passengers now came out one by one. Edward consulted his watch nervously. Perhaps Red had missed his flight at the last minute. To make doubly sure, he decided to have Mr Rosenzweig's name called out. Just as he was walking over to the information desk, Red appeared in the arrival lounge, grinning all over his face. In his left hand he carried a small leather suitcase, in his right a large metal case with stout locks. Since their last meeting Red had grown a designer beard; he wore casual clothing.

'I thought you might have missed the flight.' Edward welcomed him, stretching out his hand.

'Not just yet, please. I've got a good grip on the case and

I'd like to put it down as soon as possible. Maybe straight into the car boot, assuming you drove here.'

'Of course, but we've got to go some distance on foot,' answered Edward, his eye on the metal trunk. 'Why didn't you take a trolley?'

'I was delayed at the customs, since I had to declare this thing as merchandise. My DIY tool box. Do you follow me?' He glanced down. 'Luggage trolleys are not padded and I've got some sensitive items inside. I prefer to carry it; it's easier that way.'

That made sense to Edward. 'Come, let's take turns.' He reached for the handle. Red pulled it closer. 'No, let's just walk a little bit faster.'

They moved off.

'Did you have an enjoyable flight?' Edward asked.

'I always enjoy my flights. As soon as the plane takes off, I fall asleep. I find flying just too boring for words.'

'Did the papers arrive in good order?' Edward enquired discreetly.

'No problem; everything's in good shape,' grinned Red. 'I just think it's a pity you had to make a Jewish businessman out of me. I may not be able to carry it off.'

'Don't worry. We've found you a very modest hotel. No bar, no night-life. It doesn't matter whether you're a Jew or a businessman. The hotel is strategically situated between Hyde Park and Regent's Park: Lincoln House Hotel, Gloucester Place, near Oxford Street. I don't know whether you'd like to hire a car . . .'

Avraham Rosenzweig, alias Red, shook his head vigorously. 'No, no! I just hate driving on the left. I can still recall the London tube system. Surely you don't want me to chase around the streets of London?'

Edward laughed, looking around as casually as he could. 'No, you can use the underground as often as you wish. For business travel, my colleague Walter is at your disposal as chauffeur.' With a quick glance Edward saw they were followed by the man in the motor-cyclists' gear. 'The nearest tube station to your hotel would be Marble Arch.'

They had now arrived at the parking floor. Edward wove his way purposefully through the parked vehicles. Red followed him, cursing gently as he raised and lowered the metal case, to avoid knocking mudguards and side-mirrors with his luggage.

They finally reached Edward's car, a black, oldish four-door Rover. Edward opened the boot, Red lifted the metal case and placed it inside. From the way the car sank, Edward could guess how heavy it must be. He gave Red a sympathetic look. 'These are tools of the trade that I can't do without,' Red said curtly. 'I've made almost all of them myself. That's my problem!' Deftly, he tossed the other case inside.

As Edward revved up the engine, a large motor cycle sped by. Edward pointed at the cyclist. 'That's my colleague, Walter. He came along so that he could see what you looked like. When he picks you up from the hotel, he'll be bringing you a similar helmet. All these helmets are radio-linked.'

'Why doesn't your colleague remove it? Is he shy, or just ugly?' asked Red in his direct manner.

'Both.' Edward was serious. 'Besides, he's not really interested if he's recognized or not. So you'll just have to put up with my own face.'

By this time, Edward had driven the Rover on to the road. Thick traffic raced by. At last, a car made way for them. It was stop and start all the way past the building sites, along the M4 in the direction of the city.

'And you still won't tell me who I'm working for?' asked Red abruptly.

Edward was roused from his thoughts. 'No. I've been quite clear on this point. I think I've told you often enough that this is irrelevant, so far as you and your assignment are concerned.'

Edward's tone was slightly edgy. Red threw up both hands, as if to calm him down.

'OK, OK! I only thought you might be a little more relaxed here in London.'

There was a longish pause.

'How's Lucy?' asked Edward after a while.

'Fine, thanks. Lucy's always fine. At least, so long as I'm near,' Red added. 'She's a sweet girl. She asks no questions and that suits me, as you'll appreciate.'

'Where does she think you are right now?'

'I told her I'd be doing a sort of round trip, visiting old friends and so on.' Red stroked his stubble, pulled a pair of sun-glasses out of his breast pocket and put them on.

'So all this time Lucy has never even asked you what you do for a living?'

'No, she never has. But to understand that, you'll need to know how we met.'

'Is that a secret?' Edward looked into the side-mirror and changed lanes.

'No, it's not a secret. It all happened some years ago now. I used to go shopping down in the village every fortnight. I'd then call in at Roy's Bar and knock back a couple of whiskies. That day it was damned hot and I'd had more than a couple. As I came out into the street, I realized I was not in a fit state to drive. So I got inside the car and tried to sleep it off. Then, suddenly I saw this young girl standing there, on the other side of the street, surrounded by suitcases. She looked as if she'd just missed a Greyhound coach. I jumped out and offered her hospitality if she was prepared to drive me home. I can't recall much else. Next day, I woke up to a wonderful aroma of ham and eggs. Not in my own bed, but on the couch in a strange apartment. Lucy had rented it and I found out that she had been waiting for the Indian the previous day; he was supposed to drive her to her new apartment. We spent the day together and decided we liked one another. At some stage I asked her what the hell she was doing in that ass-hole of a place, and she simply said, 'My life till now has been shit and I've had enough.' I never enquired further about her life and I was happy to have a reason not to tell her anything about mine. So two people without a past met and they both just live for the present.'

Edward had now turned into Park Lane. The evening sun was setting over Hyde Park to their left. Edward pointed in that direction. 'There's a road called Broad Walk that runs parallel to this street. You see the trees over there; that's where we meet whenever we need to. It's roughly ten minutes' walk from your hotel. We shall always meet on Broad Walk between Hyde Park Corner and the underground garage. Will you please make a mental note?'

Red nodded and murmured: 'Broad Walk . . . underground garage . . . Hyde Park Corner.'

'I'll put you down at the corner of George Street and Gloucester Place. We shouldn't really be seen together. You are now on your own. In the glove compartment you'll find enough money for the next few days, a street map of London and confirmation of the hotel reservation. A firm called Barthley and Sons Ltd made the reservation for you.'

Red opened the glove compartment and took out a large envelope, which he opened immediately. Inside, he found ten thousand pounds, the street map and a hotel reservation confirmation for Avraham Rosenzweig, New York, for an indefinite period.

He gave a satisfied nod. 'How far do I have to drag my luggage?'

'It's only a few yards from the street corner to the hotel. By the way, you'll find a phone number on the back of the street map. That's how you can reach me or my answering machine. Walter and I check it regularly. Just in case you ever need to contact us.'

Red grinned. 'I won't find that number in the phone book, I'm sure!'

'Hardly,' answered Edward coldly and drew over to edge of the pavement. They got out and Edward opened the boot. Red placed both cases next to him on the pavement.

'When will I be hearing from you again?'

Edward handed him a small leather holdall that had been lying in the boot. 'This is yours now. Inside you'll find a mobile phone, two additional headphones and a battery charger. Please remember, you're to keep this on your person, switched on at all times. Otherwise, you can do as you please.'

They parted with a firm handshake. 'To a successful partnership!'

Edward climbed into the Rover and drove off. Red pulled the strap of the holdall over his shoulder and, with a sigh, grabbed hold of his metal case.

# 16

The hotel, as Edward had said, was only a few yards from the road junction on the left-hand side. An undistinguished house with three or four paved steps up to the entrance. It was rather tight and narrow inside. Red was always reluctant to leave his case unattended, but he found it impossible to drag it down the narrow stairs to the reception desk in the basement. "Reception" proved to be something of an overstatement. It turned out to be a tiny little bar, behind which an Asian lady was sitting. To the left of the reception desk was the entrance to a small breakfast room; above it hung a sort of ship's bell, which would have made a deafening din in that small, enclosed space.

The registration procedures went quite smoothly. Red, alias Avraham Rosenzweig, had to make a down payment, since the room was booked for an indefinite period. He then forced himself back up the stairs, grabbed hold of his case and dragged it one flight higher, to his room.

This was just as tiny and narrow as everything else in the hotel, but somehow quite friendly and comfortable. He quickly unpacked his leather case. As a rule, he never packed much clothing when travelling. If something went missing, he would buy it on the spot.

He opened the metal case briefly to take out his own mobile. It was guaranteed bug-proof, developed and tested by the Israeli secret service – a souvenir from a successful job during the Gulf War. He put the case in the cupboard, unopened.

He considered whether to lie down for a bit or to go for a

short walk to revive himself after the long flight. He decided
to go for a stroll, put Edward's money into his wallet and both
mobiles into his jacket. He then left the room.

Downstairs, at the reception desk, he enquired if there
was a good restaurant in the neighbourhood. The Asian lady
mentioned a few. Red decided upon Le Gavroche in Upper
Brook Street, which was apparently near the hotel and quite
easy to find.

As he left the hotel, the sultry air hit him; he could
hear the gentle, distant rumblings of a thunderstorm to the
south-west of the city. Red lingered as he passed the Churchill
InterContinental, casting an envious glance into the foyer. At
Oxford Street he caught sight of the bus stop sign for Marble
Arch. Edward was right; his hotel was strategically placed. He
decided to make a slight detour so as to familiarize himself
with Edward's agreed meeting point in Hyde Park.

He noticed some lightning flashes in the distance and
descended into the pedestrian underpass at Edgware Road,
where Oxford Street widens out into Bayswater Road. He
strolled along Bayswater Road, away from the centre of town,
observing the crowds coming in the opposite direction. They
all gave the impression that they were hurrying back home
before it began to rain. Lights were switched on everywhere,
as the thunder clouds brought on the darkness.

At the traffic-lights a few hundred yards on, Red walked
over to the other side of the street into Hyde Park. A cluster
of black clouds was now hovering over the Park, the sky
illuminated by powerful flashes of lightning. He asked an
old man the way to Broad Walk. Apparently there were
a number of routes. The man waved his arm in several
different directions, so Red decided to take a short cut across
the Park.

He was now walking at a brisk pace because of the threatening storm, but still managed to take in the surroundings. As
usual, whenever he prepared himself for action, he sketched
out a careful plan of the location in his mind. Significant

features were noted and stored in his mental file. Trivial aspects were ignored. This was the system Red had himself developed in situations where he had no time to prepare himself beforehand by studying a map or a street plan.

As he neared Broad Walk the first drops of rain splattered. He spoke to a young woman who had just opened her umbrella, awkwardly battling against the gusts of wind, and was pleasantly surprised to learn that Upper Brook Street was only one block away from Park Lane. Quickening his pace, he left the Park. As he arrived at the corner of Upper Brook Street, the rain came down in buckets. A few yards along a row of houses to the right he saw the sign, *Le Gavroche*. Only a glass panel distinguished the entrance to the restaurant from the surrounding buildings.

Red needed all his powers of persuasion to get a seat in the tiny restaurant. If they really were completely booked out, as the head waiter had assured him, a client must have cancelled at the last minute because of the oncoming storm. Ordering an apéritif, he then began to study the menu, ignoring the expensive prices; even for Londoners they must have been near the upper limit. He decided on a four-course meal.

Even before soup was served one of the mobile phones rang. Edward announced himself at the other end to enquire if he had found the hotel to his liking, asking him in the same breath to meet him at five p.m. the following day at their prearranged meeting point. Once the conversation was over, he took out his own mobile, dialled a multi-digit number and then left a message on the answerphone at the other end.

'This is Red speaking. Today is Tuesday, twenty thirty hours, London time. I had hoped to get through to you at this time. It's all going according to plan. They have found me a small, third-class hotel, but everything is OK. I shall find us both something better in the area tomorrow. Stand by to fly over in about three days' time. I'll phone again tomorrow evening. But please don't try to contact me. I can't be sure, but I might be involved in some important negotiations, in which case I must *not* be disturbed.'

Red switched off and replaced the mobile. At this moment, the waiter came to the table with a plate of soup; it had an exquisite aroma of garlic.

# 17

Red woke the following morning to bright sunshine. He ate, with some distaste, a rather sparse English breakfast in the basement room, having persuaded himself to take breakfast in future at a fast food restaurant he had noted close to the Marble Arch bus stop.

To while away the hours until midday, he decided to revive his local knowledge by studying his own street map of London in some detail. Around 11 a.m. he quit the hotel and made off in the direction of Marble Arch, from where sightseeing tours by double-decker left every quarter of an hour.

Red sat down in the last available seat on the open deck of a white and red bus and looked around at the other passengers, all of them devoutly listening to the monologue of the tour guide. He was soon absorbed in thoughts of his own. Could this assignment in fact be connected with the Royal Family? In his mind he conjured up the well-known faces of the English ruling party, the Opposition, the Army, the Royal Household and business leaders. Perhaps it might be a person who was expected to visit London in the next few days. The longer he thought about it, the more convinced he became that this new idea could be the right one. He simply had to discover what organization Edward belonged to – evidently one that was ready to shell out a cool million to eliminate the target person. It was not a simple case of a cuckolded husband or a jealous wife. That was obvious. This was a high-level matter – but how high?

After about an hour and a half's drive through the city, he got out again at Marble Arch. He selected one of the numerous food shops in the area and bought two generously-filled sandwiches. He wandered down Park Lane, munching as he walked, and put on his sun-glasses, even though it had just clouded over. At about two thirty, he walked into the elegant foyer of the Dorchester Hotel. His eyes slowly adapted to the indirect lighting inside, through his dark glasses.

'I shall need a double room as from next weekend for an indefinite period. But I'm only interested in a room with a view over Hyde Park.'

With an engaging smile, the young dark-haired girl at the reception desk shook her head. 'I am very sorry, Sir. But we are completely booked, especially on the Park side.'

Red moved his sun-glasses towards the tip of his nose and returned her friendly smile. Simultaneously, his left hand discreetly moved towards the young girl's right hand; he slipped a fifty-pound note into her fingers. She blushed, skilfully dealing with the note. 'I'll see what I can do, Sir!'

'You're in luck, Sir. We've just had a cancellation for a suite. Would you kindly . . . ?'

'Well, well! I thought so!' Red pushed his sun-glasses back on to the bridge of his nose. 'The reservation is for Mr Rosenzweig, Avraham Rosenzweig.'

'Would you kindly complete the reservation form and sign it?'

Red picked up the form, filled in Avraham Rosenzweig's personal details and handed it back to the young girl.

'We welcome you at the Dorchester as from Saturday, Mr Rosenzweig!'

He gave a friendly nod and left the hotel. Relying on his memory, he then set off in the direction of Piccadilly. Half an hour later he reached Old Bond Street and headed straight for Sulfa, the gentleman's outfitters, where he had once bought clothes some years ago. Feeling the quality of the various suiting materials, he remembered all those smart clothes hanging in his wardrobe back home, waiting for him to lose a few pounds of weight. Red selected two suits to try on. As he entered the cubicle, one of the mobile phones rang. He swiftly drew the curtain and answered.

'Yes, please.' His face clouded over. 'I did ask you especially not to contact me . . .' He was interrupted and waited patiently. 'OK,' he replied, quickly and quietly. 'So you arrive on Saturday. A suite at the Dorchester has been reserved under the name of Avraham Rosenzweig. You'd better put that down. I'll be along sometime. Bye.'

Visibly annoyed, he put the mobile back and applied his mind to the matter of clothing. He decided on a lightweight two-piece suit. His bill included a couple of matching shirts and a hideously expensive silk tie. He crossed over from Sulka to Bally, the shoe shop, where he completed his purchases with a pair of summer casuals.

Red took a taxi to Park Lane and asked the driver to wait for him near the car park, where he assumed Edward would leave his vehicle. There was no parking space available, so Red slipped the driver a twenty-pound note and asked him to park further up near the footbridge and wait for him there. In Hyde Park he found Edward at the agreed meeting place.

Edward greeted him. 'Did you have a pleasant day?'

Red pointed at his feet. 'I have been walking everywhere. It's good for the figure.'

Edward drew him aside so as to make way for a group of Japanese tourists, clustered around their tour guide.

'Red, our boss has asked us to set up a number of different plans so that we're prepared, in the worst case, to move into action at short notice. At this point, it looks as if we have time on our side. Walter will pick you up at your hotel at two p.m. He will drive you along several blocks, past a couple of buildings that I'd ask you to take note of very carefully. We shall then evaluate whether it's possible to arrange a natural accident in that area and then select the best alternative.'

'Edward, don't you find this all a little clumsy? I mean,

couldn't we simply agree when and where I carry out the job?'

Edward shook his head. 'I understand, please believe me. But this job is . . .' He paused. 'Let's leave it at that; that's how it has to be. Later, perhaps, you'll see why. Put it like this, this is not a straightforward task – neither for you, nor for us.'

In his choice of words, Edward sensed how badly he concealed his own feelings. The closer they came to zero-hour, the more anxious he felt that he would rather get someone else to do the dirty work.

His reactions were not lost on Red. He badly wanted to find out who it was who had commissioned the assignment. With a friendly gesture, he took hold of Edward's arm.

'OK, my friend, I'll go along with it. Is there anything else?'

By now Edward had pulled himself together. 'No. You go off with Walter tomorrow and I'll get in touch by mobile. What are you doing tonight?'

Red shrugged his shoulders.

'I can recommend the Grill Room over there at the Dorchester. Or do you prefer French cuisine? In that case, I'd suggest Chez Nico at Ninety, opposite the Grosvenor House Hotel.'

Red stared at Edward in surprise. Was he being followed, or was it simply by chance that Edward had recommended a restaurant in the Dorchester Hotel? And why did he mention his preference for French cuisine?

'But you do like French cooking, don't you?' said Edward, laughing.

'Are you spying on me?' asked Red testily.

Edward shook his head. 'No. What makes you think we are?'

'Because I went for a meal last night at a French restaurant.'

'I know.'

'So I'm being followed.'

'No, of course not, nor do we have any reason to. When I rang you yesterday evening, you talked so quietly that I could overhear one of the guests at the next table order his meal. A dish with *sauce provençale* doesn't sound very British to me!'

Red was still not convinced. 'So that's your explanation,' he replied. 'To be frank, I don't think it would do our working relationship any good if you feel you have to stick chewing-gum on the soles of my shoes.'

Edward stretched out his hand. 'Don't let that spoil your stay here in London! Things will soon start up in earnest.'

Red shook Edward's hand. 'It would be a pity if we both had to keep watch on each other. Maybe Chez Nico would not be such a bad idea, after all.' He turned round and made off towards the Park Lane underpass, Edward still gazing at him with an amused look on his face. Why should he need to keep tabs on Red?

Upon reaching the other side of Park Lane, Red stopped. He could just see Edward walk into the Park Lane garage, then break into a run. As he joined his taxi, he jumped inside and asked the driver to wait. He passed the bewildered driver another twenty-pound note and mumbled some excuse about having forgotten the address. Minutes later, Edward emerged from the garage in his black Rover. Red indicated the vehicle to the driver. 'Follow that car!'

The traffic was too dense for the taxi to move into line immediately. Red cursed to himself. His face lit up again as soon as he noticed Edward had changed direction and was now about to overtake them.

'Should we keep close on his tail?' asked the driver, changing down into first gear.

'No, keep a couple of car lengths' distance. But don't let him out of your sight!'

The taxi driver let the Rover move ahead and swung in four vehicles behind, in the slow-moving traffic. It moved in fits and starts along Knightsbridge, Old Brompton Road, Cromwell Road and Talgarth Road, towards Slough. When they hit the M4, they began to clock up the mileage. Red consulted his mental road map. The motorway bypassed Slough in the direction of Bristol. The Rover turned off the motorway after a few miles, and the taxi drew back a little. Suddenly, after a few bends, there was a long stretch of road; Edward's car had vanished.

Red ordered the driver to turn round and they slowly crawled back. At a bend to the left he caught sight of a narrow road. He told the driver to halt and got out. He sprinted along the road, lined with thick hedges on both sides, of his height. Just a hundred yards on he came to a large field, through which the road passed, and at the end of which were four houses. Edward's car was parked outside one of them. Red returned to the taxi and ordered the driver to take the route back towards London.

On the journey Red tried to figure out Edward's strange behaviour. Why all that drama? Standing by, accident scenarios, an utterly pointless rendezvous in the Park. As they turned off the M40, Red made up his mind. 'Take me to the nearest car hire.'

'Avis or Budget?' enquired the driver.

'I don't care!' came the reply.

# 18

Edward got up the next morning at six o'clock, as usual, and had breakfast with his mother. When he left home, at seven, he sensed the warm air; he felt sure that there would be another thunderstorm. He drove cautiously along the rather bumpy country road towards Marlow. Shortly after Marlow, he took the M40. In a little while he arrived at George Street, where he turned right into Gloucester Place. He stopped briefly outside Red's hotel. Leaving the engine running, he jumped out and ran up the steps to the hotel entrance. He rang several times at the intercom by the front door. A female voice answered in a disgruntled tone. 'Yes, please?'

'Has Mr Rosenzweig left?'

'Mr Rosenzweig had already left when I came on duty.'

'At what time was that?'

'About six o'clock, Sir.'

Edward quickly turned round and ran back to his car. He might have guessed.

He drove off towards Marylebone Road and dialled a number on the car phone.

'Morning, Red, did I wake you up?'

'No,' came the answer over the receiver. 'You know perfectly well I've been following you one hundred yards to the rear. Why do you ask?'

Edward gave a grin. 'It was you, wasn't it, who was banging on yesterday about chewing-gum and shoe soles?'

It was some minutes before Red replied. 'Edward, I underestimated you.'

'OK, Red. Let's leave it at that!' Edward laid up the receiver on the magnetic holder and shot off. In the rear-view mirror he saw a black Mercedes, which got slower and slower and finally headed off in a different direction.

# 19

Walter was already waiting for him at the office with the message that Sir David had called an urgent meeting for 11 o'clock. 'Perhaps it's going to speed up more quickly than we thought.' Walter moved his chair to an upright position and put both feet on the desk. 'Work it out. During school holidays William and Harry have spent more or less all the time with their father. Diana came back from the *Jonikal*, but, so far as I am aware, there are no plans for a visit to Balmoral.'

'Have Arthur and George managed to find out about any of Diana's other engagements in the meantime?' Edward had switched on his computer and was entering all the code numbers and code names. It was some time before it gave access to the data he was searching for. 'All I have in her calendar for the current period are an art exhibition and her date at the opera.'

'Yes, Arthur mentioned something about plans for a long trip, though he didn't know exactly when. But he'll be at Sir David's meeting.'

'Do you think George will last out?' asked Edward suddenly.

Walter removed his feet from the desk and stood up. He walked, with some hesitation, towards the window. 'I think we'll have to keep an eye on him.'

Edward examined the data on his screen. 'I'll work more closely with him, so that I can keep him under better control.' He flicked over to a new page. 'Have you read the latest file on old Al Fayed?'

Instead of replying, Walter came over and looked over Edward's shoulder. 'Who is this chap Dartevelle?'

Edward turned back a few pages. 'So far as I can recall, he's one of Al Fayed's lawyers.'

Walter slapped him on the shoulder. 'That's right. I have read or heard his name before. Perhaps the old man has something like a marriage settlement in mind for his son.'

'Maybe. Arthur should check that out.'

Edward's phone rang. He lifted the receiver. 'Yes?' He nodded and hung up. 'The meeting has been put forward. I smell something's burning. I won't be able to write my report until this afternoon.'

'Any new information?' asked Walter as they left the room.

'No, not so far. Only that Red tried to tail me this morning. I had a feeling he would, after yesterday's meeting.'

'And?'

'Nothing.' Edward gave a laugh. 'I saw through him and he knows it.'

'Is my meeting with him at twelve today still on?' Walter enquired. Edward just gave a nod and shut the office door behind him.

# 20

Sir David was waiting impatiently for Walter and Edward, George and Arthur having already taken their seats at the round table.

'Gentlemen,' began Sir David, as soon as Walter and Edward had arrived, 'I have to give you certain information that from now on will have an important bearing on our task. As from now we have support from an unexpected source, which should prove to be very useful. I have just learned that the Special Air Service, for some time now, has an undercover colleague in Mohamed Al Fayed's inner circle. Our SAS colleague will pass on information to us at all times, with immediate effect. His special brief, so far as we are concerned, is to pass on the latest data concerning Princess Diana and this Imameddin fellow. Direct contact between this colleague and ourselves has been approved at highest level. But . . .' – there was a pregnant pause – 'this person's mission is quite different. Absolute discretion should be exercised as a matter of priority. If his cover were blown, years and years of work would be wasted.'

Edward put up his hand. 'Sir David, if direct contact is such a risk, how can we be sure we don't come to grief?'

Sir David welcomed the question. 'A relevant point. You will all find specific instructions on your computer message desks as from tomorrow. By then they should have been agreed with our contact man via the SAS. You will appreciate that this might take a little while.'

# 21

At two o'clock sharp, Walter arrived at Red's hotel on his large BMW motorbike. As previously agreed by Edward, he was wearing a leather suit and matching helmet. A twin helmet was attached to the pillion by a leather strap.

After his frustrating experience that morning, Red had carried on driving in his hired car and had made a second trip around town. He had driven down the Haymarket and bought a classic trench coat at Burberry's. Wearing this coat, he had returned to the hotel and was now waiting outside. Walter beckoned him over and passed him the helmet, glad that he could not be seen grinning at Red. He cut an amusing figure with his classic coat and the black helmet. Walter switched on the radio for him.

'My name's Walter. Edward will have mentioned that we are planning a little round trip for today. Is the volume OK?'

Red gave a nod. 'Sure, I can hear you loud and clear. But couldn't you get hold of a leather suit or something similar for me next time we are to go for a drive?' He had obviously noticed the reactions of pedestrians hurrying past; they were turning back at him, with smiles on their faces.

Walter pacified him. 'You don't look half as bad as you think. Besides, it's quite a good idea for you to look smart – we'll be calling at an art gallery and also be visiting the opera.' He had meanwhile started up the motor. 'Take a seat. Hang on to the leather straps on both sides on my jacket and hold on tight.'

Red swung over on to the seat behind Walter and took hold. 'Everything in order?'

'OK.'

Walter raced through the London traffic with incredible speed. Red clung on to his jacket. He had not bargained for this sort of driving.

'How long have you been working with Edward?' asked Red, trying to distract himself.

'I can't remember exactly. It must be nearly five years now.'

'In the Falklands as well?'

'No. I was apprenticed as a motor mechanic and took part in motor-cycle rallies.'

'I can well believe you,' Red let slip. 'And how did you get into this job?'

Just behind a church, which Red glimpsed from a frighteningly acute angle, Walter drove into a narrow street.

'Well, that's a long, boring story. Besides, we're already there.' Walter drew his motor-cycle up to the pavement and switched off the motor.

'Keep your helmet on, so that we stay in touch. We are now in the London art gallery district. In this area alone there are at least ten or more galleries within a radius of a few hundred yards. We'll concentrate on that building.' Walter pointed across to the opposite side of the street. Red's attention was drawn to a narrow, older-style four-storey building. At street level, two imposing windows extended along its full width, separated by a small entrance.

Red nodded.

'I'll wait for you here. Go in and take your time. We think it has good prospects. Besides, it's got a very old lift.'

'I understand,' said Red. 'Will our target be arriving alone?'

'No, always with other people. I don't know precisely what Edward has told you. But on occasions like this, our target never appears without company.'

'Bodyguards?'

'I said "company"; that must suffice. Now you can remove your helmet. I'll wait here.'

Red handed Walter his helmet and entered the gallery. The interior, as seen from the street, looked quite modest but, inside, turned out to be a most impressive venue, displaying the works of talented young artists. Red strode casually through the rooms, studying a number of the objects with interest. Apart from himself and an elderly but visibly well-to-do lady, the only other person present was a smartly-dressed woman in her mid-forties, evidently responsible for sales and advice. Red slowly wandered over to the lift, which he had immediately spotted at the far end of the rooms.

'Are you interested in anything in particular?' enquired the saleswoman.

Red made a gesture, as though he wanted to go upstairs.

On the first floor the atmosphere was a little livelier. A number of small groups of individual exhibitors were standing near a young man, apparently some sort of guard. Red focused his attention on an imposing oil portrait to the right of the lift. Pretending to study its brushwork and draughtsmanship, he sat down on a stool opposite, sunk in thought.

He was reflecting on ways and means of arranging a fatal accident. His impression was that the rooms were well-attended. The lift was indeed quite ancient and must have a number of weak points. But would the target person use this tiny four-man lift? Only in case of leg or knee injury or old age, he considered. The staircase was also hardly appropriate for a contrived accident.

Red was suddenly aware that his own creative abilities must be brought into play. This gallery was not ideal for an accident. He shook his head and stood up. No, it was totally unsuitable. Why not a large hotel? Perhaps the target person did skiing or other risky sports – activities which offered better opportunities. Here, he decided, you could only use poison or firearms to be effective. And for that they did not need his know-how.

Red left the gallery. Across the street, Walter was holding the helmet ready for him. Red put it on and gave vent to his concerns.

'OK, if you want to treat me like a child, carry on! That's fine by me. It's you who are paying. But you're not making use of my expertise and I'm not simply here for a joy ride. What's the big event in that gallery, anyway?'

Walter quickly turned down the volume on his receiver. 'Red, If you can't speak to me normally, I'll have to switch off. I didn't choose the shop and I've never been inside. You take that up with Edward.'

'Then you go inside and take a look. Am I supposed to rip the paintings off the wall or knock down figurines? You asked for a perfect accident, didn't you? Then organize some balloon trip and I'll fix a gas explosion, or else arrange a helicopter flight and I'll slash the blades. But please, please, not an art gallery!'

'There'll be a reception at the gallery shortly. Our key figure will be present . . .'

Red interrupted him. 'Very well, I'll repeat myself. Nothing will work there. Now where do we go?'

Walter mounted his motorbike and revved up. 'Jump on. We're off to the Opera House.'

'The Royal Opera House?'

'No, the English National Opera. Covent Garden is being renovated at the moment, so far as I know.'

'But that would be ideal. Building sites are always perfect. Bring our target along and I'll guarantee you one hundred per cent success.'

Walter moved off. 'I'll go into that suggestion. Perhaps it's feasible. But first we call by at the National Opera.'

They were both silent during the journey. Red had not quite calmed down and Walter was deep in his own thoughts. It would certainly be simpler to get Red to arrange an accident

of some description here in London and find an excuse to
entice Princess Diana to the spot than to fix something at
short notice around her timetable. But how could that be
realized in practice?

Walter stopped at the Post Office opposite the English
National Opera. He switched off, but Red made no sign that
he wanted to dismount. Instead he talked, this time a little
more relaxed. 'Walter, I don't really want to intrude. But it's
pointless for me to look over the opera house now. Unless
you can tell me which entrance my target will use, which
seat he'll be sitting on and whether he'll go on stage.'

'I simply can't,' admitted Walter. 'At least not now.'

'In that case there's no sense in casing the joint. I am used
to working fast; I am familiar with most types of equipment.
It makes no difference to me if an arc light crashes, if a steel
frame collapses or the electric wiring snaps. But I have to
know the answers to specific questions, such as where, how,
when and why. Do you get me? I think Edward has got it
wrong. He didn't engage me as a circus clown, did he?'

'Certainly not. You can assume we can also do this type
of work on our own. Well, we needed an experienced
practitioner who, for special reasons, could not be engaged
from inside . . .'

'In that case you should treat me with more respect,'
grunted Red. He slapped Walter on the shoulder, trying
to placate him. 'Can I make a suggestion?'

'OK.'

'Take me along streets or routes you know this person uses
regularly. Even outside London, so far as I'm concerned. I
shall look them over and tell you within a couple of days how
we do it. And you leave it to me whether some dilapidated
patio falls down just by chance, or a bridge collapses due to
metal fatigue, or else a tank unexpectedly crushes the person's
automobile, simply because the driver is drunk or has gone
berserk with the controls.'

'That's fine, Red, but let's move. You've simply got to

understand that I cannot and will not show you any place that might provide a clue to that person's identity.'

Red laughed. 'That's your problem. I think it's too stupid for words!'

'You're not the only one who shares that view.' Walter looked over his shoulder and drove off.

'Take care, Walter! Otherwise I might just be able to guess who's behind this job!'

# 22

The mobile rang just after eight o'clock and woke Red up. Half-asleep, he groped around, and picked up the wrong one. Leaning out of the bed, he eventually grabbed the smaller phone. 'Yes?'

At the other end of the line, Edward greeted him. 'Not tailing me from behind, then?' he asked, sarcastically.

Red was not inclined to start a dispute at this time of day. He simply said nothing, as though he did not quite understand.

'Walter told me last night that you were a little unhappy. Maybe we should meet today and thrash this matter out together, in peace and quiet.'

Red gave a healthy yawn and leaned back on the pillow, the mobile clasped to his ear. 'I've nothing planned for today, that is, unless you've added churches to my list.'

Instead of an answer, Red detected that Edward was covering the mouthpiece and was now speaking to someone else. He could not understand one word. Then Edward came on the line again. 'OK, Red. Let's meet for lunch.'

'To be frank, I'd rather eat in the evening. But a sandwich or a salad would be fine by me. Why not make me a proposal that might wake me up?'

'Let's go out to Greenwich. I know an old pub on the Thames there. Then I'll show you round the Royal Naval College, where I did some of my training. I shall see that they give us a quiet room, in case we can't have a reasonable discussion at the pub.'

'Very well. At what time shall we meet there?'

'Have you still got your Mercedes?'

'No.'

'Then I'll pick you up around half past eleven, assuming you'll have slept out by then.'

Red refrained from answering and mumbled, 'I'll be waiting for you at the corner.'

He pressed the "off" button and tossed the mobile behind the pillow.

Now that he was awake, Red decided to go for a stroll in the fresh air. He got up and drew aside the curtains. The sky was overcast and grey but there was no sign of rain. He took a shower, put on one of his new shirts, his two-piece suit and his new loafers, leaving the hotel with his trench coat under his arm. This time, he made off in the direction of Regent's Park, which evoked pleasant memories for him. Crossing Marylebone Road, he noticed that Madame Tussaud's had just opened. Although he had been in London several times before, he had never managed to visit the waxwork museum, either for lack of time or else because of the crowds of tourists. At this time of day – just after ten – the queue was negligible. Perhaps he would recognize his future victim in the first room, or even one of his previous victims.

# 23

Edward had now completed his report on the computer. There was a knock at the door and George walked in. 'Am I disturbing you?'

'Come in and sit down. I've just put the finishing touches to my report. You can read it through. Our partner is getting impatient. I shall be meeting him for lunch today.'

George drew his chair up and sat next to Edward at the desk. 'Can I take it that our conversation is absolutely confidential?'

Edward looked at him with astonishment. 'Has there ever been any need to ask?'

George shook his head. 'No, of course not. But I am in a dilemma and need your help. Who else should I talk to? I can't talk to anyone outside these four walls; besides, Arthur, and even Sir David . . .'

'No, George, it's good that you came to me. I can imagine what's bothering you.'

'Diana!'

'I know. And I hope you've noticed that I'm not wildly excited about carrying out a job under these circumstances, without some reservations. You must be aware of the danger she exposes us to, as well as I am. OK, when it comes to espionage or terrorism or weapon dealers and political fanatics, it's a different situation altogether; the danger is evident and can be evaluated. Diana is on a higher level and, besides, she is also a highly attractive and desirable woman. I can understand why men run after her. I can well understand why she has lovers. After the loneliness of all those years, love is a sort of drug for her. I can also understand why she has left Charles. The problem is her role in this country and especially the role of her children, who will represent Great Britain at the head of the Royal Family.'

George stared at Edward with astonishment.

'I never knew . . .'

'. . . that I felt that way?' Edward asked. 'I ask myself repeatedly, why. Why? At what point do we reach the pain threshold, beyond which we can go no further? Who knows if her liaison with this Egyptian is not just a passing affair like all the others? In two or three weeks' time we may all be laughing. But who is the next on her list? Just suppose this is not simply a trivial affair. Imagine the damage that she will then have caused the Crown, the country and the rest of us. Sometimes I think that when she married Charles, we all hoped and prayed for a change in the monarchy and made a saint out of her. And then the media and the Royal Family reduced her to the level of a whore.'

Edward said all this in a quiet, almost impassive voice. 'We Brits have a tendency always to praise a person to the skies and then send them to hell. Diana is the peak of perfection. Perhaps that is her mortal offence. And what is worse, she has no chance to escape from the limelight. If it weren't for the children and the media, her life would not be in danger.'

'But does it have to be our department . . .' George broke in, 'Does it have to be *us* who pull the noose tight?'

For the first time, Edward avoided George's eyes. He turned to his computer and fiddled with the keyboard. 'One has to take a balanced view of the case as a whole. Action can only be sanctioned and executed at the very highest level, so that as few people as possible are involved. And I am very glad we have found Red and that it is not us who . . .' He left the sentence unfinished.

The emotion in Edward's voice had not escaped George's notice. He stood up and took hold of Edward by the hand.

'Thank you for being open with me,' he said quietly. 'It's of great comfort to know exactly how you feel.'

'It's a mad, mad world,' Edward replied. He stared at his hands. 'This same hand sealed our contract with Red.'

## 24

Red was hurrying along the last few yards of Gloucester Place, when he spotted Edward's Rover parked at the corner. He had lost track of time among all the waxwork figures and underestimated how long it took to get back. Panting a little, he jumped into the car and took a deep breath.

'Maybe you should have taken the Mercedes, after all. Tailing me is easier than running after me,' Edward joked. He realized that his joke had not gone down too well. 'Sorry, Red. I didn't mean it like that!'

Red said nothing. They took half an hour to cover a mere ten miles. Edward made a slight detour to point out the *Cutty Sark*, the finest tea clipper in the world, now a tourist attraction moored at Greenwich. They then drove round the Royal Naval College and stopped at the Trafalgar Tavern.

No sooner were they inside than it became apparent that there was no chance they could talk discreetly. The pub was packed tight. They made their way over to a couple of unoccupied stools at the bar. Edward sat Red down and called to him above the general din. 'We have to help ourselves to beer, so please make sure nobody takes my stool. I'm going to the car to make a quick phonecall.'

Red simply nodded and took a look at the people round about. It was only twelve o'clock but already the beer was in full flow; he had the impression that a number of the drinkers would have to write off the whole afternoon.

It was not long before Edward returned. 'Everything's under control. We'll proceed to the College afterwards. I still have one or two contacts from the past.' His eyes twinkled knowingly. He shoved Red rapidly into the dining room, where two seats had just become vacant.

'If you fancy some fish, I can warmly recommend Fisherman's Pie,' said Edward, consulting the menu. 'I recall this place from old times. Unfortunately, I don't visit Greenwich very often these days.'

'Then I'll join you in whatever you choose,' said Red and passed the young waitress a couple of empty plates from their table.

# 25

The creaking door opened on to a modest-looking room. It was not clear what its function was. Four square tables, each with four wooden chairs, were distributed quite arbitrarily around the room. Apart from that, there was no furniture to be seen. The two large bay windows had been furnished, not with blinds or curtains, but with a film of matt foil, stuck to the lower window panes. Everything was covered in layers of dust; the room was obviously hardly ever used. Edward took in Red's sceptical look; a little embarrassed, he took out a handkerchief from his trouser pocket and punctiliously flicked some dust off the table and a couple of chairs.

'I hope no conclusions about the educational standards of this establishment can be drawn from the amount of dust everywhere,' grinned Red. He cautiously sat down on one of the stools that had just been cleaned, nervous that it might not hold his weight. Edward went over to one of the windows and looked outside.

'Nothing much has changed, even out there,' he stated. He then turned round and sat down on the other stool he had dusted. Despite the outside temperature, it was almost chilly inside the room.

'Can we talk without being disturbed?' asked Red, evidently with some misgivings.

'Don't worry, we're on our own here in the wing. I use the College from time to time for confidential meetings. I have never been disturbed. We can't accept any risk, especially in this case.'

'Good, then let's start.' Red crossed his legs. 'I imagine

Walter will have given you a blow-by-blow account of my problems.'

'Of course!' Edward assured him. 'And not without justification. But I must kindly ask you for a little understanding.' He leant his arms on the table top. To be quite honest, our department was quite surprised to be given this assignment. As you've worked out, we're basically office executives. We work out ideas, concepts, strategy and so on, but, apart from some high-profile exceptions, we're never the executioners. But this case happens to be one of those exceptions.'

Red butted in. 'You still refuse to disclose your own identity and give me the name of our target?'

'No. I am under strictest orders. There are reasons. And please don't keep asking me all the time. You will find out at the very earliest at the end of the assignment, when you'll realize why it had to be the way it is. I tell you quite frankly, in all these years I have never felt so helpless as I do in this case. Let's leave it at that. It's a highly unusual case; it has so many emotional and problematical aspects.'

'OK, OK,' said Red, calmly. 'But one thing you've got to admit, in all honesty . . .'

'And what's that?'

Red looked at him squarely in the eyes. 'Is the IRA behind this?'

'No!' shouted Edward. He was clearly shocked at having raised his voice; he continued in a normal tone. 'I was not lying to you when I said I worked for the UK. Remember?'

Red nodded.

'You made Walter a sensible proposal and he drove you down a number of roads and along certain routes. Did you draw any conclusions?'

Red laughed. 'The trip with Walter was a mystery tour. We didn't see Buckingham Palace or Windsor Castle, nor did we go anywhere near Downing Street, Whitehall or the City. We didn't pass by any barracks or industrial sites . . .'

Edward broke in impatiently. 'Forget the target; concentrate on strategy.'

'I understand you. Now you try to understand me. I have to try and build peoples' characteristics into my plans, their typical patterns of behaviour or their normal reactions. All that's a blank till now.'

'That's clear. In that case, we have to work out a compromise. Obviously we won't we able to draw on the full range of your expertise and artistry. I've instructed a colleague of mine to get hold of the following data: the technical specification of two makes of helicopter, a yacht and three or four motor vehicles. These are, in military jargon, the moving parts that come into close contact with our target.'

Red was breathing a little more easily. 'Well, we're coming to the heart of the matter. You've got to be more precise about the makes or models in question. Some data I may already know and have at the back of my mind. You won't be thinking of an airbus, I imagine, for a plane crash, or the *Royal Yacht Britannia* if we have to sink a ship?'

'*Britannia?*' Edward let slip.

Red grinned. 'Don't worry, my friend. I have all her specifications, but that's because of my collector's mania. That yacht does offer one or two interesting possibilities. Unfortunately not for long. She'll be decommissioned soon.' He made a curious gesture with his hand. 'And it can't be detected by satellite! But I assume we are targeting one single person and not the entire crew.'

There was a brief pause.

Red took up the thread again. 'You've mentioned several times that the target is always at the centre of the media's attention. Is that because of frequent television appearances or continuous hounding by the paparazzi?'

'The latter,' replied Edward.

'Badly?'

'Very.'

'For us, it's ideal,' Red assured him. 'That makes the job easier.'

# 26

When Edward called by at his office later that evening, he was pleased to read on his computer news file a comment that the Press report on Prince Charles with his two sons on the River Dee had been distributed worldwide. He quickly flipped through the list of the names of newspapers and TV stations that had broadcast the news and nodded with satisfaction. He hoped Charles had joined in the fun and had not been preaching about nature and the environment. Edward then entered a short message into the computer. In his mailbox he found the phone and code numbers of the SAS agent. That meant they now had a mole in Dodi Fayed's bedroom. A mole under the nose of the rat! He smiled at the thought and shut down the computer.

Just as he was about to leave, there was a knock at the door. Arthur waved some papers at him. 'Confidential minutes!' he announced, shoving them in front of Edward.

'Do I have to look at all this today?' he moaned.

'No, but there is one you simply have to read.' He pulled out a sheet and passed it to Edward, who cast a quick eye over the page and then started to read it word by word.

Sitting down on Edward's desk, Arthur waited in excitement. Edward's reaction was unambiguous. 'That's a knock-out blow!'

'I thought it would interest you. It's hot news, not a day old.'

Edward leant back in his chair and gazed into the light on his desk. 'If old Al Fayed speaks so openly to third parties about Di and Dodi's wedding, that can only mean that it has all been agreed within the family circle. So it was not such a mad idea to bring along the lawyer . . .'

'. . . Dartevelle!'

'Dartevelle, in fact, is probably drawing up a marriage contract.'

'Apart from this, there is a phone conversation in the minutes between Charles and Camilla Parker-Bowles, in which he openly says he'd like to know the details of Diana's wedding plans. He apparently has no objections; in that case, Camilla and he would be able to . . . Then he waffles on about abdication, and so on and so forth.'

'Are there any further hints about Diana's future marriage plans in the other phone calls?' Edward picked up the rest of the papers and flicked through them quickly.

'I didn't see any other references. There was only a record of a phone call between Diana and her brother, Charles Spencer. All pretty harmless stuff. Diana mentioned a long talk she'd had with her butler, Burrell. But she gave no clue as to the contents of her discussion.'

'Very well then.' Edward laid the minutes to one side and stood up. 'Then we can go.'

'Did you speak to Red?'

'Yes, in some detail. We've cleared the air, I think. We'll start planning next week. He needs to dig a little deeper into some technical matters. But you should find it all in your mailbox. It's your job to collect all the supporting data he needs.'

Arthur screwed up his mouth. 'A very easy job! You'll have it on your desk on Monday. And what's our guest doing this weekend?'

'He's free. We haven't arranged anything together. He can do whatever he likes. Perhaps I'll ring him up or invite him to my place, since he has already found out where I live.'

'Ah! Loyal companions!'

Edward could only manage a tired smile at this remark.

## 27

Lucy entered the arrival hall at Heathrow Airport, dressed like a tourist on a month's holiday. Her suitcases and travelling bags were stacked on a luggage trolley, which she was evidently wheeling with some effort. As soon as she caught sight of Red, she abandoned the trolley, rushed up to him and threw herself into his arms.

'What time did you get up? It was so sweet of you to come and meet me! It would have been awful if I'd had to find the hotel with all this luggage. I'm so much looking forward to being here in London with you.'

Red gave her a kiss. They drew apart, hesitant, and walked back to the luggage trolley, hand in hand.

'How's business, Red?'

'Nothing much has happened so far. I'm bored and I've been overeating.'

Lucy looked at him from the side. 'You have put on some weight. And I see you've bought yourself a new suit.'

They reached the trolley; Red took over the job of pushing it. Lucy hung on to his arm.

'You look tired. Didn't you sleep well?'

A smile spread slowly across Red's face. 'Please, darling! I had to get up at the crack of dawn to pick you up. But joking aside – I've tried out some nice restaurants nearby, that's why I'm late; besides, my business colleagues here in London are early birds, and the contract negotiations are not going too smoothly. First they can't decide on this and then they can't decide on that. I have the feeling they don't really care how long the negotiations last.'

Lucy snuggled up to him. 'Now I'm here, so you can cheer up.'

In the garage stood the black Mercedes, which Red, of course, had not returned. He crammed her luggage into the boot and had to place one of Lucy's travelling bags on the rear seat, as she had brought so many of her belongings with her.

'Do you remember that time when I was supposed to join you in Stockholm for three days and in the end spent almost four weeks with you?' She laughed, walking over to the driver's seat. She suddenly realized it was a right-hand drive. 'Gee! I didn't know they drove on the left over here.'

Red opened the passenger seat door and got inside. Lucy was wavering.

'Get in,' he called, 'you drive. You'll be all right. Besides, I'm at your side.'

Lucy started the engine, groping for the gears. She put it into reverse.' I don't think I'll ever get used to this. Why don't you take over?'

'Quite simple, my darling. I've been driving a lot these last few days, so you've got to take over. And here you have the chance of practising under my supervision.'

'Does that mean I have to wait patiently for you each evening?' Lucy had reversed out of the parking space and drove out of the garage slowly, still rather unsure of herself.

'I've still got to sort out one or two matters.' Red cleared his throat. 'I was very surprised to find out that my London colleagues had booked me in at a small hotel, under a false name.'

'A false name? What odd colleagues you must have!' came her reply.

They had now reached the main road; Red simply told her to keep to the left and drive in the left-hand lane.

Lucy followed his instructions. 'What a strange feeling. Please continue.'

'Well, they had booked me in at this little hotel under

the name of Avraham Rosenzweig. Can you memorize the name?'

'I'll try,' she replied.

'You've got to, because I have checked in at the Dorchester under the same name.'

'And I thought, when you mentioned it, that was the name of a business colleague who had reserved the hotel for us. It sounds Jewish.'

'So it should,' explained Red. 'When I arrived I wasn't aware I was supposed to represent an Israeli businessman by that name. But this was just a front. Our partners in these negotiations are not supposed to know that an American is involved as well. So I'm here in London as Avraham Rosenzweig, a Jewish businessman, who can only afford a small room in a cheap hotel and not even a hire-car. That suits me fine.'

As Lucy was concentrating more on the unusual way of driving, she found it difficult to take in everything Red said. He bent over and kissed her on the cheek. 'I lead a double life over here in London.'

He leant back in the seat. Fortunately Lucy never asked questions when he told her tales. Gently, he placed his arm over her shoulder. 'Your driving's fine; I don't know what you're on about.'

'Please take your arm off; it makes me nervous!'

Red did as he was told. 'Turn right at the next set of traffic-lights.'

# 28

The Dorchester was at its busiest. The drive was chock-a-block; the two revolving doors only impeded the stream of guests in each direction. Red handed the keys to his car to the attendant in top hat and livery. Inside, there were signs of festivities and obviously some conference was in full swing. People with flowers and cases of document folders were in evidence. The small tables, chairs and sofas were all occupied. Red and Lucy weaved their way through the crowd to the reception desk, picked up the key to the room and went up by elevator to the top floor.

Their suite was at the end of the corridor. Red's attention was fixed on the windows and the view beyond. He was happy to see that part of Broad Walk could be seen between the treetops. Lucy immediately strolled through the rooms and inspected everything. Red followed her into the bedroom. She threw herself on her back, on to the bed, and beckoned to him. It was clear what she meant. 'Come over here, darling!'

Red bent over and gave her a kiss. 'Let's wait till the luggage has been delivered.'

'I bet you we both come before the bellboy comes!' she answered temptingly. She rapidly pulled up her skirt and started to undo Red's belt and trousers. 'Come, please, darling. I want you so badly!' she whispered.

Red removed his jacket. Slipping off his shoes, he slid into bed beside her. Slowly, he lay down on top of her slender body. With his left hand he ruffled her hair, with his right he caressed her naked thighs.

'Come!' she whispered again.

Lucy was right. As the bellboy knocked on the door with
the luggage, Red hurried off to the bathroom, throwing the
bathrobe over his naked body. Then he let the boy in.

'Please put everything down here,' he said. The bellboy
went off and Red pulled the door to. He threw off his
bathrobe and tossed it over the back of a chair. Lucy was
waiting for him, impatiently.

That evening they decided to take a taxi; it dropped
them off at Orso, an Italian restaurant which the driver
had recommended. They ordered spinach and potato soup
with champignons as a starter, followed by roast lamb with
potatoes and vegetables. The waiter recommended a bottle
of Brunello di Montalcino to go with the food; it was not
to Red's liking but to Lucy it tasted excellent. A delicious
orange tart, served with a raspberry coulis, made up for the
disappointing wine.

After such a filling meal, neither of them felt inclined
to return to the hotel, so Red asked the waiter for information about nightclubs. He recommended the Drill Hall, a
popular London entertainment theatre, and told them how
to get there.

They discovered, only after a long walk, that the Drill
Hall was closed in August. Disappointed, they jumped into
a taxi. They were determined, however, not to let the
bad experience spoil their good mood and turned into the
Dorchester bar for a goodnight drink.

# 29

At the Dorchester the next morning, they had just ordered breakfast in bed when the mobile rang. It was Edward, who wanted to arrange a new meeting. To avoid any comment that might allow Lucy to identify the caller, Red replied curtly. She took no notice and slowly left the living room.

'Good, I'll be punctual.' The conversation was finished.

He put down the mobile and walked slowly across to the window. Perhaps there were now real signs of action. He wondered how he should put this to Lucy.

Suddenly he felt her hand from behind, stroking his hips. He had not noticed that she had moved there. Her other hand stroked his shoulders. Lucy's body nestled against his back, her hands searching underneath his bathrobe. Red could now sense that her body was naked. Slowly he turned round, embraced her and pulled her gently down on to the soft carpet.

Once again, they came more quickly than the room service. As breakfast arrived, Lucy slipped off into the bedroom and Red opened the door. The waiter pushed the trolley into the room and was about to serve breakfast on the sofa table.

'Leave everything on the trolley, we'll cope with all that,' said Red. The waiter disappeared and Lucy emerged. 'I'm dying for some coffee,' she said, with a yawn, stroking her tousled hair. 'Come on, let's have some breakfast before we shower.'

Red pushed the trolley up against the sofa table and began

to lay the table for breakfast. He now brought up the subject of the forthcoming meeting with Lucy.

'I didn't come here yesterday only to find out that I'm a straw widow today,' she said, visibly upset.

Red settled into a chair and grabbed some toast. 'I'm sorry, but what else could I say? Tomorrow we continue with very tough negotiations at the office and Edward and I . . .' He paused as he realized he had accidentally identified him by name.

'Edward?' queried Lucy, now astonished. 'Isn't that the son of your former wartime buddy, the one who visited us recently?'

Red had the situation well under control. 'Of course,' he said with a laugh. 'Edward offered me this job whilst he was over. I'd completely forgotten you met him at my place.' His expression suddenly changed, as he continued, now in a serious tone. 'Under no circumstances should he find out that you are with me here. He thinks I'm still at that cheap hotel.' Red pondered for a moment and added. 'No, it wouldn't be right if he saw you here in London. Business is business and, besides, our private life is too precious, isn't it?'

Lucy nodded with a smile. 'Of course, darling! I am not interested in your business, either; you know that. Just tell me when to expect you.'

'I'll be back in two or three hours.'

'What time did you arrange to meet him?'

'He's picking me up at my hotel at twelve.' Red glanced at his wrist-watch. 'We have plenty of time to have breakfast and take a shower.'

They finished breakfast. As Red went into the bathroom, Lucy wandered around the rooms. She saw Red's jacket lying on the sofa and cocked her ear towards the bathroom. The water was still running noisily. Quietly, she slunk over to his jacket. With her nimble fingers, she went through the pockets. As quick as lightning, she pulled out the reservation slip for Barthley & Sons Ltd in the name of a certain Avraham

Rosenzweig. Before she had time to read the name of the addressee, she heard the water being switched off. As quickly as she had removed and unfolded the note, she popped it back inside the inside pocket and replaced the jacket on the back of the sofa. Red now came back into the living room. She embraced him, kissed him, then disappeared into the bathroom.

Red dressed and waited until Lucy returned, her hair dripping wet and her body wrapped in a bath towel.

'Darling, I must run off now. I hope to see you in two hours' time. So don't run off. I'll give you a ring if I'm going to be late.'

'Fine.' Lucy stroked Red's hair, pulled him close and gave him a tender goodbye kiss.

When Red had left, she went towards the window and looked down on to Hyde Park. She placed her brow against the windowpane, a dreamy look on her face.

She woke with a start from her dreams. In the distance, she saw Red appear between the trees. Hadn't he said that Edward would be picking him up at his cheap hotel? She saw Red stop and wave to someone. Then Edward appeared between the trees. They greeted one another and walked slowly back along the route Edward had taken.

Why had Red lied to her? Why hadn't he mentioned that he would be meeting Edward in Hyde Park? She shook her head, deep in thought, and began to dress.

## 30

Edward and Red had reached the statue of Achilles in Hyde Park. Red halted and came up close to Edward.

'I agree. You find me a room and a fast computer. I have brought my laptop with me and also my programs and diskettes. When can I move?'

'It will be a small apartment. The PC will be delivered tomorrow afternoon at the latest. The technical data should then be available.' Edward hesitated for a second. 'We should retain the hotel room.'

Red agreed. 'And what's the plan now?'

Edward's features relaxed. 'Actually, I planned to invite you to a meal and show you around London, if you felt so inclined.'

'I do, but I've been wearing these new shoes for too long. Would you mind if I went back to the hotel room, put my feet up and did some reading?'

'No problem, it was just an idea.' Edward thought for a moment. 'If you're a little unsteady on your feet today, let's just go across to the restaurant at the Hyde Park Hotel over there. The cuisine is not French and the service is not perfect, but the food is very good and it's typically British!'

'That's OK by me.'

# 31

Edward stood at the corner of Gloucester Street and George Street again the next day, waiting for Red, who was dragging along his metal case ready to move in to the town apartment and use it as an office. It was not far from Gloucester Street. Normally Edward and his colleagues, who lived outside London, used it whenever they stayed late at the office or had to find accommodation nearby because of some official engagement. It was situated on the ground floor of a small street in the neighbourhood and consisted of a tiny living room with a kitchen area, a bedroom and a bathroom. A rusty old sign with the name "Brown" was fixed to the door. The same name was attached to the doorbell.

As soon as Edward left, Red started to unpack the computer unit and removed the hard disk from its housing, apart from one holding screw. He took some diskettes from the trunk and saved them on the hard drive. He then summoned the operating program and entered a code to protect the data from unauthorized access. He finally saved all his work and laid down, dressed just as he was, on the bed.

He was startled by a ring at the front door. Glancing quickly at his watch, he realized he must have fallen asleep. Outside stood Walter, clad as usual in his motor-cyclists' kit; he had brought Red a second leather suit. 'Try it on; I'll wait outside.'

Red put the suit on; he had to admit that Walter had a keen salesman's eye. It fitted as if Walter had it tailor-made for him.

This was their routine for the next few days. Walter would

pick him up just after lunch and they drove together up and down the highways and byways of inner and outer London. He would stop every now and again, allowing Red to survey the surroundings – stretches of roadway or approach roads that were regularly or, at least, often used by their target. Red's task became increasingly obscure, since the choice of streets, bridges and avenues seemed to be completely arbitrary. He narrowed down the total of about ten possible venues to one or two. He made sketches of each of them, paced out distances and entered them in the computer the next day. Edward would appear each day at about eleven o'clock to discuss the previous day's findings.

Evenings were then spent with Lucy, who would always complain that Red's negotiations lasted all day.

All Wednesday afternoon Walter drove Red around the streets of London in the baking heat. A meeting had been scheduled with Edward afterwards back at the flat, the objective being to decide on the precise scene of the accident.

Edward was waiting outside the front door. It took some while for Red to remove his leather gear and take a shower. Edward had meanwhile made himself at home in the flat, flicking through the newspapers scattered round about.

'Did anything of interest happen today?' asked Edward casually, as Red emerged from the bathroom.

Red snorted through his nose. Edward suddenly noticed that the face of his American friend had turned puce.

'You know what?' shouted Red. 'I'm fed up, I repeat, *fed up*!' He pulled up a chair and sat astride it. 'We've got to decide here and now what we do and when and where we do it. I've been driving round the streets of London for days now, I've had them pointed out to me. But I ask you, what's it all about?' He took a deep breath and then continued. 'We've looked at about six or seven buildings now on the computer, so I can fix the accident tomorrow. So just tell me where, bring the goddam target along, and I'll bump him off on the spot! I'll have earned my fee and the job will be over for both of us!' Red had placed both arms on the back of the chair and glared threateningly at Edward.

Edward was wondering how he could convince Red that even if a location had been agreed it would not be that easy to lure Princess Diana there. He stood up, then sat down on the table.

'Red, I know that my answer will not be what you want to hear. I am also of the opinion that we should agree on one or two locations, perhaps even today. But the rest will simply take time. It does not lie within my competence to entice our target to the spot, either tomorrow or the day after tomorrow. I already mentioned at the outset that you were to stand by for some time. Nevertheless, we have achieved one aim. We have identified certain suitable locations. We can now agree on the location and at the same time plan an alternative. Then I shall set all the wheels in motion, so that our target stops there or drives past. But until that point the message is: wait, wait and keep on waiting.'

Red jumped up and stood up close to Edward. 'I'm just sick and tired of waiting. It should be bloody well possible to get this person to the spot we've chosen. Otherwise, we have no real strategy. You're doing it all wrong. And why all this goddam secrecy? Maybe I'll change my plan when I know who the target is. Walter told me he or she travels by public transport. God, it's not that difficult to arrange a different type of accident. It doesn't have to be by motorbike, car or aeroplane. But it'll only work if you reveal the cards in your hand.'

Edward felt that Red must have reached some low. He had to let off steam, so he gave him the chance. That was the only way they could finally thrash things out in peace and quiet.

He started gently. 'I must add something else. I can't ever promise you that we'll succeed in getting our target to our ideal location, or even that we can carry out the job successfully. I have the right of veto up to the very last minute.'

He had scored a bull's-eye. Red's right hand, spread out flat, thumped the table.

'That's enough! Then I'll do the job, but it's got to be right now! That means tomorrow or the day after. I'm not going to waste one more day. I've had enough of that goddam motorbike. I'm fed up in this dump here. Just cut out the excuses. I can't take any more.' He pointed to the computer at the other side of the table. 'I have all the data, do you understand? Either we go ahead now or I quit.'

Edward gave a provocative smile, wondering if he could make a quick getaway. 'That is precisely what you can't do, Red. Be good, and sit here patiently until we call you. And you'll be there when you're needed. Now do you understand?'

Red was speechless. He stared at Edward, shaking his head. Then he pointed with his index finger, in the direction of the door. 'Get out!' he shouted. 'Just get out!'

Still smiling, Edward made a slight bow and left the apartment without a further word. Red slowly slumped down on to the chair. It was obvious that Edward had deliberately provoked him. This made him more annoyed. He rang up Lucy and warned her that it might take a little longer; the talks were still continuing.

# 32

The weather outside had not yet cooled down. Red walked through the streets, deep in thought. How much longer would these goddam Brits push him around? He realized he had no means of putting pressure on them. Even if he threatened to chuck it all in, it would not have any effect on Edward's superiors. They would find someone else and ask him to return the money they had already advanced him. Besides, he ran the risk that he would receive no further commissions. His was a small world and word would get around very quickly. He had to find a way of forcing the job through. His route took him past a pub – the Marquis of Granby. A large blonde poured out a Guinness and smiled as she poured out a second and then a third. As soon as he felt he had drowned his sorrows, he settled the bill and made off towards the apartment. He would not go back to Lucy tonight.

A delightful aroma wafted in his direction through the open door of a small restaurant, the Pierre Victoire. He found a free table near the door by a window, and without a moment's hesitation, sat down. A young waiter brought him the menu; Red chose the red house wine, a dish of mussels in Pernod and garlic sauce and a grilled salmon steak.

His mood improved with the meal, which he decided was quite delicious, and he wondered how to straighten out relations with Edward the following day. After a second bottle of wine and a third slice of banana tart, he thought he had found the solution. He would invite Edward to this restaurant tomorrow. A good meal would patch things up between them.

Red succeeded in bringing Edward along to the Pierre Victoire the following day; he was evidently back in favour. Edward was impressed by the meal and made no allusion to the row the day before. He asked Red to leave the room at the Lincoln House Hotel and to spend the night at the flat. How would Lucy react to this bit of news, Red wondered. He tried to think of a suitable excuse; Edward had hinted that zero-hour was not far off.

So he checked out of the Lincoln House Hotel, moved into the flat and spent the afternoon entering and evaluating computer data.

# 33

One of the mobiles bleeped. Red woke up with a start. Half-asleep, he groped around for the light switch by the bed, picked up the mobile and pressed the answer key. Before he could even utter a single word, he heard Edward's voice at the other end. 'We're ready! Pack everything you need. It's a Gulfstream IV.'

'Shit!' Red shouted. 'Why that plane?'

Edward gave no reply. 'I'll be there in half an hour. We'll be flying off immediately.'

'Where to?'

'I'll tell you later.'

The line went dead. Red was breathing heavily. At last they were off. His brain began to work like a computer. Without any hint of nervousness, he got out of bed, stretched, did ten knee-bends to get his circulation going and looked at his wrist-watch. It was 2.48 a.m. He only had a quarter of an hour. He went to the bathroom for a cold shower.

At 2.56 a.m. he started to dress. He considered whether he had time to prepare some coffee but abandoned the idea, as the minute hand of the clock jumped from 57 to 58. He went over to the table and switched on the computer. He then took out the metal case from the cupboard and placed the diskettes inside. He copied the file from the hard drive on to one of the diskettes and shut the computer down. He pulled out the electric plug, picked up the screwdriver which lay to one side, removed the final screw from the hard drive housing on the frame and the contact plugs. Then he took the laptop out of the metal case and put the hard drive inside.

The sound of a passing car could now be heard outside. He picked up the case and the laptop, glanced carefully around the room once again and turned off the light. He stepped out into the night.

Outside, a large limousine was waiting for him. Red was unable to make out the model, as it was dark and the car head-lights dazzled his eyes. The passenger doors opened and he heard Edward's voice. 'Get in, quick! The boot's unlocked.'

Red went round to the boot and opened it. Inside were several pairs of overalls, two briefcases and two travelling bags. He laid the metal case inside, but kept the laptop in his hand. As he opened the car door he saw Edward inside, behind the driver's seat. He did not recognize the driver or the other passenger. He shut the door and held on tightly to the laptop inside the car.

Edward gave the order to move. He shook Red by the hand.

'When things get moving, they sure move fast,' said Red, pointing at his wrist-watch.

'I'm sorry about that,' came the reply. 'The timing is not my choice.'

'And where are we going?' queried Red.

As usual, Edward ducked the question. 'That's Walter in front.' He gave Red a friendly greeting. 'We're going by plane, as I already told you.'

'When do we return?'

'This evening, at the latest.'

Red nodded and looked out of the window.

'Shall we keep quiet until we're at our destination?' Red asked with amusement.

'Until we're inside the aircraft!' came the curt reply. Edward seemed extremely nervous. Red cast a glance outside again; the car appeared to have reached the suburbs. He decided to take advantage of the time and catch up on some rest. He shut his eyes. The monotonous noise of the engine lulled him to sleep.

He came to as the car suddenly swung to the left and

quickly braked. A glance at his wrist-watch told him that he had actually been asleep for half an hour. In front, a gate was opened. At this distance, Red was able to recognize the shape of an aeroplane, which he thought was a Learjet 35.

Edward prodded him gently. 'We're here!'

The car drew up close to the plane; the turbines were already running. Red, Walter and Edward got out. They went round to the boot, took out their luggage and packed it inside the hold in the tail of the plane. Behind Walter, the door slammed to. This was obviously not a standard aircraft. Inside, it was furbished on Spartan military lines and had been left in a rather neglected state by its previous passengers. Behind the co-pilot's seat, highly modern technical equipment was fixed to the side, with an additional seat. The equipment was presumably designed to give all-round land and air clearance.

'We're sitting over there.' Edward pointed at a row of four seats. There were about eight to ten seats inside. Before Red had time to sit down, the plane moved off.

For the first time that day, Red scrutinized Edward's face. He sat in the next seat and was tightening his seat belt for take-off. Red shoved his laptop under the seat and moved the back of his seat into a more comfortable position.

The aircraft had now reached the runway; it turned round sharply. The light was switched off and the engines revved up. The plane accelerated. As they took off, Red tried to identify whether it was a military or a private airport, but they immediately pitched to one side and flew in a long curve. He was unable to make out anything in the darkness.

The light came on again. Edward then took out some faxed sheets and handwritten notes from his inside jacket pocket.

'We're flying to Nice,' he said curtly.

'Nice?' Red replied with astonishment.

Edward nodded. Red pushed the back of his seat a little further and made himself comfortable. He had a number of people filed under Nice – industrialists, artists, bankers, politicians and businessmen.

'OK, who are we gunning for?' he asked, in a tone that left no doubt that he expected a proper answer. Edward looked away, gazing into the distance beyond, as if he wanted to savour every minute of secrecy that kept them apart. Now, suddenly, he felt the need to overcome all restraint. He felt it was the right moment to divulge the identity of their target.

'Great Britain runs a huge risk of conflict between its national and its international interests. We have been given the task of eliminating those problems and protecting the throne from danger . . .'

'Dodi!' Red interrupted, looking Edward straight in the face. Edward slowly shook his head.

Red drew himself up. 'Do you mean to say you want to send your beautiful Princess back to her Maker?' The tone of his voice was bemused and frightened. Edward merely nodded and glanced down at his papers.

'Holy Smoke!' Red thumped the arm rest, his right fist clenched. 'At first I thought it could be her, but then I thought: No, dammit, it's got to be Prince Charles or her lover. But Di! You can't despatch a beautiful girl like that! She brings hope to millions and millions of people in your country.'

'That depends on one's point of view,' Walter butted in for the first time; his voice could be heard clearly without a loudspeaker. He relaxed his seat belt and looked at Red. 'Do you have any problems with that?' he asked.

'Problems?' Red shrugged his shoulders. 'What sort of problems do you mean?'

'Emotional problems.'

'Me?' Red looked at Edward. 'Did our agreement mention anything about emotions? No, I just can't figure it out. You have a beautiful figurehead and then you want to do away with her. Why?'

Edward removed a page from the bundle of papers and began to quote. 'The Gulfstream IV is now standing at Nice. It will pick you both up at Olbia tomorrow and return to London. Have arranged that the aircraft is parked to the side of Nice airport. Head for Nice, please not Cannes. The landing strip there is sixteen hundred yards long. Use appropriate aircraft.'

Red interrupted. 'So it's Cannes not Nice?'

'We fly to Cannes if the weather holds. Our ultimate destination is Nice,' explained Edward.

'I hope you guys know what you're doing,' said Red with a sigh. He took out his laptop from under the seat and switched it on. There was a whirring noise and its pale-green screen lit up a few seconds later.

The plane had now reached its scheduled height. To the east, dawn was breaking.

Red repeated his thoughts out loud. 'OK then, Gulfstream IV.' He typed some data and waited for the bleeping noise that indicated he had hit the right spot in the file. 'Year of construction?'

'Year of construction,' repeated Edward, flicking through his papers. 'Sorry,' he said slowly, still searching. 'The year of construction is unknown, at least so far as I know. Is that important?'

'Everything is important if you want to see a good job done. And that's what you expect, isn't it?' Red stared at his screen. 'Which route does the plane take?'

'We don't know,' replied Edward, rummaging around deeper into his papers, as if he might find a few additional scraps of information on the aircraft in question.

At last, Red found what he was after. 'Aha, it's the Al Fayeds' private jet, isn't it?'

'You mean to say you've got his plane stored on file?' asked an astonished Walter, squinting at the laptop screen.

'I've recorded every VIP's private plane in case it could be useful in my work some time. These people often hire out their aircraft to other VIPs. So a small number of aircraft covers quite a large number of people.' He chuckled quietly and flicked deeper into the file. 'If I were to ask you where you ideally want the crash to take place, are you going to tell me or not?' Red looked at Walter, then at Edward.

'Does that lie within your area of competence in this particular case?' asked Edward cautiously.

'Of course,' replied Red. 'But I'll consider any special requests and I might or I might not take them into account. So I gather you have no firm instructions. Let me give you some advice. Avoid the Mediterranean. There are too many private yachts around at this time of year. They will all race to the scene of the accident for survivors. The water's quite warm, so anyone who's injured will stay alive for some time. Besides, you don't know how experienced the pilot is. He might glide to safety and keep the plane afloat.' He turned to Edward. 'You may remember that I told you about my flop in Germany some time ago. I failed to take the plane's gliding skills into account. By my reckoning they were for it, but the pilot handled it beautifully.' He consulted his screen again.

'I'll see if there's any drink on board,' said Walter, moving towards the cockpit.

'What do those two over there know about the mission?' asked Red, pointing his head to the area behind Walter.

'Nothing. Anyhow, they have been hand-picked, so they are one hundred per cent reliable. We engage them only for top-secret missions,' answered Edward.

'So they are your own people?' asked Red.

'Yes.'

'Good. I'd like to speak to one of the pilots afterwards.'

Walter returned with a bottle of mineral water and three plastic cups. 'There's nothing else on the plane,' he explained, apologetically.

'Then you should ask your guys at Cannes for replacements. A few snacks would do no harm, either,' Red complained.

'There is an alcohol ban on all our aircraft,' explained
Walter. He poured everyone a drink, then shoved the bottle
into the net behind his seat and was about to sit down
again. Red indicated that he should remain standing. 'Wait
a moment!' He entered some data into the laptop and waited
until the machine threw up the information he wanted.
'Ask the pilot about the basic weather situation over the
South of France and what changes are forecast in the next
twenty-four hours.'

Walter returned to the cockpit.

'The South of France?' asked Edward, full of interest.

Red took his time to reply. Edward admired his cool.
There was no indication that he had been planning murder
for the last half-hour.

'Yes, the South of France,' repeated Red suddenly. 'As
a rule, this type of aircraft has the choice of two routes
for London. Either the pilot stops at Nice and then flies
diagonally across the Rhone-Saône valley to London via
Paris, or else direct to Marseilles, then up the Canal du
Midi, over Bordeaux, and up the west coast of France.'

'How do you choose which route to take?' asked Edward,
taking greater interest.

'The route is determined by the passengers' own prefer-
ences, the weather, tower control and the pilot's mood. Wait
and see what Walter says. Then we'll know more.'

Red took a look through the window and returned to
his computer. Outside, daylight was visible. The sun dazzled
Red, then Edward, according to the flight of the aircraft. It
was a little while before Walter returned. He had made a few
notes and passed Red a slip of paper.

'I don't understand any of this, but here's the data the
co-pilot dictated to me. I hope I took it down correctly.'

'For an examination in navigation, it wouldn't do,' grinned
Red, 'but for my modest requirements, it'll do.' He put
the slip of paper on the arm rest. Without consulting his
computer, he continued. 'So, we shall have westerly winds

and clear skies on either route but no bad weather fronts. The outlook for tomorrow is roughly similar. Perhaps the wind will increase in strength; there's a band of stormy weather from the Atlantic following close behind, which is due to reach France during the course of the late afternoon or early evening. If I were the pilot, I'd select the Rhone-Saône valley route. But, as I said, there are always other factors to reckon with.'

Uneasily, Edward took in the news about the stormy weather front. As a former Marine, he preferred to be on water during rough weather than in the sky, especially as he had a tendency towards airsickness.

'I'm more or less certain the pilot will choose the eastern route. But let's wait and see.' Red closed the file and called up another. 'Let's look at the lie of the land. The Gorges de la Nesque would be ideal or the area around Mont Ventoux. Do you know the area?'

'Is that the mountain range you can see from Aix-en-Provence?' asked Walter.

'No, those are the Luberon mountains. But you're in the right area. The Gorges de la Nesque and Mont Ventoux lie further to the north. It's a very lonely area – ideal for a plane crash. It would take a long time to reach the scene. Besides, there is a high risk of fire in this area after the long dry period, so the chances are that the aircraft and the surrounding countryside would be scorched by fire.'

Edward listened to Red with astonishment. They had sketched out quite a number of scenarios together the previous week. Casual comments about life and death were normal topics between them both. But now, as plans became more concrete, he had an uncomfortable feeling. In the last ten years he had worked on strategies to eliminate terrorists and political fanatics, but to be standing suddenly at the centre of the action was a totally new experience. Was he really equal to the occasion? He thought of George, aware now how well he understood their feelings. It was fortunate Walter had been assigned to them, not George. He stood up, without saying a word, and went forward to the cabin.

Walter observed him. Sir David had reasons for choosing Edward's department. He was certain that Edward had the nerves to see their mission through to the end. And Walter was grateful to be on the job. Edward was always very consistent and utterly reliable. You could learn a thing or two from him.

'If they fly the other way, we'll quickly have to work out an alternative,' warned Walter. 'That's the tourist route. Canal du Midi, Carcassonne, Toulouse. I hope they don't take that route.'

'Carcassonne? That's a real tourist trap, north of Corbières. It's like any other town but La Cité is an old fortified citadel, newly renovated, situated on top of the mountain. It's a tourist attraction for us Americans and the Japanese, like Buckingham Palace in London, Neuschwanstein Castle in Germany or the Church of the Holy Sepulchre in Jerusalem. Even French tourists flock there like mad. If the Gulfstream drops down there, we'll have one hundred dead bodies on our hands. Not a good idea, wouldn't you agree?'

Walter shook his head. It was amazing how sensible and matter-of-fact Red was when at work. What a pity he had only known him as a pillion passenger touring the London streets. He was not really the killer type. Walter was also joining the ranks of Red's admirers.

'There should be no real problems on the technical side,' added Red casually. 'Do you happen to know whether the plane is in a hangar or is standing in the open?'

'I've no idea. On the fax, so far as I can recall, it mentions that it's in the open.'

'And how, then, am I supposed to get to work on it? I imagine the Gulfstream will be under tight security, just like any other aircraft at every airport around the world. What makes you think it's not the same here?'

'You noticed that we took overalls with us. We shall resurface as maintenance men.'

Edward returned from the cockpit.

'Red has just enquired how we find the plane at Nice and where it's located,' explained Walter.

Edward sat down again in his seat and dug into the files. He found the relevant page at last.

'We are to meet this man at Cannes; he will give us a letter of authority signed by Mohammed Al Fayed, permitting us to board the aircraft in order to instal equipment inside. The document is genuine; only the date has been altered. And there is another name . . .' He rummaged around again in his papers. 'Pierre, a night watchman, who we should find out about. If he's there, we'll have to adapt our style a little; he knows that new fittings have recently been installed, since it was he who opened the door to the genuine maintenance men.'

Red broke in again. 'Obviously we've got to do this on our own. So, which of you has any idea about flying?'

They both shook their heads.

'In principle, the plan is not as complicated as all that. I only have to make a small adjustment; it won't be detected after the plane crash, even if it's gone over item by item. We only need to cross the Gulfstream's flight path. This procedure will take place outside the safety zone and has to be agreed on and approved by each of the pilots. As soon as we have reached a certain distance from the plane, I can interfere with his altitude control so that he falls into a tailspin. After the initial moment of panic, the pilot will try to regain height, since he won't have a clue what's happened. The plane won't react. He'll try to correct, applying the techniques he has been taught and has practised for cases like this. Then he'll have signed his own death warrant. Everything he does will have exactly the opposite effect. And when he's realized it, it'll be too late.'

Edward had followed Red's description with the closest attention. 'That means we can't fly to London tonight but have to spend the night at Cannes or Nice and tail the Gulfstream.'

Red gave a nod. 'Right! Only we fly off from Nice and Diana flies from Olbia. Ideally, we should both take off simultaneously, since we're a little slower than the Gulfstream. Before then we have to know which route the Gulfstream pilot has recorded. It shouldn't be a problem for your pilots to find that out. Then we take the same route. At the appropriate moment, we announce a change of direction, for example because of some suspicious noise we've suddenly noticed. We ask permission to land at a convenient location, forcing us across his flight path. Then we'll get really close. We'll have to make a landing, or else we lose all credibility. We won't be noticed, because by then the news about the Gulfstream crash will be topic number one in the flight tower.'

'Sounds convincing,' Walter said languidly, consulting his wrist-watch. 'We've got a good hour yet.'

'I need that time for preparation.' Red was already at the computer again, entering data. 'I have to fish out the diskettes from my case as soon as we land.'

'I have one question, though,' said Edward. 'If I understand you correctly, you'll give some signal when you cross the flight path. Is that correct?'

Red nodded.

'We have the transmitter on board here, obviously,' Edward continued, 'but the receiver has to be installed into the Gulfstream, which will become obvious sooner or later.'

Red grinned. 'That's the trick! I make use of the radio transmitter we installed in the Gulfstream. I've been working on this problem for some years and then suddenly hit on the solution. I only need to know the frequency of the Gulfstream. But that's no problem, especially as we'll be flying the same route together for at least some of the way.'

'I never thought it would be so simple.'

Red leant over towards Edward. 'Believe me, we're all dupes. Nuclear power stations are safe; the hole on the ozone layer is harmless; our allies are our friends. Absolute rubbish! They are leading us by the nose, so we don't live in a state of fear. It only needs a false gesture or a badly-installed valve to throw the whole world into confusion. This brings me back to the subject of my work: technical weaknesses, human imperfection, natural events. Get what I mean?'

'I think I can guess.' Edward re-sorted his papers and put them back inside his jacket. He then leaned back in his seat and closed his eyes.'

## 34

At that moment Sir David was holding a meeting with Arthur and George. Glancing, as usual, at the frosted-glass panel above the door, he sat down in his chair. He removed his gold-rimmed spectacles from the case and put them on.

'Did Edward and Walter get off on time?'

'They set off just before four,' answered George. 'So they should touch down at Cannes in about an hour's time.'

'Cannes?' queried Sir David in astonishment. 'I thought the plane was at Nice.'

'You're quite right, Sir. But Edward felt it would be a little too risky to land there. They land at Cannes and then take a hire-car to Nice.'

'Did the business of Mohammed Al Fayed's letter of authority work out all right?' This time Sir David looked straight at Arthur, who nodded eagerly.

'It was by pure chance that I found this document. Henry referred to it . . .'

'Who is this Henry?'

'I apologise. I assumed you had already read the information from the SAS on computer. Henry is the code name of our SAS agent. The technician from the firm that fitted the air-conditioning left the document behind in Al Fayed's plane. Quite by coincidence, our agent took the flight after the installation work was completed and picked up the paper. Edward will receive a doctored version of the same document in Cannes, through a middleman.'

Sir David betrayed some signs of nervousness. 'I did ask

you, gentlemen, to involve no one else in this affair without my permission. We are playing with dynamite!'

'We have followed your instructions, Sir. Our middleman doesn't know Edward's identity. All he has been told is that a friend of Al Fayed wants to pass some information on to him as soon as he arrives at Cannes.'

Sir David intervened. 'Suppose the middleman opens the letter?'

'Edward and I discussed that last night. In that case he will pretend that he's the maintenance man for the air-conditioning. And if in fact the letter is secretly opened, it will contain only the letter of authority permitting Edward or a fitter to instal or carry out repairs on the new air-conditioning equipment. For practical purposes it is only an identity pass for airport control.'

Sir David seemed to be happy with that explanation. He pulled a folder out of his bundle of files. 'You must get in touch with Edward after this meeting as a matter of urgency. He may well need the support of both of you. Is there an aircraft on stand-by?'

George had reservations. He intervened. 'Pardon me, but won't we attract attention if we book two machines within a short space of time, both with the same destination?'

Sir David looked at George over the rims of his spectacles. 'Very good, George. Alright then, if we have to fly, we should fly by a scheduled flight. It wouldn't take that much longer, would it?'

'I've never flown from London to Cannes,' answered George. 'Presumably the flight is via Paris.'

'Would you kindly find out if there are direct flights to Nice or Marseilles. I have no idea. I am sure you will make the right decision, if the worst comes to the worst. Perhaps you don't have much choice. Now I should like to raise a totally different issue.' He opened the file. 'Some time tomorrow morning, Princess Diana's plane crash will hit the headlines. We shall be called in as a matter of routine. In that event we shall work as normal and, I trust, discover nothing suspicious.'

'Edward is very reliable,' assured Arthur. 'The American was given a first-class reference by the CIA; he has considerable experience and discretion. We've done some research on him and found no weak points. At Edward's request, we've kept our distance from him here in London.'

'Very well. Edward must have his reasons.' Sir David consulted the file again. 'How do we finally get rid of this American?'

'Immediately after the accident he'll fly with Edward and Walter to Heathrow and we'll escort him back on the next flight to New York. Red has spent the last few days in our London apartment. We shall remove all evidence today and bring his belongings from the flat to the airport. Edward insists that Red should leave the UK as soon as possible.'

'I agree. Please contact Edward immediately and find out if he needs you both.'

## 35

The layer of cloud beneath the aircraft thinned out and the shimmering blue of the Côte d'Azur to their left and the slopes of the Provençal Alps on their right became visible. Edward woke up just as the plane began its descent. Red had shut down his laptop and looked out of the window. The surface of the Mediterranean glistened in the morning sun. Yachts, both large and small, were anchored in the bays.

'St Tropez,' Red said, pointing down. 'They go to bed at this hour!' On the horizon, silhouettes of islands emerged through the morning mist. Red jerked his head to the rear. 'Those must be Corsica and Sardinia. Your Princess must be asleep somewhere over there. Or maybe they're still awake, engaged in intense erotic foreplay.' He gazed, almost in a dream, across towards the islands. 'I'd love to know what she's like in bed. A little whore or Her Royal Highness? I imagine *she* knows a thing or two! I just can't think what you guys have against her.'

Edward hesitated before replying. Walter chimed in.

'It wouldn't be such a problem if she were a tennis star or a film actor. But you know who Dodi is. His father is public enemy number one for us Brits and, what is worse, one of Kashoggi's bosom pals. One can overlook the playboy image, even the fact that he's two-timing Diana and this Kelly Fisher girl. But it's impossible, he being a Muslim and her an Anglican. The rumour is that she'll convert to Islam. She has to if they get married, otherwise Dodi's a dead man. So that's what she'll do. Just imagine. Prince Charles succeeds to the throne. Or else he abdicates, in which case we jump one generation. Then it's William's turn. Princess Diana is his mother and that won't change. So the King's mother is married to a Muslim and has also converted to Islam. And his stepbrother, also a Muslim . . .'

'Is it true that she's pregnant?' asked Red, who was aware of the rumour from the newspapers.

'Yes, very probably. It seems that someone from the practice of a certain Doctor Coxon – a London internist – was somewhat indiscreet. We know for a fact that Diana has an appointment with her as soon as she's back in London. The rumour is certainly not without foundation.'

'But you seem to have put two and two together in such a clumsy way. Why the mad rush and the final OK only tonight?'

'We'd already been given final approval before you were called to London. There was some delay only because we believed – and of course hoped – that the affair would blow over. But yesterday we were given the information that Diana would be coming with Dodi to England or else Scotland, to Balmoral, where the children are spending their holidays, and would be making an official announcement about their marriage plans. They were then to fly back to London and give a Press conference. We've now reached the point of no return.'

'Poor Diana!' Red commented, with genuine sympathy. 'No sooner is she in her seventh heaven than I shoot her out of the clouds. But that's how it is sometimes. It's best to quit when things are going well. That's true of your Princess, though the timing's not her own.'

They had now passed St Raphaël. The plane was rapidly losing height. Red, Walter and Edward prepared for landing.

'I don't suppose we'll be getting a decent breakfast, will we?' asked Red.

'Not at Cannes airport, at this time of day. But in the town you can order breakfast at any hotel,' Edward replied. 'I shall first contact the messenger with the letter of authority. We're supposed to meet at the airport. Why don't you drive off to some hotel; I'll follow later. You can phone me and tell me where to meet you.'

Walter gave a nod and Red looked out of the window again. There were some maniacs out swimming at this hour of the day!

'Take seats for landing!' announced the pilot over the loudspeaker.

# 36

At that time of day on a sunny Friday morning, Cannes was still half-asleep and there was hardly anyone in sight as the taxi dropped Red and Walter at a small hotel, situated one block away from the sea. Red, who spoke French with hardly a trace of an accent, asked for some coffee and a couple of croissants, although they were not resident guests. With some reluctance, the proprietor agreed.

The breakfast room had a view over the sea, but it was stuffy inside. There was a lingering smell of cold, stale cigarette smoke. It also served as a guest lounge during the evening. Part of the table had been scantily laid. Taking all the time in the world, the proprietor himself brought out some milk and croissants from a small room nearby.

Red and Walter had sat down at a table for four by the window and were looking out to sea. The islands were no longer visible at this level. Huge aeroplanes thundered over the beach, heading for Nice airport.

Walter had imagined Cannes to be quite different. This was certainly not the familiar backdrop for the Film Festival as he had seen it on television. Red had already switched on his mobile in the taxi and tried, without success, to get hold of Edward.

'Suppose we don't make contact?' asked Walter, dunking his croissant into the coffee.

'We'll reach him alright,' said Red with a laugh. 'He just has to remember to switch on his phone. He's bound to, if he's missed our call.'

## 37

Edward exchanged a few words with the pilot at the airport,
then took a taxi to the hotel Arthur had indicated. It was
set back some distance from the beach – a typical establishment used by commercial travellers, servants or chauffeurs
whenever their employers or bosses were staying on the
Côte d'Azur.

Edward asked the taxi to wait and entered the foyer. At
the reception desk, he enquired after a guest by the name of
Gaston Pallma, who, he was told, was registered there. After
searching through the list, the young receptionist eventually
located him. With a brief glance at the clock, she dialled the
room number. Gaston picked up the receiver immediately;
he must have been waiting for their signal for an hour.
Edward left the reception area and moved towards the
foyer. With a jolt, the ancient lift opposite was galvanized
into action. Edward's eye fell on the indicator above the lift
door. Evidently, his man's room was on the third floor, or, at
least, the lift stopped there. He took a few steps towards the
gates, which were suddenly thrown open with some force.
A stout, dark-haired man of about fifty got out, holding a
white envelope in his hand. Seeing Edward, his face lit up.
With a small bow, he briskly handed him the envelope, and,
in a high, singsong voice, uttered a few words in French,
which Edward did not understand. He turned back to the
lift, activating it with another jolt.

Edward gave a friendly nod to the young receptionist, left
the hotel and jumped into his taxi. He opened the envelope
and cast his eye over the letter of authority. He noted in

particular that the date showed no signs of having been
tampered with. Henry was obviously a master at forgery.
Now relaxed, he pulled the mobile from his pocket to ask
Red the address of the breakfast hotel. He gave it to his driver,
who started the engine and drove back up the same street.

## 38

Red and Walter had eaten their croissants and drunk their cups of coffee by the time Edward arrived. He joined them at the table and ordered breakfast.

He made sure that none of the other five hotel guests could overhear him, pulled up closer to them both and said, quietly, 'We wait for half an hour, then go back to the airport and change; then we pick up Red's case and fly back to Nice.'

Walter nodded. 'Should all three of us fly there together?'

Red butted in. 'If they let the three of us in, yes. What does it say in the letter of authority?'

'It only says that he authorizes such and such a firm . . . and so on.'

'Fine. There is no restriction on the number of people in the letter.' Red spoke in an undertone. 'I think it makes sense if you both come along since I need as many pairs of eyes as possible to keep watch, depending on where our plane is located.'

The hotel proprietor placed Edward's breakfast on the table. 'Do you wish to settle now?' he asked, in an uncompromising tone. Edward paid. His mobile phone rang. It was Arthur, who wanted to know whether he should join them, with or without George.

'No, that won't be necessary but if I want you, I'll let you know. At the moment, there's no need for you to come,' Edward assured him and placed the phone back.

Looking at Red, Walter asked, 'Do know your way around these parts?' A smile spread across Red's face.

'Let's say I once did a job here some years ago and had to

look around the place. Anyhow, I just love France, and the French, and especially good food. But the area around the Côte d'Azur is not my idea of France. It's a mixture of all nationalities, full of very rich people or people who just want to be rich. For some of them it's important to have spent at least one holiday here. No, when I think of France, then it's got to be the Pyrenees, the Canal du Midi or the Atlantic Coast. Or else the Yonne or Nevers in central France. And of course there's Paris!' Red's eyes lit up.

'Then why don't you simply move to France? You're free to stay or live wherever you want, aren't you?' Walter asked.

Red pointed to Edward. 'Ask him. I have a kingdom of my own; I'm absolute ruler over a couple of thousand square yards. I built it up, bit by bit. Why should I give up all of that? Besides, you only really envy something if it doesn't belong to you. I'm sure France would bore me stiff after only six months.' He looked out of the window towards the sea. A large white yacht sailed past. 'Dreams fade away fast.'

## 39

At Cannes the day had begun. The taxi dropped the three men at the airport. Their pilots, meanwhile, had made their way to the airport restaurant, where they were sitting, playing cards. After a search, Walter found them and asked for the keys to the plane. Red and Edward accompanied him to the Learjet.

They opened the hold and changed. The only one whom the overalls fitted exactly was Walter.

'An ideal mechanic's figure,' he grinned and took a few steps, as though he were sashaying along a catwalk.

Red was busy rummaging around for some diskettes in his metal case. 'Can I sit in the plane for a couple of minutes? I just need to work something out.'

'Of course,' replied Edward and opened the aeroplane doors. 'It has just occurred to me that we don't have the keys to the Gulfstream.'

'We don't need any; I've got my case here!' Red sat down in the front seat and switched on his laptop.

'How long will you need, Red?' Edward enquired.

Red shrugged his shoulders. 'I don't know yet, but it could be about half an hour.'

Edward looked at Walter. 'Perhaps we should leave him in peace. If you finish earlier, Red, we'll reach each other by mobile. We shan't be far.'

They wandered slowly around the plane and stopped at the barbed wire fence surrounding the airfield. Edward was the first to break the silence. 'I know how you must feel, Walter. Don't think I've forgotten. I've always admitted, quite openly, that I would only do this job if I were convinced there was no other way. And now I am convinced it's got to go ahead. But she still has a chance. It could be that she's just bust up with Fayed. Perhaps the Kelly Fisher affair will alter things at the last minute. But if not, Walter, we see the job through. There's no other alternative.'

'I know.' Walter leaned on the fence near him, looking up at the clear blue sky above. 'And I fully support the decision, you realize that. Otherwise I wouldn't have joined you out here.'

They stood at the fence for almost a quarter of an hour in silence, each absorbed in his own thoughts.

# 40

Lucy got up as the first rays of sunlight filtered into the room. She wondered whether she should wait for breakfast until Red arrived. On the other hand, it was best to get out into the fresh air on a bright and sunny day like this; but on the other hand, Red would surely need no convincing that with a woman there was an alternative way to start the day. She had never had any reason to complain about his sex drive.

Unable to make up her mind, she went to the bathroom to take a shower. Pausing in front of the large mirror, she contemplated her body. In her opinion, she was still quite desirable. But did Red also think so? She felt her full, firm breasts and her slim hips, wondering if Red slept with other women when he was away on business. He still looked marvellous for his age. She rejected the idea. He was simply not that type of man and besides, she was not jealous and in fact had no right to be.

Taking her time, she showered her body, in the fond hope that Red would perhaps suddenly appear and start to make love to her in the warm spray, as they had done so often before. After a good ten minutes, she turned off the water. Perhaps he might still turn up – or had he spent the night with Edward and goodness knows who else?

There was no sign of Red. Lucy slowly dressed and ordered breakfast for two. There was still no sign of him when breakfast was served. She could make no sense of her earlier observations. After all, Red was highly skilled at the game of hide-and-seek.

The room service had sent her the *Daily Mail*. She cast her eye over the headlines on the front page and hastily flipped through the rest of the paper. Her feeling of disappointment became more intense. Over the last few days, Red had been working round the clock and had hardly spent a single night with her. What annoyed her most of all was the fact that she still hadn't a clue what had brought him here to London.

The phone rang at last. It was Red at the other end of the line.

'Where are you?' she asked, reproachfully. 'I've been waiting to have breakfast with you and I'm almost starving.'

Red explained that he was already on the street, waiting to be picked up by his business colleagues. He was off to Birmingham for an information meeting and would be back the next day, most probably late at night. Immediately, Lucy realized he was lying; she could hear the noise of an aeroplane in the background, taking off above Red's head. She jumped off the sofa, sprang to the window and threw it open. There was no trace of a plane outside. So he must be somewhere outside the city. She shut the window again, giving nothing away to Red.

'Very well then, till tomorrow evening.'

Red still had the phone to his ear when Edward and Walter returned to the plane. 'I was just about to phone you,' he called across to them. 'I can now save myself the bother.' He replaced the mobile and stood up. 'So far as I'm concerned, we can start. But I'll have to call by at a shipbuilding yard.'

Edward stared at him incredulously. 'A shipbuilding yard?'

'That's what I said. I can find the spare part I need either here or at the maintenance stores at Nice airport; it's also used on yachts. But I don't want to attract attention.'

Edward hurried over to the pilots in the restaurant, to pick up the aeroplane key and give them instructions for the following day.

The three of them then drove by taxi to Nice, making a slight detour to the harbour. Red got out to do his errand.

'He's a devil of a chap!' said Edward.

'He's a devil alright!' added Walter, gazing out of the window.

The driver knew instantly which gate to drop them at. Red had told him they were aircraft maintenance personnel who were engaged to carry out repairs on a private jet. He instructed the driver, however, to halt a good two hundred yards from the gate. Edward paid and the three of them, dressed in overalls, got out. As soon as the car was out of sight, Edward took the letter of authority from the breast pocket of his overalls.

'Let me take that,' Red called out, taking the sheet of paper from Edward's hand. He pointed to his metal case and turned to Walter. 'You carry that; Edward can carry my laptop. It'll look more convincing if we allocate the equipment amongst ourselves. OK, let's go!'

Red strode confidently towards the gate. He noticed that the security officers had already caught sight of them and suddenly walked over to the wire fence and waved to a couple of workers, also in overalls, standing near a medium-sized aeroplane.

'Hi, folks! Great weather today!' he greeted them. 'Hope it stays fine over the weekend. Now wave, both of you,' he hissed at his two colleagues. Edward and Walter did as they were told; the other workers actually waved back.

'We're already half-way there!' Red said with a grin. 'We now belong to the rest of the gang.'

He turned round the corner to the security building and knocked furiously on the windowpane. The security officer pointed to the door. Red walked over. It opened before he had even reached it. Edward and Walter waited apprehensively, near the window outside.

'Pierre!' Red called into the shed through the open door.

'Pierre's got the day off,' came the reply.

'Pity.' Red entered the building and plucked the letter of authority rather awkwardly from out of his pocket. 'We have to attend to the air-conditioning so that they won't be sweating inside this weekend.'

One of the security men took the paper. 'Do you know where the plane is?'

'We'll soon find out,' said Red cautiously.

'I'll give them a call and find out for you.'

The security officer picked up the receiver and dialled a short number; a fellow security man prepared their identity passes. 'Are there just the three of you?' he asked, by way of confirmation. Red nodded and, going over to the door, called out, 'Come in fellows, we're about to be decorated!'

They were each given a plastic identity holder, printed with the word "Service", an individual number and an official stamp. A register was put in front of them and they were asked to enter their names and sign.

Red scribbled an illegible signature and passed the book to the other two. 'It's your turn now,' he said, secretly winking at them both. Edward entered some sort of cypher in the last column, Walter used an actual name – Mouton – that they had seen on a roadside hoarding somewhere along the way .

They still had to find out where the Gulfstream was. At long last, the man at the other end of the phone gave the required information. 'Yes? I shall tell them, thank you.' The guard hung up.

'You realize that the plane is scheduled to take off at twelve?'

Red turned to Edward angrily. 'No, we didn't. Then we'll have to look sharp. Where is it located?'

The security officer stood in front of a map which recorded all the parking slots and pointed to one just at the edge. 'Here.'

Red glanced at the map. 'And where are we?' This time the guard pointed to a spot at the bottom of the map.

'OK. Thanks!' Red tapped his forehead with his right index finger, turned around and practically shoved Edward out of the security room, leaving Walter trailing behind with the heavy metal case.

Red told him to turn to the right, without loosening his grip on Edward's shoulder. They slowly disappeared from the view of the security men, behind some high bushes. From the direction of the runway, aircraft engines could be heard preparing for take-off. To the rear, Walter was gasping at the weight of the case. A twin-engine plane thundered past, over their heads. Instinctively Walter ducked, Red let go of Edward and plugged his ears. He then stood still and waited until the plane was far enough away.

'What sort of goddam outfit do you belong to?' he screamed, standing aggressively in front of Edward. 'I have never worked with a bunch of amateurs like you in my whole life. OK, I'm being paid, very well paid. But I'm not paid to spoon-feed you lot. First, I'm supposed to examine lifts, then we make plans all day and suddenly it's on – and you think I can pull the rabbit out of the hat just like that! I understood that the flight was tomorrow and that I had time to prepare the plane today. And then what happens? Damn all!' Red tapped the glass of his wrist-watch. 'Only one hour to reverse the Gulfstream's flight controls. I can't do it, I tell you. You've got to find some other goddam fool. Anyone can see it's a load of bullshit!'

He gesticulated menacingly at Edward. 'I'll tell you one thing; I'm now going to do things *my* way! I don't need you!' He turned round to Walter. 'In fact, I don't need either of you. I can wipe her off the face of the earth without your help.' He took a deep breath and looked up into the sky.

That was the moment Edward was waiting for. 'Have you finished?' he asked curtly. 'In that case we can talk as adults again.' He paused and stuck both hands in his trouser pockets.

'It is most annoying, of course, that the plane is booked to depart at twelve. But no one was to know. A member of the Al Fayed family has obviously decided to go off on a trip somewhere. Or else, perhaps, Diana has also made up her mind to leave for London today. Our information that the plane is making a one day stopover here is scarcely twelve hours old. And it's *your* job to make sure when it does leave that it will never land in London!' His voice was firm and authoritative.

Red was still looking up into the sky overhead. He rocked on his heels, waiting for Edward to continue. But Edward held his peace.

He slowly shifted his gaze downwards to the ground, then over to the smaller planes parked there. What a pity, he reflected; the plan was such a good one. He walked up to Edward and took the laptop out of his hand, then turned to Walter. He stood there in front of him for a moment and shook his head. He took hold of the heavy metal case, pushed a rather nonplussed Walter to one side, and walked back the way he had come.

'What is this all about?' Edward called after him. Red turned around as he strode on. 'Quite simple; I'm off!'

'But you can't do that now!' Edward was about to make off after him but was restrained by Walter. Red turned round again. 'I advise you to stay there on the airstrip for a little while, or else there'll be some awkward questions to answer at the gate.'

Edward and Walter saw Red slowly disappear behind the private aeroplanes. Walter sidled up to his colleague. 'Let him go; he'll be back. Princess Diana has been given an extension.'

Edward reached for his mobile and dialled a London number. After a while, Arthur came on the phone.

**43**

When Sir David, Arthur and George met again that morning in the large conference room, everything seemed to be going according to plan. Arthur reported that support from George and himself had not been necessary at Cannes, at least, not for the time being.

Sir David gave George a reproachful look, glancing towards the frosted-glass pane over the door. 'You have been rather neglectful,' he said.

'I'm sorry, Sir!' came the response. George jumped up and turned on the debugging device.

'Gentlemen, we must now consider in detail the steps to be taken after the death of Princess Diana. Have any of you given thought to the matter?' Sir David looked at them in turn.

'Arthur and I have gone through the general check list for sudden death of members of the Royal Family or Downing Street. I have taken down the key points. You will presumably fly to the scene of the accident, together with Prince Charles. It is up to him to decide whether or not to take the children. A commission of inquiry will then have to be set up to investigate the accident. Half its members will come from our department, the remaining half from Scotland Yard plus, in this case, aviation experts, including a representative of the aircraft manufacturer. The national sovereignty of the country in which the accident will have occurred is a material factor. Then we have to provide information for the media. In this regard, we should perhaps draft an official Press statement now. It would be for you to enquire at source as to the extent to which the regret and concern of the Palace may be integrated into the text of the draft. In any event, statements on behalf of the Government should be drafted. The check list does not envisage an official Press conference. It is a decisive factor if the body is found at the scene of the crash. If so, it will be brought over with Prince Charles in attendance. If not, he will fly back after participating in an extensive search of the area. As is customary, flags will be flown at half-mast. The role of Buckingham Palace in this matter has yet to be defined. A visit of condolence to Prince Charles by Downing Street would appear to be somewhat superfluous; however, members of the Spencer family should be located. We should limit our involvement to Earl Spencer, in order to avoid any embarrassment to her mother or her stepmother. Other formalities, such as the organization of the funeral arrangements, can be left to Earl Spencer. Strategically speaking, that would be the best solution for our department. For us, the important question is who should represent the Palace at the funeral. Our position is that it would be adequate if it were restricted to Charles plus the children. If he were to refuse, it would be awkward for the whole of Great Britain.'

'Very good; it all sounds quite straightforward. But why should *I*, in particular, fly with Prince Charles?'

George became a little embarrassed. 'Without wishing to cause offence, of course, our view is that the function of travelling with Charles does not call for a top-level personality; otherwise the event will be given too much prominence. As you appreciate, the media will take a keen interest in who turns up with him.'

Sir David had not failed to observe a sudden blush spreading over George's cheeks. It made him smile. 'That was most delicately put! You're quite right. Perhaps we . . .'

A sudden bleeping sound could be heard. Arthur jumped up. 'There's a call for us. I'll be back as soon as I can.' He left the room.

Sir David held his head in his hands. 'Now, where was I?

Ah, yes, perhaps we should agree what should be done with this fellow, Red. You said Edward would arrange for him to fly back to the States straight afterwards?'

'That is correct, according to Edward's instructions. We have already put his luggage together and can bring it to Heathrow at a moment's notice.'

'And the second limb of the journey?'

'The same as before.'

Arthur stuck his head into the room. 'Excuse me, Sir David, but can you come to the phone urgently, please? Edward is on the line.'

Sir David got up and went into the ante-room.

'Red has gone to ground in Nice. Apparently the setting-up time was too tight. Edward and Walter are here at Nice airport,' Arthur reported, excitedly.

Sir David grabbed the mobile. 'Edward, come back as soon as possible. Report to me as soon as you're back.' He gave Arthur the phone again and returned to the conference room. Arthur followed a little later.

'George, please go back to your office. Contact the CIA again and try to find out a little more about this chap Red. He is getting odder and odder every minute. He has already cashed in on half a million pounds; he can't just break our agreement and disappear without trace.'

'Disappear?' asked an astonished George, unaware of the contents of the phone call. 'It appears that he was given too little time to do the preparatory work on the aircraft. Apart from that, I have no further details. But if Edward gets in touch again, you should relay the call to the office,' Arthur said.

'Please also find out, as a matter of urgency, what our internal plans are, so that they can be put into operation at short notice. No matter what, Princess Diana must not set foot on British soil ever again!' The excitement in Sir David's voice was unmistakable.

George nodded, silently collected his documents, and left the room.

## 44

Red rushed past the security hut with a friendly wave, and immediately chanced upon a vacant taxi driving by. He signalled the driver to stop.

'You don't have to switch on the meter. I just want the entrance to flight departures,' he shouted into the cab and sat down on the back seat.

'That's not on,' replied the driver.

'Of course it is; I pay well!' Red took his wallet from his overall pocket and flashed two UK fifty-pound notes in front of the driver. 'If you change them, they'll buy more than a couple of meals,' he grinned, as he tossed them over the seat. The driver took them, without saying a word, and put his foot down on the accelerator.

The journey hardly took two minutes. Red jumped out and hurried back to the airport building with his luggage.

The young lady at the reception gave a smile as she saw him coming. 'What can I do for you, Monsieur?'

'When's the next flight to London?'

She entered some data into her computer and consulted the screen. 'The British Midland midday flight is about to be called. The BA flight is half an hour later.'

'A direct flight?'

'They are both direct flights.'

'Are there any vacant seats?'

'There is plenty of room on both flights, Monsieur.'

'Then I'll take the first. Where do I book the flight?'

She pointed to another counter with her ballpoint pen. 'Over there, Monsieur!'

'Thanks!' Red turned round and went across to the reservations counter. Another lady welcomed him.

'A seat on the next flight to London – one way!'

The lady nodded. 'Smoker?'

'No.'

'Window seat?'

'That's fine.'

She typed in a few details. 'What name, please, Monsieur?'

'Avraham Rosenzweig.' She typed the name on to the computer keyboard. The printer began to whirr. Red pulled out his wallet. 'Can I pay in sterling?'

'Oh, it would be easier if you exchanged them at the foreign exchange counter over there, so that I can accept francs. I shall put the ticket on one side. You have plenty of time, Monsieur!'

Red dragged his luggage across the hall to the bank counter, exchanged some notes, and dragged the luggage back again. 'I am so sorry, Monsieur!' she said as he returned, realizing how heavy his cases were. Red paid and took the ticket.

'Would you kindly make your way to the check-in in the course of the next ten minutes?'

Red nodded and followed the signs.

# 45

Lucy had just finished breakfast. She asked room service for the Yellow Pages of the London telephone directory. She took the phone off the glass table and sat down on the sofa, holding the phone in her hand. She fished a ballpoint pen out of her handbag, opened the bulky book, searched under the heading "H" for the London hotels and dialled the first number in the column – 723 3386. The voice of the young lady at the other end of the line announced the Crown Royal Norfolk Hotel.

'Please can you tell me if Mr Avraham Rosenzweig is still booked in?'

'Would you spell the name, please?'

Lucy spelt it out and waited. It was some while before the reception came back. 'I'm sorry, but we have no record of a gentleman by that name.'

'Excuse me, I must have got the wrong number.'

Lucy then dialled the next hotel and got a negative reply. She then dialled the next number. It took a full hour until she finally struck lucky with the Lincoln House Hotel.

'Mr Avraham Rosenzweig? So far as I know, he has already checked out. One moment, please!'

Lucy tapped the table nervously with her ballpoint pen and waited. She then heard the receiver being picked up. 'I was right, Madame, Mr Rosenzweig is no longer here.'

'Could you tell me, please, when he left?'

'I'm sorry but I'm not allowed to give that information.'

Lucy replaced the receiver and sat back in the sofa, thinking hard. Where had Red spent the night when he left her on her own? She made up her mind to solve this riddle as soon as possible.

## 46

It was a good hour later when Edward and Walter arrived at Cannes airport. Red was nowhere in sight, nor had the two pilots caught a glimpse of him.

Edward had pulled himself together. He tried to contact Arthur in London but got hold of George instead. 'Arthur is still with Sir David,' he was told. 'I have heard the bad news. Do you know what the plan is now?'

'No, Sir David just told us to return as quickly as possible,' Edward replied.

'He is absolutely determined that Princess Diana should not return to England alive.'

Edward could hear George's voice failing, so he changed the topic of conversation.

'You can do two things for me, please. Firstly, would you find out how I can get hold of our two pilots. I have given them my mobile phone number and asked them to call me early tomorrow morning, because we all thought we wouldn't be flying back until tomorrow. I need that right now. Secondly, would you please find out if Red left Nice by plane and what his destination is. He's not around here at Cannes airport.'

'I'll do that straightaway, Edward.'

'Thanks.' Edward pressed the 'off' button and attempted to contact Red again. He had obviously switched off his own mobile.

George came back quickly. 'I located the pilots and rang them. They'll be with you as soon as possible. I've made no progress so far with Red. But I'll have the information by the time you've arrived in London. By the way, that chap is a slick operator.'

'I am aware of that. Why do you mention it?'

'He has removed the hard disk from our computer. We cleared out the apartment this morning.'

'You've got to be bright to think about that in the first place.' Edward ended their conversation. 'Our crew is on its way,' he called across to Walter, who was standing some yards away. Walter came over and looked at Edward, helplessly.

'What do we do now?'

'Just wait. What else can we do? Either Red is handling this thing on his own, in which case we wait till we know the outcome, or else he really has flown off, in which case the question is, where to?'

'If so, then he's certain to return to London. His clothes are there.'

Edward laughed out loud. 'Walter,' he said mischievously, 'can anyone be so naive? Someone like Red only needs his blessed case and his laptop, nothing else. Besides, he has removed the hard disk from the computer we lent him, so that none of his data falls into the wrong hands.'

'When are the pilots due?' asked Walter, consulting his wrist-watch.

'I haven't a clue, but I don't think they'll be long. Let's wait in the restaurant and order a bite to eat. Who knows what's going to happen today and when we'll ever get our next meal.'

## 47

Edward was not far wrong. No sooner had they ordered their food when both pilots arrived at the restaurant with their flight cases.

'Take your time eating. We have to carry out the usual checks first and warm up the engines. That'll take a little while. Also, we have to announce our time of departure,' the chief pilot explained.

'We'll be at the plane as soon as we can,' Edward assured him.

'What do we do if Red fails to surface again?' asked Walter cautiously, when both pilots had moved out of sight.

'Then I'll fly over to the States and shoot him myself. I'll find him, wherever he is,' Edward growled.

'But seriously, what happens next?'

Edward shrugged his shoulders and gave no answer. What was to be done? This question had been nagging him for more than an hour. His worst fear was that Red would do the job single-handed and that, as a killer, nothing could hold him back. But then he secretly hoped to hear that Princess Diana would cancel her marriage plans with Dodi at the last minute, or that her pregnancy was merely a rumour or a ruse, or even that Dodi would suddenly revive his interest in Kelly Fisher, that dumb American pin-up.

'What are you thinking about?' Walter enquired.

Edward just murmured something incomprehensible to

himself. The meal was being served; he was happy not to have to give a proper answer.

Edward had ordered grilled octopus. Walter was looking forward to his lamb *à la provençale*. It had a glorious flavour of thyme.

## 48

Red had made a curious impression on the British Midland passengers. Clad in his overalls and holding his laptop, he was nearly shown straight into the cockpit. The stewardess was astonished to see him produce his boarding card. Most of the other passengers were businessmen and, despite the heat, rather well-dressed. Their stares had no impact on Red; he was used to far worse.

The plane was only sparsely filled. It rolled punctually up to the edge of the runway. The stewardess was walking down the aisle, checking the overhead lockers and the passengers' seat belts. She noticed Red's mobile sticking out of his breast pocket.

'Have you switched off your mobile?' she asked him, with a friendly smile. 'Please check. Thank you!'

Red was annoyed with himself that he could let anything like that happen. He had been working for years on various methods of interfering with a plane's electronics by mobile phone. He was aware of its potential.

He called for an English newspaper and languidly flicked through the pages. He had since realized that he had been too aggressive to Edward. But in the last few hours before the job was due to start, his nerves had hit the tolerance barrier. Besides, he was no longer so young; he had to admit that to himself often enough in recent years. Quite apart from that, it would have been amateurish if he had tried to fix the plane in one hour flat. He would need to stress that point to Edward once again.

Red wondered what he and Walter were up to? Would

they look around for him in Nice or Cannes? He felt uncomfortable that he had not at least left a message for them at Cannes. They were both nice guys. He judged Edward to be the brighter of the two, but Walter as being more reliable once the going got tough on jobs like this. But – and Red was quite certain about this – neither of them was the killer type. So they would be needing him again.

He was even more worried about what might happen next, since he did not want to abandon the job. All that was necessary was to find out Princess Diana's very next engagement after her visit to London. Edward should find out as quickly as possible. It was clear that it would be some time before a chance like the Gulfstream crash would again present itself. But he had carried out too many jobs not to realize that there were usually alternatives. If Diana were to drive to that castle in Scotland, she would go either by helicopter or fast car. The job would be simple enough if only one knew what type of transport was envisaged, even though the crash would take place on British soil.

Red closed his eyes, but inner tensions prevented him from falling asleep this time. He looked out of the window. There were mountains immediately below. He tried to find out what part of France they were flying over; taking a bearing on the sun, he calculated the direction of the flight path. As his eyes fell on the hilly landscape, he realized he had fallen in love with the country.

## 49

Edward and Walter had no idea that they were only a few miles' flying time behind Red. They whiled away the time planning theoretical scenarios. Diana would touch down in England tomorrow some time or other. In fact, the current information sheets mentioned only London, but it was quite possible that she might fly to Aberdeen, which meant that they would be short of time to carry out the necessary preparatory work.

'Do you happen to know the road between Aberdeen and Balmoral?' Walter asked. Edward shook his head.

'I have been there once or twice on my motor-cycle,' Walter continued. 'The area would certainly offer a number of opportunities for Red, I imagine, assuming, of course, that he does surface again. But I think it's only practicable if Princess Diana were to break her journey in London.'

Edward tapped Walter on the arm. 'You're not aware of Sir David's new instructions. Diana must on no account set foot on British soil. That means that the accident should not take place in England.'

'OK. So that makes our task virtually impossible, whether it's London or Aberdeen. Of course, we needn't take his instructions too literally. Our chances are best only if she has no contact with the Press or her children. At least, that is my opinion. Alternatively, we'll have to shoot down the aircraft before it lands.'

Edward snapped his fingers. 'You're right, that could be our solution! If the plane is unexpectedly shot down over the Atlantic . . . A bang, then she goes out like a light, for ever!'

'Nonsense!' Walter interrupted him. 'That's a harebrained idea! Not all the wreckage sinks to the bottom. They would fish out the smallest pieces and would easily establish that the plane had been fired on. Then the hunt would be on.'

'So what? Then there would be speculation but still no proof,' Edward retorted. 'Don't you understand, Walter? If the accident is timed to occur after the official announcement of her engagement, there will be even more suspicion of dirty business.'

'Maybe, but . . .' Walter had to admit that he saw no other solution for the time being. He was keen to know what his London colleagues had worked out in the meantime. As they came closer and closer to London, the more his brain throbbed with the refrain: *Diana must die, Diana must die, Diana must die*!

Edward noticed the change of expression in Walter's face. He decided to speak to him about it. 'When I was over in the USA with Red the other day, I suddenly experienced a curious turbulent feeling inside. My mind was in a whirl, so I tried to concentrate on other things, but my head was turning round and round. I don't know if you've had that feeling. I have been trying now for some time to work out what the cause was. At any rate, I've been through a lot in life. I fought in the Falklands and have seen men killed in action. I've worked on assassination jobs. And then, all of a sudden, I felt strange. I don't know if Red noticed, at least he gave nothing away. I passed it all off as jet lag symptoms. But I was ashamed of myself. Yes, I felt genuine shame! But I have no idea what caused it.' He paused, looked out of the window, then continued. 'I have been turning that experience over in my mind ever since and I think I might have hit on the reason. It was George who once told us that in his opinion Princess Diana lacked the image of an enemy of the people. And just this morning Red even asked us if we really wanted to eliminate our "beautiful Princess". I think that's the heart of the matter. We identify with her. She's a woman who wants something from life; she wants to *live*. And we're assigned to eliminate her only because her ideas aren't ours, nor those of the Royal Family, nor of other British subjects, all of which could lead to complications. She doesn't conform to the standard image of an enemy. You fire back spontaneously if a soldier has you in his sights. If a terrorist takes people hostage and threatens them, you give the order to shoot to kill. In this scenario, the action takes place at a totally different level. At the end of the day, though, the message is the same: kill or be killed.'

Edward turned round and glanced at Walter, who had buried his head in his hands. He grabbed him by the arm. Walter gave a jump and looked up. 'I think we all feel the same,' Edward whispered. 'We must move ahead; we'll see it through!'

## 50

The plane touched down shortly afterwards. A car was waiting for them. As soon as the driver took the motorway towards London, Edward made another attempt to contact Red. This time, to his utter surprise, Red replied.

'Damn it all, where are you hiding?' Edward shouted angrily. 'We didn't bargain for that kind of behaviour.' He waited for Red's response and quickly looked at his watch. 'OK, then, in half an hour.'

He switched the phone off. 'We're lucky; Red's in London. He took a flight back and had turned off his mobile. We meet him in Hyde Park.' He gave the driver the necessary instructions.

'What else did he say?' asked Walter.

Edward shook his head. 'Nothing, but it was he who asked for a meeting. I had the impression he felt a bit sheepish that it had come to this.'

The driver made good progress through London; he obviously knew the area well. He made a detour to avoid a few road junctions that were notoriously congested at that time of day.

At the end of Broad Walk they found Red waiting. He greeted them in the same gear in which he had left them – in blue overalls, weighed down with his metal case and laptop.

They were not surprised, therefore, at his first question, which was whether his clothing was still in London.

'We put your clothes in the car,' explained Walter. 'Do you want to change first?'

Red shook his head. It was obviously more important for

him to think over the next steps with them. 'Let's leave that
till later,' he said. 'But I'd like to deposit the case in your car
for the time being.'

Edward glanced at Walter. 'Would you see to that, please?
We'll walk along a bit; you can join us later.' Walter took
hold of the heavy metal case without a murmur and carried
it to the underground garage where their car was parked.
Red and Edward made off in the direction of Hyde Park
Corner.

'Please let me explain,' Red immediately volunteered. 'I
think we've come to know each other well enough, so there
ought to be no reproaches on either side. As soon as I am
aware of the full facts, you'll understand, I set about my work
extremely carefully. I don't think either of us fully appreciates
what could be at stake for us both. You might be moved to a
slightly quieter department. But your boss, whoever he may
be, would be involved in the biggest scandal that has ever
happened in Great Britain. I personally have got quite a bit
at stake too. Now, I'd like to bring you into my confidence
with some information that nobody else knows, apart from
Lucy and myself. And I'd be grateful if you would keep it
to yourself.'

He stood still for a moment, making sure they could not
be overheard. 'I'm planning to retire once this job is over
and done with. I'd like to quit this prison and enjoy some
freedom with Lucy; she has no idea what my work actually
is. I made up my mind to do so following your last visit,
and, to be frank, I was encouraged by a remark you made at
the time about my retirement. Now, I don't want to jettison
my whole future by acting too hastily, nor can I afford to.
Believe me, the conditions for an air crash in France were
exceptional. But I would have had to work on it for at least
three hours non-stop. Three whole hours – and not just one
miserable hour – with the chance that the pilot or someone
else might suddenly turn up unexpectedly and catch us at it
red-handed. Do you realize what that would have meant? The

end of the road. The whole plan would have blown up in our faces. So let's establish one thing: it didn't happen. And let's just ask ourselves the question, in all seriousness: what do we do now?' Red stared at Edward, who had taken this all in quietly. 'Or have you reached some other conclusions in the meantime?'

'No,' answered Edward in all honesty. 'We have thought about one or two alternatives but they are too risky and therefore impracticable. But the question is: what is practicable?'

Red was still standing at the same spot. 'I don't know if this is the right place to continue our discussion. Maybe we should return to that little apartment I had . . .'

'It has since been cleared,' interrupted Edward.

'And what about my belongings?' Red enquired.

'They are packed up somewhere for you to pick up. We assumed you would fly back as soon as the job was finished. There's no need to worry. We'll find you another hotel for tonight.'

'That's unnecessary. I'll handle that. Let's arrange to meet and talk some place tomorrow. Then we'll solve the problem.' Red looked round and saw Walter coming towards them.

Edward started to explain. 'Red would like to talk to us where we can't be disturbed. We might drive out to Greenwich again . . .'

Red interrupted him. 'No, we'd lose far too much time. Can't we simply send the driver away and go off somewhere?'

Edward looked at Walter again.

'OK,' said Walter. 'I'll send him home and drive the car towards the Knightsbridge exit. Wait for me there, please.'

He hurried back to the underground garage.

'How many men have you got on this job?' asked Red abruptly. To his surprise, Edward answered this time without a moment's hesitation.

'Five in all. But apart from Walter and myself, they only

know you by name. No one's tailing you, nor have I given anybody any data or descriptions whatsoever that might lead to your identification. Unless, that is, the CIA . . .'

'Not so loud, man!' hissed Red.

'You're quite right. Perhaps we should change the subject. In any case, you need have no concerns in that area.'

They continued their stroll in silence and arrived some moments later at the Knightsbridge exit. The noise of a car hooter could suddenly be heard. It was Walter, who was waiting for them both. Edward went over to the driver's door and opened it.

'I'm sorry, but I need some time with Red on his own. One of us has to . . .' He made an unmistakable gesture with his hand. 'I'll report back as soon as possible. We'll see each other later today.'

Walter got out, allowing Edward to take over the steering wheel. He gave him a friendly slap on the shoulder. 'Do your best and make sure you come up with the right solution. His case and clothing are in the boot.'

Red thanked him with a wave of the hand and eased himself into the passenger seat, laptop in hand. 'Poor Walter,' he said with a laugh. 'A great guy, I'd say.'

## 51

Edward threaded his way through the dense traffic.

'This gets worse and worse every day,' Red observed. 'I couldn't stand it here for long. How can you possibly get to work if you need so much time for even the shortest journey?'

'If you work here or have to attend a meeting, you go by tube. It's the most reliable form of transport,' Edward commented. This reminded him of the reason why they were meandering painfully and aimlessly through the London traffic.

'But what do you suggest we do now? I would guess we only have about twenty-four hours, at the most.'

Red opened his laptop and switched it on. 'I've already made a start. Let's consider the facts as we know them. Your Princess will be picked up in Olbia tomorrow by the Gulfstream and will be flying to London . . .'

'Stop!' Edward was drumming his fingers nervously on the steering wheel. 'One or two questions need to be answered. We don't know whether she's flying to London and from there to Balmoral to join the children, or whether she's flying direct to Aberdeen.'

'OK. But she won't be walking from the airport to the Castle. And if she flies via London, she'll be travelling from there by car or some other form of transport, won't she?'

Edward gave no reply, so Red developed his train of thought further. 'The question now arises as to what type of vehicle she'll be using in London, or else in this place called Aberdeen. That means I'll have to work on a maximum of two types of motor vehicle. How close is your man to the Princess?'

'Why do you ask?'

'Well, I'd be grateful if I knew as soon as possible where she lands and what type of vehicle I have to plan for. Ideally, I'd like to know precisely at what spot the accident should take place and how. Do you get the point?'

Again, there was no reply.

'Let's assume your Princess is to be picked up at Olbia some time in the late morning. In that case, we have to know where she's flying to – at least two hours before departure. I'm happy with two hours, plus flying time to London, provided the vehicle is easily accessible. That means you have to find me some place I can operate from without being disturbed. If she flies to Aberdeen, on the other hand, we have to add on our travelling time. This means that the time available in Aberdeen would be pretty short.'

Edward broke in. 'I've another idea. We should find out if we have a say as to what type of vehicle picks her up. Whether in London or Aberdeen. Which would give us time to work on both vehicles tonight and then we could simply drive one of them to the airport where she lands.'

'That would obviously be the best and the simplest solution,' agreed Red.

Edward steered the car to the kerb and grabbed his mobile. Arthur answered. Edward outlined his latest idea and asked him to sound it out.

'Edward, that's ideal,' said Red, now a little happier. 'If we can possibly get the vehicle ready on the spot tonight, we can either drive or fly to Aberdeen. We would gain a lot of time and would have prepared for all possible contingencies.'

'Always assuming we are not detected as we approach the vehicles. I don't foresee any problem in London. In Scotland, it won't be so simple. Prince Charles might send his car to pick her up. In that case, we wouldn't get anywhere near.'

'Aha,' Red grinned, 'so Charles is not involved in your scheme!'

Edward was annoyed that he had let the cat out of the bag; he ignored the remark. 'We can't take anything for granted, of course. Perhaps it'll be a pushover. We'll soon find out.'

They emerged through the traffic jam at last. It occurred to Red that he simply had to ring Lucy. 'Maybe we should take a drink together whilst we find out what options are available. I must say, I'm almost dying of thirst!'

Edward agreed.

## 52

Walter was astonished to find that only George was waiting in the large conference room. Sir David and Arthur had withdrawn, having asked George to let them know as soon as Edward and Walter arrived. George got up and phoned them both from the ante-room. He then sat down and joined a very exhausted Walter.

He gently broke the ice. 'Jolly bad luck, what?' he said. 'On the other hand, I must frankly admit I'm glad it didn't quite work out. I always hoped . . .'

'It will!' Walter butted in resolutely. 'We'll have it over and done with as soon as possible, then we'll all go throw up and life will just carry on as before! So, please contain yourself!'

George stared at him in amazement; he had never heard Walter speak like this before. 'Where's Edward?' he enquired.

'He's on his way here, with Red.'

'Red? I thought he had gone to ground.' George jumped up, shocked; this meant that the job could be brought back to life.

'*Had* gone to ground! Red arrived here in London before we did. Didn't you find that out? He took an ordinary scheduled flight.'

George shook his head. 'That may well be, but we've heard nothing. Perhaps Arthur has the information. That means we're back on course, doesn't it?'

'Yes, we carry on as before. Edward and Red have just driven off to talk things over and agree on tomorrow as the day for action.'

'What sort of a man is he, this chap Red?' asked George.

Walter stood up and went over to the drinks table. He helped himself to an orange juice. 'If you set eyes on him without knowing what he does for a living, you'd never believe he was a professional killer, or at least sent people to their death. On the other hand, when he comes to the point, he's so matter-of-fact that your spine tingles. He unpacks his computer and describes in great detail exactly how he'll kill a man by accident, without raising any suspicions, in just the same way that a carpenter might tell you how he assembles a piece of furniture you've asked him to make. And the extraordinary thing about him is this: you soon forget that it's *you* who commissioned him to do the job. You understand? With him, you lose all sense of being personally involved in the act of murder. And I know from Edward that he shares my feelings.'

George stared at Walter. How would he ever forget that he had played a role in the execution of a death contract? Even if he was only a small cog in a big wheel, he would still be party to the assassination.

Sir David's arrival jolted him out of these thoughts. They both noticed that he had already put on his gold-rimmed spectacles, which for him was highly unusual. Also, he had brought no files with him, only a piece of paper, which was folded. He appeared to be in quite a state. 'This fellow Red, or Rosenzweig, has flown back to London. Find him at once!' he demanded.

'Excuse me, Sir,' Walter broke in, 'but Edward is now sitting down with him, reviewing the situation.'

'And why was I not informed about this before?' asked Sir David angrily. He sat down in his usual seat and glared at Walter.

'Pardon me, Sir, but I have only just arrived. Edward and I separated, and I had to take the tube.'

With a wave of the hand, Sir David indicated that they could both sit down again. 'Has anyone thought about the next step? Do either of you realize what a fine mess this chap Red has landed us in by walking out on the job?' He banged the table with his fist. 'Our instructions are crystal clear: Princess Diana must on no account set foot on British soil again. So how are you going to prevent her now?' He paused and signalled to George to bring him a drink. George poured him some mineral water. Sir David drank half the glass and put it on the table with a thump. It was quite obvious that he had been vigorously attacked and placed under pressure.

'The object of the exercise was not an assassination, but a straightforward accident that would raise nobody's suspicions. I must now ask you to carry out our objective without further delay, no matter what it costs or how it is to be executed. You cannot seriously believe that Princess Diana will avoid the glare of publicity when she arrives tomorrow, having spent a whole week with this man Fayed. You know as well as I do what rumours have been spreading throughout the media in the meantime, which we well know to be fact! The photographers and the journalists will be queuing for miles. And I can already see the headlines in the *Sun*: "Princess Di to marry Dodi, Princess Di pregnant, stepfather of Prince William, Heir to the Throne, involved in arms deals!"' His face was now even paler than usual. 'Gentlemen, you must see to it that these headlines never get into print!' He jumped up and hurried out of the room as quickly as he had come in.

# 53

It was already dusk when Red entered the suite at the Dorchester. The rooms lay in comparative darkness; Lucy was nowhere to be seen. As he undressed, he inhaled the smell of overalls still clinging to his body, so he decided to take a shower. In the bathroom he realized that Lucy had already put on her make-up for the evening. Some articles of clothing hung over the bathtub and on the edge of the bath stood a bottle of nail varnish she had forgotten to close. Coming out of the shower, he caught a glimpse of his three-day-old beard; it had grown quite bushy in the meantime. He deliberated whether to shave it off, but finally thought it best to leave it on until he was back home. Lucy would probably only return later that evening; he therefore decided to eat at the Dorchester and leave a message for her at the reception.

He dressed and looked around the room before leaving. He had to take Edward's mobile with him at all cost, since it had not been clarified whether the car that was to pick up Diana at the airport tomorrow could be made available that evening. He had to prepare himself for a turbulent night. As he consulted his watch, it appeared more and more unlikely that she would be taking the night flight up to Aberdeen. Red, himself, had no idea when he might be called upon in the next twenty-four hours; his only hope was that the job was practicable and that he could get it over with quickly. In case of doubt, he had a card up his sleeve – but he would keep that to himself for as long as possible.

He left the hotel suite. The lifts were in constant use, so he had to wait for quite a time until a gentle signal indicated

that one of them was on its way. As the door opened, he saw
Lucy in front of him. She was as surprised as he was.

'Red, what are you doing here? I thought you were in
– er . . . ?' She had forgotten the name of the place he had
mentioned.

Red ducked the question. He took her by the arm and
kissed her; the lift doors meanwhile closed, leaving them
both alone in the corridor. Quick as lightning, he lost no
time in adjusting to the new situation. He then slowly relaxed
his grip.

'Darling, aren't you happy to see me back in London so
soon? The timetable for negotiations was drastically altered,
since the conditions were totally different from what we had
been led to believe. So that means I'm still on call but I'm
close at hand, so now we can do things together.' Lucy,
herself, was happy that Red didn't ask any questions, so she
didn't query what 'on call' actually meant. Instead, she clung
on to his arm and went back with him to their suite.

'I was just about to order myself something to eat in the
Grill Room,' he explained. 'But we have other options!'

'No, let's relax and eat here. I've been on my feet today and
feel a little tired. I'd like to change my shoes.' Lucy slipped off
her flat-heeled shoes and went into the bedroom to look for
a pair of mules. In her new shoes she went up to Red, with
a smile on her face. 'Now you can kiss me more easily!'

As Red clasped her into his arms, he caught sight of the
Yellow Pages on the sofa table, which had not been put back.
He wondered whether to mention this to her.

'You smell of oil,' she said, snuffling around his neck.

He gave a hearty laugh. 'Impossible! Why should I smell
of oil? As a matter of fact, I have just taken a shower. Maybe
it's the shower gel or my new shirt.' He took off his jacket
and sniffed the underarm of his shirt. 'Yes, that smell could
be mistaken for oil.'

Lucy appeared to be happy with the explanation. 'Why
not put on some eau-de-toilette; the smell is not that

pleasant. Or else change your shirt and send it to the laundry.'

Red went into the bathroom and put on some aftershave. As he returned to the living room, he noticed that the Yellow Pages had disappeared from the sofa table. This, he reflected, was rather interesting; what had Lucy been searching for in the phone book, and why, especially, did she wish to conceal it from him?

'What have you been up to today whilst I was away?' he asked casually, hoping to find out by a different approach.

Lucy had meanwhile poured herself some cognac and was moving the balloon to and fro between her two fingers. 'Let me think. First of all, I had a long lie-in and then I spent some time on my make-up. And then I ate some breakfast, and afterwards I took a stroll around town. Tonight, I decided, I would dine at the Orso but my legs and feet were killing me, so I came back to the hotel. Perhaps I should have asked them to bring me something to eat in the room.'

Red took Lucy's cognac glass from her hand and drank the contents. 'Let's go eat!' He put the glass on one side and gave her a kiss on her brow.

## 54

Edward entered Arthur's office and found him on the phone to vehicle control. 'If I understand you correctly, no arrangements have been made yet.' Arthur gave a desperate look in Edward's direction. 'In short, you don't know. Thanks!'

He threw the receiver on to the telephone and gave vent to his anger. 'It's enough to make you sick! It's a pile of shit! I've been phoning and phoning. Nobody knows a single thing. Everyone says that Princess Diana is expected around midday tomorrow, but no one can tell me where she arrives and what car has been booked to pick her up.' He grabbed a piece of paper he had laid on the desk. 'The only point of reference I have is that she might have a date with Fay Marshalsea, who would be meeting her.'

'Who on earth is this Fay woman and how did you get hold of her?'

'Fay Marshalsea is Diana's former lady-in-waiting. She's the one with the twins.'

Edward suddenly remembered. 'That all sounds quite possible. But how accurate is this information?'

'Accurate?' Arthur gave a laugh and raised both arms, in a theatrical gesture. 'Nothing is accurate. Do you realize I've been phoning around about this stupid vehicle for two hours now? I have also told Henry in the SAS to be on his toes. He, by the way, is the source of our information about Fay. But not even he's entirely sure that the information about Fay is accurate; it could also be this Doctor, Ann Coxon. He picked up the data quite by chance and probably far too late; he didn't think it was relevant.'

'That means we're dangling in mid-air again?'

Arthur nodded. 'Yes, you can put it that way.'

'And what's George up to?'

'He's sitting down with Sir David and Walter at a crisis meeting. Sir David is under quite a lot of pressure. When you rang at midday today, he gave the impression that he would have liked to have taken a revolver and finished off the job himself. We should have hired a hot-blooded Italian from Sardinia. A murder on Sardinia – everyone would have bought that.'

'Arthur, we've always assumed the accident would take place here in London or in England, at least. No one could possibly foresee how the situation would unfold and that Princess Diana would be spending time abroad.'

The door opened and George entered. He was perplexed to see Edward. 'What are you doing here? What have you arranged with Red?'

'Nothing definite. He's on call in some hotel or other. I left his laptop and case in the boot. The car is parked in the garage, under lock and key.'

'In that case we could carry out a quick check on the data he's saved on file,' grinned Arthur.

Edward looked at him, crossly. 'In our situation, we should let sleeping dogs lie. We can do without the aggro and all the other problems. The whole assignment now makes absolutely no sense whatsoever. We can't jeopardize his position any further.' His voice rang out authoritatively. 'Arthur, no individual initiatives, please. Is that understood? Red entrusted his personal belongings to me and they will stay under lock and key.'

He did not notice Arthur smirking. 'If anyone wants me, I'm in my office.' He turned round and went off.

'We're all a bundle of nerves today,' sighed Arthur, as he picked up the phone again.

## 55

Walter sat at his desk, reporting that day's events on the central computer. He looked up briefly as Edward entered the room. 'Have you seen George yet?'

'I know everything. Even Arthur's had no success.' Edward sat down at his desk and also switched on his computer. He entered the various code names and code numbers until he had penetrated the very highest security level he had personal access to. He flipped through the older entries until he came to new information. But there was only one fresh bit of news – from Sardinia. Diana had dialled a number on her mobile, which sounded rather familiar. He took it down and switched into the public information file, but no trace of the number was recorded. He entered one security level higher and finally identified it as belonging to James Whitaker. Edward wondered what tales Diana had been telling this particular court correspondent she had been so friendly with over the years. He entered the minutes files but found no record of the phone conversation. He switched back to the news file and flicked further on. What surprised him was that the latest news update at five o'clock recorded no data on the excursion to Cannes.

'Walter, how far have you got?' he asked, almost nonchalantly.

'Hang on a second.'

'Take a break and update your report in the central computer file,' Edward told him.

Walter saved the text he had recorded and sent it upstream. Edward stared at the screen but nothing had changed. The last entry was recorded at 5.12 p.m. 'Repeat and double-check that you've entered the correct data,' he told Walter, who laboriously re-entered his data. Again, Edward's screen recorded no change. 'How curious,' he commented. 'I think you can spare yourself the effort on your daily report. Someone has built in security controls.' Then he closed the file and typed in a short text and sent it to the central computer. Again he switched over to the news desk. It had not been recorded. 'Forget it,' said Edward pensively. 'We've been cut off from central memory.'

'What does that mean?' rejoined Walter.

Edward shoved his chair backwards and gave the matter some thought. 'For the moment, I can't make head or tail of it. But someone has given instructions that our data should not be read by anyone else.' He suddenly clicked his fingers and jumped up. 'Walter, do you realize what that means?'

Walter gazed at him expectantly.

'This can only mean that even colleagues who have access to higher-level and top-level secret data haven't been informed about our job. The information about the liquidation of Princess Diana apparently just bypasses certain departments and certain people who might have comments of their own. And the instructions probably do not come from the top of the organization, as Sir David has always led us to believe. Walter, there's something fishy about this whole business!'

'Then let me just check what justification was given for us to use the Learjet today.' Walter entered a few coded numbers into his keyboard and called up a complete overview of the entire action plan for the day. He clicked the mouse on to the Learjet icon, which flashed up the following information: 'Bodyguard and transport Avraham Rosenzweig, Arms Salesman. Accompanying passengers: two. Objective: DST rendezvous, Cannes'.

'I think I must be going mad!' Walter interjected angrily. 'Do you know who we flew with today? An arms dealer, called Avraham Rosenzweig, to the *Direction de la surveillance du térritoire*, at Cannes. We are not mentioned by name at all; it would obviously look unconvincing if it came to light that two members of our department were accompanying an arms dealer as his bodyguards. That would make everyone suspect what the endgame was.' Walter's face had now turned quite puce; he was drumming his fingers nervously on the edge of his keyboard.

'Take it easy,' Edward drew his chair up to Walter's desk and sat down. 'Let's just summarize the facts as we know them. Firstly, we have been briefed on the job exclusively by Sir David. We can certainly rule him out as the man who pulls the strings. He simply wouldn't dare; furthermore, he's not a fanatic. At the level beyond him, we reach a dead end. But we were authorized to access the CIA, and from the CIA there must have been a lateral connection to some higher level of authority. And then we have our man Henry from the SAS, which means there will be an official exchange of information with the SAS in the whole affair. On the other hand, Sir David was able to agree the Press session with Prince Charles very quickly. Therefore, one begins to suspect lateral contacts with Buckingham Palace.'

'That leaves all options wide open again,' concluded Walter with a sigh. 'I don't think we'll ever succeed in finding out who calls the shots.'

'Wait a moment, I'm not giving up that quickly!' Edward stood up and went over to his computer and switched over to another file. He would contact this man Henry; perhaps he knew more about the background. He picked out his number and code name and dialled him. It was a little while before Henry picked up the receiver.

They swapped code names.

'Edward here, anything to report?'

'It's evening now and I haven't had anything to eat yet,' came the reply.

Henry was obviously unable to speak at that moment without being overheard.

'Then get in touch, please, as soon as you've had your meal or before you go to bed.' Edward hung up. He would have dearly loved to have known who Henry was and where he had been planted within the Al Fayed establishment.

## 56

Red and Lucy ordered a bottle of champagne in the Grill Room of the Dorchester, with oysters as a starter. But the oysters weren't to Red's taste. They were not so fresh as those from Gruisson or Saint-Jean-de-Luz.

'You don't look too happy today,' Lucy gave him an anxious look and clasped his right hand. 'I'm worried about you. You look tense and tired. I think I should take better care of you.'

'Why not?' laughed Red, throwing her a kiss across the table. 'You ought really to spoil me much more than you do already.'

Two waiters hurried over to their table. One of them cleared away the oyster shells and plates; the other brought the soup Red and Lucy had ordered. The soup was far too hot, as Red soon discovered. He laid down his spoon and dug into the bread that had just been served. He had eaten very little all day and had been on his feet for the last eighteen hours.

Lucy was wondering why he was in such a bad mood. Had something gone wrong? Or had he noticed something? She was not sure herself. She had the distinct feeling that this time things were different. Here in London, he disappeared rather more often than usual, had stayed at his own hotel, which he had then suddenly quit. He must have stayed elsewhere, since he had not slept with her for two nights. Was another woman involved?

Red seemed to sense that Lucy had also stopped eating and was simply staring at the table in front of her. 'Hi, sweetheart, a penny for your thoughts!'

As he picked up his spoon again, Edward came on the phone. Red jumped up with his mobile and hurried out of the room. Edward told him that for the time being there was nothing significant to report and that, in fact, nothing was expected to happen immediately.

'Edward,' threatened Red, 'each minute is a minute lost.' He had now reached the lobby. 'I don't want a repetition of this morning's experience ever again; since then I have also given you my own analysis of the situation. I don't take risks. Just think up something. There must be a way of finding what's on tomorrow's goddam agenda. Somebody's got to know.'

Edward assured Red that they had pulled out all the stops. However, he suppressed his real concern that he had serious reservations whether the assignment could now be carried out at all.

'OK, Edward. I'm sitting here enjoying my evening meal; after that, I'll find a hotel room. Then I'll hit the hay, so please ring me once we're definitely on course, since I'd like to catch up on some sleep before then. I imagine you'll want one hundred per cent concentration from me tomorrow, which I can only guarantee if I get enough sleep now. Period.'

Red replaced the mobile and went back to the restaurant. His soup, of course, had gone cold. He asked for it to be taken away. Lucy gave him an understanding look and stroked his hand.

'Are you very hungry?' asked Red. Lucy understood immediately; she laughed, with a shake of her head. That was her old Red!

They both stood up, almost simultaneously, and called the waiter over. Red pressed a fat note into his hand and whispered a few words in his ear. The waiter nodded and went off. Lucy and Red left the Grill Room.

'What did you say to him?' Lucy enquired.

'To be frank, I just told him your mother had died suddenly.'

Lucy burst out laughing. They moved quickly towards the
lift; the doors were wide open. Red pressed the button for
the top floor before any other hotel guest could get inside.
He embraced Lucy, kissed her, and deftly undid her bra; she
began to loosen his belt. As they hurried out of the lift on the
top floor, they nearly knocked over an elderly couple waiting
there. They ran down the corridor, and Red opened the door
to their suite. Before she had even reached the bedroom, Lucy
had dropped her dress. She flopped down backwards on to the
bed, with a laugh. Red paused for a fraction of a second, as the
question flashed through his mind whether Diana could also
be so boisterous. He conjured up her image, with her long
legs. It was sad that, possibly at this very moment, she might
be enjoying sex for the very last time in her life.

'Please hurry!' whispered Lucy. 'I want you. If I haven't
had anything to eat, I should like at least a decent dessert.'

Red dropped on to the bed next to Lucy and started to
smother her naked body with kisses.

## 57

Walter had propped his feet up on his desk, fast asleep, when suddenly he was woken by a hand shaking his shoulder.

'Walter, wake up!' Edward was standing next to him, holding a cup of tea. 'I have a suggestion.' He paused for a moment and then continued. 'Since we still don't know Princess Diana's plans after her arrival, I thought it would be a good idea if you flew up to Aberdeen with Arthur, as soon as possible. If her ultimate destination is Balmoral, then at least you'll both be on the spot.'

Walter stared at him, utterly confused. 'And what if Red is not there on time, or has simply thrown in the towel. Am I supposed to do the dirty work?'

'No. You can take your motorbike and recce the area between Aberdeen and the grounds of Balmoral Castle. You might be able to find out on the spot what vehicle has been booked to pick her up and what the arrangements are. That means we could provide Red with the data he urgently needs.'

Walter took his feet off the desk. 'Does Sir David know about this plan?'

'No, not yet. I wanted to talk to you first. I would only inform him if you agree and then we'd arrange for a plane to be laid on. So what do you think?'

Walter stretched and yawned. 'It's OK by me, so long as nobody wants me to pull the trigger.'

Edward gave him a reproachful look. 'How long have we known each other, Walter? You know I'd never ask you to do something I wouldn't do myself.'

Walter got up. 'Then tell Sir David and order the aircraft. Where do I find Arthur?'

'He's lying down somewhere a the back of the office. Let him relax till I've checked that it's all in order.' He then left the office and Walter sipped some tea from the cup Edward had brought in. He gave a shudder; it had been standing for too long and was now quite cold. He lifted the phone and dialled a number, only to find an answering service at the other end. Walter dictated into the machine. 'It's me. I've got to fly to Balmoral at short notice. I'll contact you as soon as I've arrived. You won't be able to reach me till then.' Then he dialled another number. There was no reply for a moment or two. 'Walter here. Please fill my petrol tank and make sure it's in working order. I'll be down below in about ten minutes' time.' He hung up and put his legs on the desk again. It might be a little while before Edward returned.

## 58

After Edward had obtained Sir David's approval for the Aberdeen initiative, he quickly opened the door to the conference room where Arthur had gone to take a nap. Arthur quickly came to and squinted at him. 'Are we on?' he asked.

'More or less. Sir David has agreed that you and Walter fly to Aberdeen. You can move any time now.'

'What's our brief? Are we sure Diana will be landing at Aberdeen?'

'No. But we have to cover both contingencies – you two in Aberdeen and George and me here in London. Red will join us immediately, wherever her plane touches down. If it's Aberdeen, you are to prepare the ground for him, so that he can get the job done quicker.'

'And how are we supposed to prepare for action?'

Edward reached out and pulled him up. 'Quite simple. You find out what vehicle they've put on for her and what route she'll take.'

Arthur was doubtful. 'And you think it'll work out just like that?' he asked. 'Will Arthur be taking his motor-bike?'

'Of course. It wouldn't make sense otherwise. Let's move, Walter's waiting for you.'

They left the room and walked along the long, empty corridor to Edward's and Walter's office.

Walter had already put on his motor-cyclists' gear. He had slung a second motor-cyclists' suit over one of the chairs. 'That should fit you,' he commented, casting an expert eye over Arthur. 'Not quite catwalk material, perhaps, but good enough for the job.'

Without a word, Arthur removed his trousers, placed them inside the strongbox lying on Walter's desk and started to put on the leather suit.

'Has Henry rung?' asked Walter. Edward shook his head.

'Their local time is an hour later, so they must be getting ready for bed,' Arthur grunted. 'Some time or other, that woman will have to announce when she's ready to leave her love nest and where she wants to be taken afterwards.'

'Unless this chap Dodi is hiding behind the name of Henry, he's unlikely to be the first person she tells. You can be sure that Henry will be in touch as soon as he has any information.'

'And what's our man Red up to?'

'He's on stand-by at some hotel or other here in London.'

Walter took two helmets from the cupboard and gave one to Arthur. 'I look forward to when it's all over, hopefully within the next twenty-four hours.'

Walter and Arthur were already on their way to the aeroplane, when Edward's office phone rang. He was dozing at his desk and woke up with a start. He fumbled for the receiver. It was Henry at the other end; he gave the code word.

'They have invited some friends for breakfast tomorrow morning at eight. They plan to leave about midday . . .' he whispered.

Edward interrupted him. 'Destination?'

'Precise time of departure and destination at present unknown. Over.'

Contact was suddenly broken. Edward replaced the receiver, disappointed. What else could be assumed? They would be flying from Olbia about noon, which meant that they could hardly arrive in London before three p.m., or at Aberdeen half an hour later. That would give Red a little extra time.

He dialled a short number. 'Could you please find out if

a car has recently been placed at Princess Diana's disposal
for tomorrow? I am at my desk. Thank you.' He hung up.
Should he put Red in the picture? He felt that it would not
make much sense to interrupt Red's sleep. He decided to
snatch a few hours' sleep also, making himself as comfortable
as he could in his office. He leant back in his chair and closed
his eyes.

He reflected how often during the last few weeks he had
dreaded this day. Now it had arrived, there was no turning
back. Nobody could – Red, Princess Diana or himself – none
of them. How long would it take for the official news of her
fatal accident to break? If she landed in London, it was certain
that a crowd of photographers would be lying in wait. What
was Red's strategy to get rid of her? The question had been
ignored completely when discussion focused on a plane crash.
He had to resolve it with Red tomorrow morning. No matter
how, news of the accident would spread like wildfire. Radio
and TV stations would be interrupted. Inquisitive members
of the public would rush to the scene of the accident. And
what if Diana was just badly wounded? He rejected the idea;
Red would surely do a thorough job.

Edward panicked at the thought of the media and public
interest. When and how would the boys find out about
it? Suddenly he was wide awake. What should be done?
It was inconceivable that the media broke the news on
radio or TV unprepared. Till now, no one had raised this
point. Edward visibly became more and more nervous. Her
boys! He recalled how, as a child, he had learnt about the
death of his own grandfather. He remembered how he had
suffered, even though his grandfather had been ill for some
weeks and his mother had taken great pains to prepare him
beforehand.

He jumped up. Nothing could now hold him in his chair.
Clenching his hands inside his trouser pockets, he desperately
tried to think up some way of avoiding this problem. Why
had nobody considered the children till now? It didn't make

him feel any better that their father was with them at this moment. How would Prince Charles himself react? Did he know the agenda? Edward had no idea. He thought he could gauge the Queen's reaction but could not be sure. Perhaps the brief to eliminate Diana came from some other source. She was undoubtedly a thorn in the Establishment's flesh – the politicians, ultraconservative monarchists and religious fanatics. Whoever had commissioned the job must be somewhere near the top, otherwise Sir David and his department would never have been involved in such a reckless assignment. But in his mind he always came back to the conundrum that there was no record of the job on the computer.

There was a gentle knock at the door. George entered the room. He looked tired; his eyes were bleary. 'Well?' he asked.

'Still no news.'

George slumped into Edward's chair. Edward stared at him. For him it must be far worse. George was an excitable sort of person, rather like Prince Charles. When it came to creative suggestions, he was undoubtedly the best man in their department. But when the moment came for hard-headed decision-making, George turned out to be a shrinking violet; there was always the danger that he would simply fall apart. And that posed a risk for them all. He had therefore suggested to Sir David, several months ago, that George should be sidelined in this particular assignment but had ultimately allowed himself to be overruled. George had immediately produced some imaginative ideas and had in fact made valuable suggestions, for instance, how to give Princess Diana a bad press. But recently he had generated fewer ideas. There was obviously more to this job than simply to ridicule her.

So there he sat, silent and utterly exhausted. 'Did you manage to get some sleep?' Edward asked. George gave no reply and stared morosely back at him. What on earth was going on inside his mind? Edward turned round and grabbed the telephone again. It was an age before someone responded at the other end.

'Any news?' he asked curtly. He replaced the receiver. 'Absolutely nothing!'

## 59

The Learjet speedily gained height. They had only just managed to cram Walter's BMW motor-cycle into the plane. Walter and Arthur were now sitting opposite one another in their motor cycle gear, armed with a Thermos flask of tea and a small packet of biscuits. The flight had been smooth; there was no trace as yet of the front of bad weather that was forecast from the west.

Walter ripped open his packet, offering it to Arthur, who helped himself to three biscuits.

'Surely Princess Diana will spend her first night back at Kensington Palace. It may sound stupid, but perhaps nothing will happen. Which would be a pity because of all the expense. The whole thing could have been done far more simply.'

'Are you sure?'

Arthur nodded. 'It could have been organized more discreetly, preferably without Sir David and Edward being involved. As for that chap, Red! We could easily have found someone to do the job.'

'Would you have volunteered, in that case?'

Arthur frowned. 'I would certainly have moved ahead more quickly. Once a decision is made, the results should follow. After finding out the facts, one should react immediately, not shoot off to America first and only work out a plan of action for the so-called accident afterwards.'

'How would you have gone about it?' Walter enquired.

Arthur thought for a minute or two. 'I was never consulted. But, so far as I'm concerned, the facts would have come first. Dead is dead. Of course, an accident has its advantages. But

we live in fast-moving times, so an assassination attempt is
soon forgotten.'

'As in the case of President Kennedy's assassination, when
all hell was let loose?' said Walter, sarcastically.

'The Kennedy case is a load of nonsense. We have no real
contact with the USA and, besides, that all happened over
thirty years ago. They handled it badly at the time. If they had
done more to publicize his negative side – his political apathy,
his love affairs – the whole business would soon have been
forgotten. "Exposure" is the key word; no public mourning,
no creation of a cult figure. The Americans just lost their grip
on the whole situation.'

He paused, helped himself to a biscuit and washed it down
with a gulp ot tea. 'What do you think would have happened
if that Fisher girl had been offered cash? She'd have been so
intoxicated with the smell of money that she'd have flown
straight off to the Côte d'Azur and blasted the Princess to
oblivion. She'd have wallowed in the publicity and, after
serving a prison sentence for the rash act to which she had
been driven by Dodi's emotional cruelty, she'd have walked
off, rich, famous and highly desirable. You can take it from me
– women who destroy their rivals are at a premium. She could
have seen Dodi off as well, in my opinion; which would have
exposed his dirty business deals and the whole affair would
soon have been hushed up. Old man Fayed would have seen
to that.'

Walter listened, rather bored. He knew where Arthur
stood. It was perfectly clear that he would want to leave
the department if Arthur took over from Edward. He had
often compared Arthur to Red in the last few days; Red,
interestingly enough, made the more pleasant impression of
the two.

'Shall I tell you what will happen if we do what Red is
planning to do? The whole world will be in a state of shock
– the beautiful wife, the lovely mother, the poor kids. Just
think what she's been through in the last few years. And now,

when she wants to cut loose from it all and start a new life, this terrible accident happens. She'll turn into a new icon. No, old chap, that's the wrong way. The Russians do it the right way; they demote their unloved leaders before they leave office. As soon as they elect a new President, hardly anyone remembers what the old one was called.'

Arthur was now in full flow, evidently happy to speak his mind without restraint. He took the biscuits from Walter and helped himself. Walter had to smile; he hoped that this day in Arthur's company would soon be over. He glanced at his wrist-watch. Thank God they were more than half-way there.

But Walter had been too optimistic. The co-pilot suddenly appeared and informed them that Aberdeen could not take them yet, so they had to circle around before being allocated a landing slot. Arthur pushed his seat back. 'Well, we have time for a quick nap,' he said. Walter agreed and thankfully closed his eyes.

# 60

At 5.03 a.m. precisely, the mobile next to Red gave a ring. He had spent half the night awake anyway, listening to Lucy's gentle, regular breathing. Quick as a flash, he grabbed the phone. It was Edward, who told him to be at their regular meeting place at the Hyde Park exit by six. Red mumbled 'OK', asking no questions.

Things were moving again. Red turned round towards Lucy. She had apparently noticed nothing. He waited for a moment, since he still had a little time. Edward could hardly be aware that he had spent the night just round the corner. Carefully, he got out of bed, went to the bathroom and took a cold shower to make sure he was fully awake. He quietly made his way to the living room and got dressed.

Outside, dawn was breaking but Hyde Park was still empty. He went over to the little desk, took a piece of paper from the leather writing case and scribbled a note for Lucy. He cast a final glance into the bedroom. She was still fast asleep. He put the note down by the bedside table. 'Had to rush off – shall ring tonight, latest, or will be back by then!' He put on his shoes and coat and left the suite.

There was no one to be seen downstairs in the foyer apart from the night porter and a guest with a suitcase, who was apparently waiting for a taxi. Red walked outside into Park Lane; it was now coming to life. He took a few deep breaths. It had only cooled by a few degrees during the night; he felt an approaching thunderstorm in the atmosphere. The sky was overcast, with dark clouds overhead. Avoiding the short cut, he opted for the longer route through the Park Lane underpass, so as to give Edward no clues as to where he had spent the night. He slowly ambled along the perimeter of Hyde Park, since the main gates were still closed.

Red arrived at their agreed destination just before six. Edward was nowhere in sight. He removed his coat and placed it over his arm. Today, he reflected, he had to pull the rabbit out of the hat. Basically, the situation was chaotic. On the other hand, this might not be a bad way to get the job going. No one looking back at the accident would realize that a secret mission had lurked behind the planned murder, given the absolute mess they were in.

A car drew up to the pavement. It was not Edward he saw at first, but a youngish man he did not recognize, of medium height, with bleary eyes and a haggard look. He recognized Edward at the back of the vehicle. A door was opened from inside and Red bent down. 'Have you got my case and the laptop?' he enquired.

Edward beckoned him inside. 'They're in the boot. Jump in!'

Red made room for himself on the rear seat and greeted the driver in front.

'Red, this is George.'

'There are more and more men on the job each day,' Red grumbled and shoved his coat on the rear ledge.

'No more than the absolute minimum,' Edward responded. He was obviously tense and very nervous.

'Where are we going?' asked Red.

'To be frank, we don't yet know.'

Red gave him an understanding look. 'It's as bad as that, is it? That can't be true! That means we have to improvize. How many airports are there in this goddam city?'

Edward thought for a minute. 'There are four commercial airports – Heathrow, Gatwick, Stanstead and Luton. And then there's Stolport for smaller aircraft; for the Gulfstream and similar aircraft there are several others.'

Red tapped the fingers of his right hand nervously against

his thigh. 'Is it possible for you, without raising anyone's suspicions, to influence air traffic control or airport security staff as to where Diana's plane will land?'

'I think so. We would need to use the excuse that she needs urgent protection from the dreadful media. Why do you ask?'

'Well, it would make our job that much easier. We could choose an airport that gave us a good escape route by road to the city centre. I take it Diana will be returning to Kensington Palace?'

George replied from the front of the car. 'We can assume she will, if she lands in London.'

'Fine. Then drive me to an airport that has access to London through the countryside — fields, woods, open spaces and so on — and not via the suburbs.'

'That would mean Blackbushe, Sir,' came the reply from the front.

'Then can you please drive me straight there, as quickly as possible?'

Edward butted in. 'It's not quite as simple as that. We have to give instructions to the vehicle that will be picking her up.'

'Bad thinking!' rejoined Red. 'We change her plane's landing instructions only at the very last minute. By then she'll have arranged to be picked up at some other place. And by the time he's made it to the right airport . . . we'll have got there first and she'll jump into our car without suspecting a thing. Do you get me? It's our big chance. Besides, I'd need to take a look at the surrounding area. It may not even be relevant whose vehicle she takes, provided I can choose the right spot. I've got a very good operational plan. Have you got your mobile handy?'

Edward nodded.

'I rely on your guys to find me a generator and a powerful cable winch, the type of equipment you use for self-starting a glider. They've got to be easily transportable.'

Edward gave him a bewildered look. Red laughed, digging him reassuringly in the ribs.

'No more questions now! Just get hold of them for me, pronto!'

Edward dug inside his coat pocket and dialled a number, glancing at his watch. 'I have no idea if anyone's there at this hour.' He was in luck. 'Tom, Edward here. I need a portable generator and a quick-start cable winch. Do we have that sort of thing; if not, can you get hold of these items soonest?' He turned to Red. 'What capacity generator?'

'Powerful enough to control the winch, with plenty of spare capacity.'

Edward repeated Red's request and waited for a response at the other end of the phone. He addressed Red again. 'We can lay our hands on a cable winch with pneumatic clutch, complete with flywheel and tension spring . . .'

'Excellent!' replied Red, now relaxed. 'What's the cable length?'

Edward relayed the question. '900 yards for a release height of 400 yards. It's powered by a soundproof six-cylinder turbo diesel and works without a generator.'

'Very good!' Red now seemed to be quite happy. 'Order it now! But also find out if it's fitted with an all-surface base.'

Edward repeated Red's enquiry and then gave him a nod.

'Brilliant!' Red laughed, now in his element. 'They should stay on call, with the equipment at hand.'

Edward ended his call and turned to Red. 'What's our strategy?'

'You know, Edward, you've always got to have some sort of life belt on board. I invented a sort of bait some years ago. Of course, this goes somewhat against my principles, but, as I mentioned, it's my safety net if all else goes wrong. But the end result, if you do it properly, is the same. Rest assured – I can guarantee your accident!'

'Red, you're talking in riddles . . .'

'I'll explain my method. I have set up this bait precisely for today's type of job – rapid action, anonymous vehicle, and accurate results. The bait consists of four thin, highly-magnetized iron rods, about six inches long, connected at one end by a ring and held together by a spring. The same kind of equipment is used for directing satellites in space. Folded up, it looks like a metal sleeve or a small tube that might have been dropped somewhere by accident. At the bottom end, there is a mechanical device that can be activated by a sensor, which is concealed inside one of the iron rods. If a vehicle drives over it, the iron rods spring apart and hook on to the undercarriage. I have linked the ring of the bait to the cable of the winch. It is very tough, but also thin and light. All we need is a bend in the road. It doesn't matter whether it's a tight bend or a long bend. There are only two basic requirements. On the far side of the bend there has to be either a slope or a precipice, or else a large tree, an iron pole or a concrete wall. Our job is to find that spot.'

Red gazed out of the window; he could only see houses and gardens. 'Tell the driver to get a move on, so we don't waste time.'

George, who had heard every word Red had said, despite the car noise, put his foot on the accelerator.

Edward was sceptical. 'And that should do the trick?' he asked.

'Just like my wooden board with the rear lights. Simple but brilliant, believe me!'

'What if we can't locate the ideal spot?' George chimed in.

'No problem, we'll be sure to find it. We've only got to comb the whole area. Maybe I should sit in front as soon as we've got out of this goddam town.'

Edward looked out of the window to get his bearings. 'We'll be out of London soon.'

# 61

Walter and Arthur took off for Balmoral Castle on the BMW motor-cycle as soon as they had touched down at Aberdeen. The crew was told to stay there until further notice. They quickly hit the A93 and were now driving along the River Dee. Walter, the previous week, had gathered a few rough ideas as to the scene of a possible accident by driving Red around; he now cast his eye over a number of promising places for a fatal crash.

Shortly after Ballater, he stopped. He tried to phone Edward, but without success, perhaps because of the mountains encircling the River Dee. He decided to have another go later. It would be disastrous if contact by phone were cut just at this crucial time.

After Braemar, they found a small hotel at the foot of Meall Gorn, where they had breakfast. Since they had landed, Walter noted with some satisfaction, Arthur was rather quiet. A plump landlady saw to their needs as if they were her own children. He asked for a room where they could freshen up. She hurried over to the tiny reception desk and returned with two keys in her hand.

Before Walter went up to his room, he tried to phone Edward again by mobile. He failed to make contact again, and asked the landlady if he could phone from a call box. She pointed to a small cubicle by the reception and left him on his own. Edward's mobile number was engaged. He dialled the office number but there was no answer. He wondered if he should disturb Red or Henry, but decided instead to take a shower first. Edward might be free a little later.

The landlady mentioned casually that Prince Charles was staying at Balmoral with his children. Walter decided to play the innocent tourist. She did not know, however, whether Princess Diana was also staying there. One of her guests, she volunteered, had sighted Camilla Parker-Bowles, which indicated, Walter reflected, that Diana would certainly not be driving straight to Balmoral. Besides, who knew if she wouldn't simply land in the castle grounds by helicopter. In any case, she might switch to a helicopter directly after she arrived in London or Aberdeen. He went up to the room he had been booked in, removed his leather gear and took a shower.

Two doors down the corridor, Arthur was also having a shower. He had decided to pay for his room in advance, so he dropped on to the bed and tried to catch up on some sleep. Walter would wake him up as soon as the action started.

He was aware, however, that he was too churned up inside to fall asleep. Perhaps this was his lucky break. Red might be too late, or just not turn up at all; he would then take over. Walter certainly couldn't. But he, Arthur, would waste no time in getting the job done, as soon as he saw his chance. He considered how he could trip Walter up if the right moment came. Walter would never agree to risk anything on his own; he was simply Edward's poodle. Ever since Red had given up so pathetically at Cannes, Arthur had felt the challenge to show some initiative of his own. He wondered why Sir David had hired an outsider in the first place – perhaps because he did not wish to take personal blame for any failure, just before going into retirement.

Or did Sir David wish to avoid dirtying the hands of his own staff? He, Arthur, would have no hang-ups if he found Walter in his way and had to move him quickly off the job.

Walter then came into his room. 'I got hold of Edward at last. He is now doing the ground work in London with Red. No sign from Henry yet. They're presumably all sleeping in.'

'By the way, who told you this chap Henry is really close to the scene? After all, Sir David said Henry was shadowing old man Fayed and not Dodi. So he must be somewhere near the father and can only pass on information second-hand.'

'That's better than damn all,' replied Walter. 'The main thing is that we get our data from the other side of the fence.'

'What do we do if Diana lands here and Red hasn't arrived? We must have a plan of action.'

Walter did not quite know how to answer the question. He could not imagine doing anything without agreement from headquarters in London.

Arthur could guess what was going on inside Walter's mind and continued, provocatively, 'I suggest we push her car off the road somewhere. No one will recognize us. On a bike like yours, we'll be back inside our jet within the hour.'

'Are you out of your mind? In that case you can find yourself another bike and another driver. I consider myself bound by instructions from London.'

Arthur jumped up angrily. 'Have you forgotten our instructions? The decision has been taken. Diana has to bite the dust, no matter how. And as soon as possible. We are each under orders to carry out those instructions, as the chance arises.'

Walter drew the chair up to Arthur. 'I see it somewhat differently. If you plan to go it alone, then count me out! In fact, I know just how to put a spanner in the works!'

Arthur jumped out of bed and squared up to Walter. 'Are you trying to threaten me?' he shouted furiously.

Walter put a finger to his lips. 'If you lose your temper like that, the job's over, here and now. Everyone will know what we're up to. Can't you try to speak quietly, at least?'

Arthur was angry with himself for shouting. He swore to himself he would not give away what he planned to do if zero-hour presented itself on the River Dee.

## 62

George was still driving Edward and Red along secondary roads leading from the various London airports direct to the city centre. George had selected Blackbushe airport to start with. Red asked him to halt at three or four spots, quickly jumped out of the car and jumped back in again, shaking his head.

'Absolutely impossible. Firstly, it's doubtful whether the Gulfstream pilot would be willing to land here except in case of extreme urgency, and, secondly, the approach roads are too congested and easily visible from all angles.'

Edward glanced nervously at his watch, calculating how much time was still available for Red to select his accident spot. He was also anxious as Henry had not phoned. He was impressed by how coolly Red had resumed his work after the altercations of the previous day. Unlike him, Red appeared composed and in full command of his emotions.

'Which airport are you driving me to now?' asked Red. George quickly consulted his road map. 'Farnborough.'

Red pulled out his laptop and typed in some data. He turned round to Edward with a reassuring glance. 'It's not really as bad as it might look. We're getting close to the heart of the matter. Why not give some thought to what excuse we give for diverting Diana's plane?'

'I've been thinking of very little else the whole time,' replied Edward with a groan. 'As soon as we know where she's due to land, there'll be a handful of photographers on the spot – which is a pretty safe bet – and I'll ask airport security to divert her plane to our preselected landing strip because of anticipated crowd control problems.'

Red was excited about Farnborough airport, since it was basically a businessman's venue. At exit 4 on the M3 he noted a couple of topographically interesting places where the road conditions seemed suitable but which might have caused complications due to the flow of traffic.

'The extended left curve from the roundabout would be perfect and so would the long feeder road to the M3,' explained Red. 'At the left curve, I would direct the driver towards the column at the end of the curve. On the feeder road I would prefer to crash her vehicle into the concrete supports. But that has to be calculated to a split second. The vehicle should effectively crash, but ideally not on to the road underneath. There would be too many deaths. In either case, the traffic immediately behind Diana's would have to be held up slightly, which would attract attention. So, let's drive on to the next airport, George; maybe we'll have better luck there.'

George put his foot on the accelerator. Edward looked at his watch again. The choice of airport was narrowing. Time was now pressing. Was there no other solution?

The road signs announced the route to the next airport.

'Are you sure we still have some chance?' asked Edward cautiously.

There was no reply from Red; his mind was concentrating on the road ahead.

'Isn't there some way of fixing the Gulfstream . . . ?'

'Halt!' Red shouted suddenly. George jammed on the brakes; Red surveyed the surroundings, his eyes half-closed. 'Drive off the road over there,' he ordered him, pointing to a small lay-by. George steered into the lay-by and switched off the engine. 'Everyone out!' he commanded them. They both looked around. Red had actually stopped on a long bend in the road, screened by a dense wood on one side and, on the other, by a ditch that ran along the side of the road, separated from an adjacent field by a barbed wire fence.

'Is there usually so little traffic here?' Red asked them.

George nodded. 'It's only a cross connection, but it's the shortest route to the fast road into London.'

This was a possibility, Red thought to himself. He gave them a signal to follow him. He went back along the road for a hundred yards or so and jumped into the ditch. He scrutinized the road surface like a professional surveyor and knelt down on to the road, passing his open hand over the asphalt several times, as if he were stroking it. Finally, he walked a few yards into the wood opposite, moving slowly from one tree to the next, glancing back towards the road and ducking down occasionally to view the scene from a different perspective. 'This would be ideal!' he said impassively, directing George to a spot on the road. 'Park the car exactly on this spot.'

George drove the car over the spot he had indicated.

'You see, Edward,' Red continued, pointing a few yards to their rear, 'if we set up the cable winch facing this direction and put the bait exactly where George has parked, it simply has to work. As soon as the bait has taken hold, her vehicle will be dragged this way, is forced into a skid and crashes head-on against this tree – eighty miles an hour at the moment of impact, I would guess – without braking, that is.'

He stepped to one side and whistled softly. 'Edward, come over here. If we want to, we can do a little fine-tuning. We can get the vehicle to skid between these two trees and then let it crash against this tree, head-on. The result would be better. We only need to move the winch a couple of yards to the right. The bait would stay put.' He thought for a moment. 'The car should have a sloping hood, like the latest Mercedes, or Audi, Rover, or Lancia. I don't know if you can rustle up something to Diana's liking that doesn't look suspicious. But definitely no older-style models on any account, and certainly not a Roller, please! A Jaguar sports car would also be a possibility.'

A car then drove by. Red looked at his watch. 'That was the only car in the last six minutes.' He drew their attention to the soil underfoot. 'We'll have to lay a medium-sized tree trunk across here, so that the rear of the vehicle is raised just before impact and the roof drawn forward. We need only to be careful that the cable wire doesn't damage the bark of the tree trunk we've laid across the path. That would make the whole thing look suspicious.' He looked at Edward. 'So what are we waiting for? Take George to pick up the cable winch. This is the perfect spot: little traffic, the only fast connection to central London. But please – no more colleagues!'

Yet again, Edward was impressed by the logic of Red's strategy and the accuracy of his calculations.

'How much time do we have?' Red asked him.

They both consulted their wrist-watches.

'I have no idea,' said Edward. 'Our contact man has not yet got in touch.'

'Then *you* phone *him*,' Red told him, without raising his voice.

Edward pulled the mobile phone from his inside pocket and dialled the number. It was engaged. He pressed the 'off' button and waited for a while. He tried again, but it was still engaged.

'Damn it all, then don't waste time! Drive off with George and phone from the car. I'll stay and wait for you here and take down the exact measurements. Just hand me the laptop and the case from the boot.'

Edward and Red walked back to the car. George spotted them coming towards him and got out.

'My case!' Red called out.

George went round to the boot, pulled out the heavy metal case and put it down on the road.

'We're off to pick up the cable winch; Red's staying here,' Edward explained. George jumped in again and started up.

'How long will you need?' asked Red.

'It'll be a good hour before we're back, I'd say,' replied George, as Edward got into the front passenger seat.

Red lifted his heavy case on to the verge of the road; Edward handed him his laptop from inside the car.

'If you don't find me here, I'll be somewhere up there in the wood,' Red shouted to him as George drove off.

As the car drew out of sight, Red dragged the case through the trees behind a shrub, so that he could not be seen from the road. He opened it and took out an infrared rangefinder. At that moment a car drove by. Red looked at his watch again and grinned with satisfaction. Then he began systematically to measure the bend in the road, entering the details into the computer. As quick as a flash, it traced a diagram from the input. Red could now calculate the precise spot for the bait. He took out a diskette from the case and inserted it into the laptop. All sorts of lines and squares suddenly featured on the screen. He slowly threaded his way in and out of the trees, comparing his surroundings to the graphics on the computer screen.

He thought he had found the precise spot at last. Placing his laptop carefully on the ground, he walked over to the case. He took out a pair of leather gloves, which he put on, and a tape measure, which he took to the place where he had deposited the laptop. He attached the brass ring at the end of the tape measure to a branch of the tree, picked up a stone and headed off in a straight line towards the road. As he walked, the tape measure unwound. He made sure the road was free of traffic and started to run, without taking his eye off the tape measure as it unwound. He reached the spot where George had previously parked the car, paused, took the tape measure reading, and made a small cross on the asphalt with the stone. He then rolled up the tape measure and disappeared again into the trees.

As he entered the fresh data into his laptop, the graphics on the screen immediately changed shape. Next to the lines and squares, hatched areas appeared, flashing rhythmically.

Red took a small metal box from the case and opened it carefully. It contained tiny silver chips. At that moment, the noise of a car and persistent hooting could be heard from the road. Edward and George had returned. He quickly shut the lid of the metal box and walked over to the road. Edward had jumped out, searching the surrounding area. Seeing Red pop up between the trees, he waved and ran towards him.

'Come on, Red! I've just had a call from our contact man. It's all been changed. We must fly off to Paris immediately.'

'Paris?' called Red. 'Why Paris?'

Edward stood still, out of breath, and waited till Red came closer. 'They're both flying there – Diana and Fayed. The flight was recorded at le Bourget – the airport near Paris.'

Red stamped his foot on the ground. 'Shit! It would have worked beautifully here. Now we're back to square one. Who knows what to expect in Paris!'

'I have already booked a helicopter. The jet is still with Walter and another colleague up in Aberdeen. They've both been briefed. They're flying straight to France. How and where we meet up has yet to be decided.'

Red was unable to contain himself. This was the second time in twenty-four hours that a good plan had been aborted. 'You go back to the car; I'll get my things together. Ask George to drive up to the wood so I don't have to carry the case too far.' He turned on his heels and hurried back, without waiting for an answer.

As soon as he was out of sight, Red took out his mobile and dialled a number from the file. 'Drop everything and fly to Paris on the next flight. Take a taxi to outside the town centre and hire a car from a small hire firm, nothing big but something fast and flexible. Then drive back to the outskirts of Paris, get hold of ten thousand francs without fail and wait at a parking lot till precisely eighteen hours local time. Then phone me on the dot, not a second earlier or later. And don't forget the time difference!'

Red put the mobile back inside the metal case, replaced

the little metal box and locked the case. He could hear the car draw up behind. He grabbed hold of the case and hurried over to the car.

'Why couldn't that guy have called earlier?' he snarled as he jumped inside. 'Surely he knows what's going on.'

George accelerated towards London.

'I thought your Princess wanted to see her kids and announce her engagement. I just hope she hasn't reconsidered the whole thing and now wants to go back to Charles. It wouldn't be the first time that's happened. From what the Press says, his brother Andrew and Fergie are back together again. It would be the last straw if you guys had got it wrong! So Paris, here we come!'

'According to our contact man, he understands that this is merely a shopping expedition. Tomorrow morning Princess Diana, at least, will be returning to England,' Edward explained. He had folded his hands, so as to steady the slight shaking which had taken hold of him since Henry's call.

'Does that mean we could have quietly carried on as before?' asked Red.

'No! It will be easier abroad. The UK was our worst case scenario ever since the Cannes job folded up. No, Paris will be fine. But, as you have quite correctly pointed out, we're back to square one. You may find it simple enough to use the same technique there.'

Red looked across at him. 'Are you joking? Or do you happen to have people at hand who can lend you a cable winch just like that, without asking questions?'

Edward said nothing. Red was right; they had to think up a different formula for Paris. Hopefully, Sir David could get hold of Jean-Luc without delay. Jean-Luc was absolutely first-class; he had been on the British payroll for a number of years and had frequently operated as their department's contact man in France. Edward had worked with him closely a year ago, when they had tailed an IRA member who had gone to ground in France and whom they wanted to repatriate to the UK. Thanks to Jean-Luc, they had succeeded. He realized Jean-Luc also worked for the CIA. His expertise was not in fixing 'accidents' but in close observation of people and obtaining information and materials that were needed for operations on French territory.

'Problems?' asked Red.

'No. We have a man over there whom we have worked with in the past. I thought it would be a good idea if he joined us.'

'What does that depend on?'

Edward smiled and shrugged his shoulders. 'It simply depends on whether we can get hold of him quickly.'

George drove from the side road into the main flow of traffic from the suburbs towards London. He knew this area since childhood. He could only follow parts of the conversation in the rear and gave way to his own reflections. His thoughts turned to Princess Diana, who would also presumably be driving to the airport at this moment.

His reservations about the whole plan troubled him yet again. Why was Diana so unpopular? The Press would take no notice of her if she were still a simple nursery teacher. It was her position that made her special and – to some – unacceptable. Why couldn't people show more tolerance and just leave her in peace? Everyone paid lip service to freedom of religion and belief and boasted of their tolerance. What was wrong if she married a Muslim and converted to Islam? What difference did it make if William later succeeded to the throne as defender of the Anglican faith but his mother belonged to another religion?

He had not been brought up as a religious person. But his parents had taught him to respect the notions of truth and justice. Tolerance and human values were both aspects of this tradition. Could they ever look back on their assignment as a worthy human cause? Would he ever be able to justify his part in the action by reason of his oath of loyalty to Crown and Country?

# 63

George turned into the airport approach road. The security guard cast an eye inside the car and recognized Edward, who gave him a friendly wave. The main gate was opened. George drove across the runway, towards a waiting helicopter. Red and Edward got out, handed the pilot their luggage from the car boot. He shoved it inside the helicopter, with the help of one of the ground staff, to whom George tossed the car key. George clambered into the helicopter behind Red and Edward. No sooner had the door shut than the rotor blades started up. The other pilot passed Edward a note. He read it quickly.

'Two bits of information. Arthur and Walter are already on their way by air. We meet at an airport called Vallée de Seine. They'll be flying with us from there to another destination, where Jean-Luc will be waiting for us.' Edward looked happy. 'Jean-Luc is the best man for the job in the whole of France.'

With a jerk, the helicopter took off. George, who had not yet sat down, nearly lost his balance.

'Seat belt!' shouted Red, above the noise of the engine. George sat down beside him and fastened himself in. The helicopter swung sharply to one side.

'Are we flying over French airspace in an official capacity?' Red asked Edward.

Edward shrugged his shoulders. 'I've no idea. We don't check that. We just book the aircraft and name the destination.' Conversation had now become very difficult because of the din. The three passengers picked up the sound absorbers by their seats and put them over their ears.

# 64

The helicopter pilots had flown at an alarmingly low level for the last few miles over the Channel. They reached the French coast near Dieppe and then headed for Rouen along the River Varenne.

Red glanced impatiently at his watch from time to time. Finally, he unfastened his seat belt and staggered over to the pilots. 'Can you make contact with the Learjet?' he shouted to the cockpit.

The co-pilot removed his earphones and looked at him with surprise. Red repeated his request; the only response was a nod.

'Then find out their location and also when they're due to land.'

The co-pilot gave another nod and put on his earphones again. Red could see him fiddle with the controls of the radio link. It was at least five minutes before the co-pilot turned round again. 'We'll land more or less at the same time. It's up to flight security who lands first. How important is it that we land first?'

Red shook his head. 'It's not that important. How much longer will we be?'

The co-pilot consulted his instrument panel and then a map lying on his lap. 'I would say we'll be there in quarter of an hour or so. But, as I said, if the Learjet gets there first, we can delay touchdown.'

Red clambered back to his seat.

'Problems?' Edward shouted.

'No,' Red shouted back. 'We'll be there in about fifteen minutes; the jet will land at roughly the same time.'

Edward leant over to George. 'As soon as we touch down, Red and I shall stay here. You run and grab hold of Walter and Arthur, plus the bike, and bring them on board, OK? We'll take off immediately so as to waste no time.'

George gave him the thumbs up. 'OK!'

They all looked nervously out of the window. They were flying very low indeed. In the mist on the horizon a dense area of tall buildings and church towers loomed into view, evidently a very large town. In quick succession they then followed two busy streets leading towards the town centre. From his side near the window, Red suddenly pointed overhead. Edward leant forward and caught a glimpse of the white Learjet pulling ahead of them. He sat up straight. 'Walter and Arthur are making their descent,' he shouted to George. 'They'll beat us to it!'

The helicopter lurched heavily to one side, flew in a curve to the right and then to the left. A row of runway lights was now visible. The helicopter flew over the runway, towards the tower to their right. It came back again and turned sharply to the left. As it straightened its flight path, Red and Edward caught sight of the Learjet on the ground.

Within a few seconds, the helicopter touched down. George had already loosened his seat belt. The pilot warned him by hand signal to lower his head. George opened the right-hand side door. The draught from the helicopter blades blew into the cabin, making it difficult for him to jump out. He ran over to the Learjet, bent double, welcomed his two colleagues, exchanging a few words of greeting. They then dragged the BMW from the plane.

The pilot had now switched off the engine and looked across to the jet. 'Do we set off again after refuelling?' he asked Edward.

'Yes, we just take our two colleagues on board and start up again as soon as possible.'

'Do we take the motorbike as well?' the pilot asked.

Edward gave a nod.

'In that case, we've got to secure it properly. I hope there's enough equipment on board.' The pilot jumped out of the helicopter and disappeared. The co-pilot had already got out to order fuel.

The pilot returned a little later with some nylon cord and a length of cable with snap hooks. Walter pushed his bike across the concrete path. He reached the helicopter and greeted them. 'We meet again! Who'd have thought we'd end up in France today?' The pilot climbed inside and pointed to George's seat. 'Ideally, we should lift the seat and secure the bike to it. I'm afraid it'll be a bit of a squeeze, but there's no other way.' He raised the seat and locked it.

'Let's give it a try!'

Walter, Arthur and George hoisted up the motorbike from the ground. Edward and the pilot took hold of it from above. They gradually manoeuvred it, after much shoving to and fro, into the right position. The pilot anchored it down properly.

'Let's keep our fingers crossed,' said Edward, once they were all aboard. He pointed at Red. 'May I do the introductions? Arthur, this is Red. Red, this is Arthur. Walter you already know.'

Red smiled and shook Arthur by the hand. Edward quickly sat down between Red and Walter, fastened his seat belt, and put the sound absorbers over his ears.

As they took off, he leant across to Red and shouted, 'Have you thought out a plan of action yet?'

The expression on Red's face told him that his mind was already at work. Red merely shouted back, 'I don't count my chickens before they're hatched. Let's get to Paris first. Where are we due to land?'

Edward had no idea. He scrambled over to the co-pilot.

'Which airport are we flying to?' he shouted.

'We're not flying to an airport,' came the reply. 'We've only been told to fly to a site near a place called Chavenay. In fact, there is a small airfield nearby, but we fly to the right of it and taxi round three or four miles to the east, towards Saint-Nom. They'll signal from the ground where we're to land.'

'How long is the flight?'

'Half an hour at the most, probably less.'

Edward thanked him, made his way back to his seat, and put Red in the picture.

## 65

After Red phoned telling her to come to Paris immediately, Lucy assumed that he had wrapped up his business
affairs and was planning to look over a few properties with
her. She had booked the very next flight to Paris and
withdrawn ten thousand francs from the bank; she now
made her way through the arrival gate. She told the taxi
driver to take her to Morment, a name she had casually
read on a passing removal van, without any idea where
Morment was located. Twelve miles or so outside Paris,
she found herself travelling through a little village, where
she caught sight of a vehicle workshop. She told the driver
to stop and tipped him generously to compensate for the
lower mileage. Lucy crossed the road and ran back a few
yards to the workshop. An old man lying under a tractor
gazed at her as she entered the courtyard. He crawled out
from under the tractor and greeted her effusively, removing
his beret.

He welcomed her, ogling her quite unashamedly. 'What
a luscious bloom for my humble garden!'

'Please, Monsieur, I have a problem and I was told you
could help,' she began in her heavy American accent. She
smiled at him helplessly, fluttering her eyelids.

'Bastian will always help a beautiful damsel in distress.'

'I need a car,' Lucy looked round the yard and spotted
a white Fiat Uno. She pointed to it, 'Just like that one
over there.'

'I'm very sorry, Madame, but I can't help you. It belongs
to one of my clients; it's been brought in for servicing over

the next day or two. He's back from Spain next Tuesday, by which time the car must be ready.'

Bastian slapped his hand on the tractor. 'This is the only vehicle I can let you have; the kids have gone off in my car to the seaside for the weekend.'

Lucy dug her heels in. 'Monsieur Bastian, I just need a car overnight, not for three days, do you understand me? Only one night?' She gave him an eloquent look, and continued, when she saw the smile on Bastian's face. 'You know, I don't want anyone to identify my own car in front of the hotel.'

Bastian scratched his head. With a crafty expression in his face, he looked to and fro, between Lucy and the Fiat Uno. Lucy was now positive that she was winning. If she waved some money in front of him, he was certain to make up his mind. She opened her handbag and made a point of taking out her purse. 'I'd like to repay your generosity. So I'd be grateful if you named a figure. I'm not going to bargain with you.'

Lucy sensed Bastian struggling with himself not to blurt out the answer, 'Yes'. He was obviously trying to see how much he could squeeze out of her.

Playing for time, he asked her, 'How far are you going, Madame?'

'To a suburb of Paris and back,' she answered truthfully. 'And I'd fill up the tank.'Bastian still did not look too happy. He walked over to the Fiat and opened the car door. She could see that the keys were still inside. Bastian sat down inside and stroked the steering wheel pensively. 'I just don't know, Madame, it doesn't belong to me. What if my client finds out?'

'Why should he find out? You said he's only due back from Spain in three days' time. I'll have returned the car long before then. I'll offer you a thousand francs.'

'A thousand francs?' Bastian repeated. He opened the door of the glove compartment and checked inside. 'The papers are all there.' He got out. 'You must leave me a deposit as security . . .'

'No problem,' she replied. 'I'll leave my passport behind.'

'But you'll need it if the police stop you,' he reminded her.

Lucy shook her head. 'My husband is in the diplomatic corps in Paris. He'd take care of any problems.' She handed him the thousand francs and the American passport. Bastian put the franc notes in a pocket inside his overalls and tried to spell out the name on her passport. Lucy then tossed her travel bag on to the passenger seat and got inside, eager to make a getaway before he changed his mind.

'Au revoir, Madame Broomfield, bon voyage!' In the rear-view mirror, she could see him running behind the car, waving her goodbye. She took the road back to Paris. At the edge of the village she noticed a bistro with a large parking area and a petrol station close by. She immediately drove into the petrol station and filled the tank. There was still time to spare before the six o'clock phone call. She paid the bill, drove to the car park near the bistro, and walked inside.

At that time of day it was quite full. There were about ten characters at the bar, drinking pastis and vin rouge.

Lucy sat down at a small table, ordered a café au lait and a cognac, and picked up a local newspaper from the next table, trying to make some sense of its contents. She soon gave up. Her patchy vocabulary was too limited; it was only good enough to help her to translate the titles and enjoy the photos.

## 66

Jean-Luc was sitting at the steering wheel of the Citroën, dozing gently. Its doors were open, allowing the heat to escape. He was small, a little under fifty, dressed in a white shirt and a summer suit, the jacket of which he had tossed on to the rear seat. Pop music was quietly playing on the car radio.

The Citroën was parked inside a wood at the edge of a clearing about the size of a sports field. A narrow, well-trodden path led from the car into the bushes. Jean-Luc suddenly woke up to the clatter of a low-flying helicopter. He turned down the radio, got out of the car and looked up in the direction of the noise. The helicopter loomed up at last, skimming the treetops. Jean-Luc waved with both arms and pointed to the centre of the clearing. The helicopter flew over and vanished again. From the noise of the engine, he now guessed that it had circled round the back of the wood and was about to return. It flew over the clearing again and then swung in, throwing up so much dust that Jean-Luc had to run back to the car and shut the doors.

It took some time for the rotor blades to come to a complete stop. Edward got out first and greeted him. 'You haven't changed a bit!' Jean-Luc returned the compliment. Edward turned round and introduced his fellow passengers in sequence as they emerged from the helicopter.

'It'll be a tough day for you today!' said Jean-Luc, clapping both hands together. 'Sir David has briefed me about your plans. You won't find it easy here in Paris, though.'

'But we've got Red and yourself,' replied Edward, as

though he did not really count himself as part of the team when it came to real action.

'I'm sorry, but it will be rather tight inside my car. I didn't expect a whole football team.'

Edward gave a laugh and put his mind at rest. 'Those two aren't just wearing leather suits for fun. We've got a fast motorbike on board. Red, George and I will be coming with you. Have you any idea where we're going?'

Jean-Luc beckoned to Edward to follow him to the car. The others, meanwhile, were levering the motorbike out of the helicopter.

Red eventually joined Edward and Jean-Luc; they were both bent over a road map laid out on the bonnet of the Citroën.

'Here you are, Red,' Edward explained, 'this is a small, dilapidated factory shed. We drive there and set everything up inside . . .'

'We often use it,' Jean-Luc confirmed. 'It has two advantages: firstly, it's very accessible by road and, secondly, the grounds can't be seen, since they're surrounded by a high wall. We shan't be disturbed there, whatever you're planning to do.'

George ran over and thrust the mobile at Edward. 'Henry!' he said, gasping for breath. Edward greeted him. This time, evidently, Henry was much more informative than before. Edward looked at the Citroën and pointed to the car phone. 'What's your phone number, Jean-Luc?'

Jean-Luc recited what seemed to be a never-ending list of numbers, which Edward repeated. 'Henry, you can also reach me under this new number as from now. It would be much better if *you* phoned *me*. I shall discuss matters with my team straightaway. Can you please phone again in quarter of an hour?' He waited for the reply and terminated the phone call.

Arthur and Walter had raced over.

'Princess Di and Dodi have just landed at le Bourget,'

Edward explained. 'They were picked up by two cars and four bodyguards and are driving, presumably at this very minute, towards the centre of Paris in a Mercedes 600. Their destination is the Ritz. The hotel, by the way, belongs to old Fayed. It's safe to assume they'll both want to freshen up a little . . .'

'Bonking!' Arthur butted in, with a grin on his face.

Edward pointedly closed his eyes and gave a loud sigh. 'I don't think such comments are called for at this moment. Now, where was I? Yes, they will both spend only a short time at the Ritz. Perhaps they might stay the night . . .'

This time it was Jean-Luc who broke in. He was rocking up and down on tiptoe as he talked, possibly because he was smaller than the rest. 'They will probably spend the night at Dodi's apartment at the Arc de Triomphe or at his parents' villa in the Bois de Boulogne, where, incidentally, Edward VIII once resided.'

Edward gave a quick nod of acknowledgment, then carried on: 'As I said, this is all guesswork. One thing, however, is certain. There's no record of any flight departures for Princess Diana direct from Paris or any connecting flights. In any case, they will both want to go shopping today and then eat out somewhere in the evening. That's clear.'

'So that's it, then!' Red sounded relieved. He stroked his nose with his index finger. 'The prospects are excellent. Are there enough paparazzi in town?'

Jean-Luc laughed. 'My dear friend, as soon as Di arrives in Paris, she'll be surrounded by a flock of vultures. And if she's with a lover, Dodi for instance, there'll be nobody else in sight.'

'Good, good! But we need to find out what route the lucky couple take from the shops to the bedroom. Presumably by car. Do you know?' No one answered, so Red turned to Jean-Luc.

'Where is this Ritz Hotel, anyway?'

Jean-Luc moved Arthur to one side to get a better look

at the map. 'There's Place Vendôme. Here's the apartment
at the Arc de Triomphe and there's the villa in the Bois de
Boulogne.'

'But no one goes that way on foot, so how does she get
there?' Red asked Edward.

'She'll go shopping on foot, of course, but in London
it would be a little different from here because of this Al
Fayed chap.' Edward thought for a second or two. 'Over
here, she'd be accompanied by a couple of bodyguards, and
perhaps a small group of friends from the jet set. The cars
would be directed by radio from one street block to the
next . . .'

'That is, until they get sore feet and return to the car.
OK, then they'll both go for a meal, but not to McDonald's,
obviously. How long would that take?'

Red was speaking to Jean-Luc but answered the question
himself. 'About two hours, I assume. The car will be waiting
around for them somewhere. Edward, how close is our
undercover agent to Dodi?'

The question left Edward somewhat embarrassed. 'I . . .
I've simply no idea,' he stammered. 'He was targeted at
Mohammed Al Fayed in the first instance. Why?'

'We've got to know the goddam facts once in a while!'
Red replied angrily. 'Ring up dear Henry, ask him if he's
in Paris, if he's near them, and, more importantly, if he can
order a car for us in case they drive back home after their
meal. Now get moving!'

He sounded so determined that Edward picked up his
mobile without a word and dialled Henry's number. He
tried to compose himself, speaking as calmly as he could.
'Henry, are you in a position to choose the car that picks
up Princess Diana after dinner tonight?' Suddenly he looked
serious, almost perplexed. He then relaxed and gave Red an
encouraging glance. He covered the mouthpiece. 'Four-by-
four or Mercedes?' he whispered to Red.

The answer came like a pistol shot. 'Mercedes!'

'Somebody's coming!' Walter hissed, looking over Red's shoulder.

Edward spoke into the mouthpiece: 'The Mercedes', he whispered. 'Ring me in half an hour.' Quickly, he switched off and shoved his mobile into his trouser pocket.

'Leave this to me,' said Jean-Luc quietly and walked briskly over to the two men; they were walking along the path in the wood. 'I'm glad to see you. Our helicopter had engine problems. Is there an airfield nearby; if so, how do we get there?'

The older of the two pointed towards the west. 'The airfield's over there, but I have no idea whether they'll be able to help you.'

'This kind gentleman offered to give us a lift in his car. I would advise you to turn back. We don't want to injure anyone, if we have problems starting it up again.'

The two men threw a final inquisitive look at the helicopter, nodded sympathetically and turned back. Jean-Luc waited until they were out of sight.

'Don't worry; they've gone. Well then?' He looked at Edward expectantly.

'Henry says there are at least half a dozen cars here in Paris that the Al Fayeds use. Private, business, or whatever. But he thinks there is a chance that he can pass one on to them at short notice – either the four-by-four I mentioned, or a Mercedes 280. We could lay our hands on it immediately.'

'Let's get on with it then!' Red urged them. 'What are we waiting for? The more time I have, the better. Give this guy Henry another ring, right now. He obviously won't be able to speak openly. Just tell him where we'll be waiting to pick up the car.'

Edward got out the mobile again and dialled Henry's number. 'Send the Mercedes as soon as possible to . . .' He turned to Jean-Luc for guidance, who gave him an address. 'Understood?' he asked Henry. 'I'll be in touch as soon as the car has arrived.' He looked over towards the helicopter. 'I've got to speak to the pilots. Red, can you come with me?'

Edward was the first to get to the helicopter. He told the pilots: 'Please wait here. I'll get you some food and drink. Our friend here,' pointing to Red, 'has to fly back to London tonight as a matter of urgency. The rest of our party will follow in our jet. Do you think you'll manage to take off from here in the dark?'

They nodded.

'Do you have enough fuel?'

'Yes, no problem.'

'Very good. Then thanks for everything and I wish you a safe return journey this evening. Give me your frequency, please, so that I can contact you if necessary. Our French colleague has a transmitter in his car, and I can announce our departure time so long as you stay on call.'

One of the pilots scribbled some figures on a slip of paper. 'I've given both frequencies, in case one of them has to be closed down for some reason or other.'

Edward thanked them again and he and Red went back to the Citroën.

'Walter, could you please go to the nearest village and bring the pilots something to eat and drink? Jean-Luc and I will let you know where we're going. You and Arthur will join us later. Are there any questions?' Edward asked his team.

'No!' replied Red impatiently.

## 67

There was total chaos on the streets around the Eiffel Tower and the entire *banlieue*; almost the whole of Paris, it seemed, was returning from holiday. Jean-Luc had allowed for less than half an hour for the journey from Chavenay to the disused factory shed. The four of them had already been on the road for one whole hour and still had not arrived. Henry's car would have the same problem. In these conditions, Red deliberated, central London traffic was virtually a motor race by comparison. Nervously, he glanced at the clock on the dashboard; its hands were moving slowly but surely towards 6 pm. At last, Jean-Luc turned off the main road and on to a road that led through a derelict and dilapidated industrial district. The roads were full of unrepaired potholes; whole areas were in need of asphalting. Red crossed his fingers, in the hope that his laptop in the boot would survive the potholes. It would be the last straw if the computer let him down now.

'If necessary, can we tell Walter to get going?' he asked suddenly.

'What do you mean?' asked Edward.

'To mingle with the paparazzi,' came the reply. Edward gave it a thought or two.

'I see no problem, but we have no press cameras on board.'

'That's no problem,' Jean-Luc volunteered. 'I can get hold of a complete Canon set with a long-range lens, plus all the extras. One of my close friends is a photographer. I've borrowed his gear for my own investigations. It wouldn't look suspicious if I handle this one in the same way.'

'Then you should be able to get hold of a special Paris numberplate for the motorbike?' Red enquired.

Jean-Luc shook his head. 'A Paris numberplate is very difficult to get hold of. But I can get one from Bordeaux. I would think that would be alright, so long as it's not an English one?'

'OK. When can we get both those things?'

'If Edward doesn't need me, I'll drop you here at the factory shed. I should be back within the hour, traffic permitting.'

'That will be fine. How do I get back to the helicopter tonight?' asked Red.

Quite right, Edward was thinking. He had not considered that. He was anxious not to be seen with Red under any circumstances, in case anything went wrong. He tapped Jean-Luc on the shoulder. 'Could you get hold of a second car for a couple of hours? George will drive Red back to Chavenay after the accident and return immediately.'

'Yes, of course. In that case, George should come with me when I pick up the camera and the numberplate. I have another car, a Renault. We'll bring it along.'

'Do you think I'll be able to find my way back to Chavenay?' asked George, studying Edward's reaction intently.

Red turned round to them both in the back of the car. 'I don't see any problems. We'll take the map Walter's using. I'll find my way out of Paris; to return to Paris, you just follow the 'Centre Ville' signs. At the city centre you should agree to meet at an agreed landmark – the Eiffel Tower, the Arc de Triomphe, or whatever.'

'That's fine! I would have had problems finding my way back to Chavenay by night, without a road map.'

Jean-Luc slammed on the brakes. 'The entrance to the shed is so well concealed that I've now driven past.' He reversed a good two hundred yards and turned the steering wheel sharply to the left. The car almost spun round on the spot.

In front lay a narrow approach road; at the end was a small industrial area, on which stood a number of buildings and a factory shed. Jean-Luc set the car in the direction of the shed, where the BMW was already parked.

Walter and Arthur had covered the ground much faster and had meanwhile given the place a thorough going-over. As soon as they heard the sound of the Citroën's engine they emerged from the shed. Jean-Luc parked near the shed door. Red jumped out and grabbed his metal case and laptop from the boot. George shifted from the back seat to the passenger seat, ready to drive off with Jean-Luc.

'You haven't heard or seen anything of the Mercedes, have you?' asked Jean-Luc. Walter and Arthur shook their heads. 'It would be advisable, perhaps,' said Jean-Luc, turning to Edward, 'to place one of your men at the roadside entrance. The gate is hard to find, especially for someone who has never been here before.'

Edward looked to Walter and Arthur for suggestions. Walter raised his hand. 'Perhaps it would be less obvious if I stood outside with my bike.'

'OK, Walter.' Edward pointed in the direction of the entrance gate. 'You'd better get there quick.' He paused for a moment. 'By the way, prepare yourself mentally for a bit of socializing on your bike this evening with the paparazzi.'

Walter gave a nod.

'Is there any food or drink anywhere?' asked Red casually. 'I simply can't recall when I last had anything to chew.'

George stuck his head out of the car window. 'Jean-Luc and I will bring you something. How about some pizza? OK?'

There were no objections.

'Jean-Luc, please give me your car phone number, in case we have problems,' asked Edward. Jean-Luc handed him his visiting card.

'Investment adviser?' queried Edward, teasing him. 'Who do you invest with?'

They both laughed. Jean-Luc jumped into the car with George.

'Halt!' shouted Red suddenly. 'Who's got the road map now?'

'Walter.'

Walter, who was just about to start the motor, groped inside his breast pocket, pulled out the map and passed it to Red. He then revved up and drove back to the entrance gate. Jean-Luc started up the Citroën and followed him.

Red, Edward and Arthur waited until both vehicles had driven out of the narrow gate, then moved into the shed. The roof was leaking in places. Here and there, big puddles of water reflected the sunlight as it shone through the large windows, some of which had glass missing. Edward tried out one of the light switches by the main door. Three neon tubes flickered overhead; the rest of the shed stayed dark, although there were one or two lights hanging there.

'That should be enough,' Red decided. 'I've got a powerful torch with me.' He put his case on one of the three long tables and opened the locks. Undetected, he took out his mobile and slipped it into his trouser pocket. He glanced at his wrist-watch and pointed at a small clock at the end of the shed. 'Is that a toilet over there, do you think?' The door happened to be locked. He looked around and found a window with no glass inside. He swung over the window-sill, into the open, and landed in a small inner courtyard, overgrown with weeds and scrub.

From behind a large bush he pulled the mobile out of his pocket and waited. The hands of his watch jumped from 5.58 p.m. to 5.59 p.m. Red took a few paces away from the shed, keeping an eye on the window. There was a rustling noise from behind. He quickly turned round and spotted a cat; terrified, it shot off into the bushes.

To the second, his mobile began to bleep. Red answered. 'Please take this down. Buy yourself a road map of Paris and the suburbs. To the west of Paris you'll find a place by the name of Chavenay. There are two roads leading to

Saint-Nom from Chavenay. Take the northern road. That
leads to the road from Feucherolles to Saint-Nom. Opposite
the road junction, you'll see a narrow parking bay in a hollow.
Stand by for me there from 10 p.m. onwards, local time. Now
repeat, please!' Red listened and nodded once or twice. He
quickly switched off, so as to avoid any further questions.

**68**

As Lucy left the bistro and came out into the open, she felt her eyes smarting because of the cigarette fumes that had hung about in heavy clouds inside. She crossed the car park and walked up a narrow, gentle uphill path that led to a small wood at the top.

Why did Red suddenly want to give up everything and move to this country? The thought obsessed her. She had been sure he would want to move to France in his old age. But she had never considered joining him. That depended on so many other factors. They had become very close over the years and Red was not such a bad chap, after all. But did he really believe he could live in safety outside his mountain stronghold? Everything pointed to the fact that he was about to conclude some deal he was now involved in. He had previously mentioned two jobs. She knew Edward, who was one of his partners. But who were the other two characters who had visited him? Who had engaged him for the Paris job? She could not make head nor tail of it. Glancing at her watch, she wondered why she had to phone him so punctually? She decided not to climb any higher, though she felt there might be a good view over Paris from the top. She returned to the petrol station and asked if she could use the phone. The girl at the cash desk directed her to a small room nearby, where the telephone was. She dialled Red's mobile number on the dot, at six o'clock, took down his instructions and went over to the cash desk to pay. She bought a street map of Paris and asked for Chavenay to be pointed out to her.

What on earth was she to do for the next four hours?

His business was obviously taking up more time. It was hardly worthwhile taking a trip to the centre of Paris. Lucy had noticed, however, that Versailles was on the route to Chavenay, so she decided to break her journey there. She might even have time to visit the gardens, which she had so often read about. She climbed into the Fiat and worked out her route from the map, skirting Paris at some distance because of the traffic.

As she neared Versailles she noticed that all the sightseeing attractions were shut down, except for the park. With the help of a tourists' guide, she set off with the idea of strolling round the Grand Canal. But she had failed to take the map's scale into account. As soon as she realized how immense the park was, she decided she would walk along a small section of the canal and then turn back.

At a small restaurant near Versailles railway station, she wolfed down a dry baguette, topped with a runny Brie, which she washed down with half a glass of red wine. As she got up she felt hungrier than ever.

It was getting dark outside, as Lucy headed for Chavenay. Soon after Saint-Nom, she came to the road junction Red had mentioned and drove into the little parking bay where they had both agreed to meet. She locked the doors from inside and adjusted the seat to a comfortable position. How could she tell how punctual Red would be?

## 69

Edward and Arthur had meanwhile seated themselves next to Red's case on one of the tables, as there was nothing else to sit on. Walking towards the window, Red had spotted a small, shaky oil barrel. He now rolled it over to the table and produced from his case a small piece of cloth that he normally used for cleaning his hands. He spread it out over the barrel and sat on top. Without a word, he reached for the laptop and switched it on. He then unfolded the road map and searched for Place Vendôme in the street index. It was only a few yards from the Jardin des Tuileries and the Place de la Concorde. He marked the rough spot where the Ritz Hotel would be. Then he looked for the Arc de Triomphe, where Jean-Luc had said the Al Fayed apartment was located, and finally the Bois de Boulogne. He very quickly identified Mohammed Al Fayed's house and marked both spots.

How would Di and Dodi drive to any of these three locations after their evening's tête-à-tête? Red tried to reconstruct the situation and traced all the routes back to the Avenue des Champs Elysées; he was sure they would spend the rest of the evening together somewhere near. Most of the quality restaurants in Paris were in the eighth arrondissement. He was also sure that the bodyguards would be more concerned with the paparazzi than the vehicle itself. It was likely that only one driver would stay behind inside the car.

Red wondered what Henry's function was if he could decide on the car they would take that evening. Was he head chauffeur, a private secretary, or one of the senior bodyguards? He must surely occupy one of these posts. Therefore it was

logical, Red considered, that Henry would also have a say
in the choice of chauffeur. He could imagine that Princess
Di might wish to drive her own car herself; Dodi, on the
other hand, was the type who preferred to be driven. But
if they travelled together, they would undoubtedly take the
chauffeur.

'When are you going to call your man Henry again?' Red
asked Edward.

'We had agreed I would call as soon as the Mercedes
arrived.'

'Am I correct in assuming that the person who decides
which car takes them home tonight also decides on the driver?
Do you follow me?'

Edward lowered his gaze, as he pondered the question.
He took his time, evidently trying to imagine himself in the
same situation, as Red had done. Arthur merely reacted with
a twitch of the mouth.

'I don't think it's written down anywhere that the man in
charge of the vehicles is also responsible for the choice of
chauffeurs. On the other hand, I think it's quite likely, since
car and driver are one and the same thing, so to speak.'

Red bent over his map again. 'Paris has quite a few
bridges; and bridges are ideal for accidents. Plenty of open
spaces, lanterns, and lots of pillars and statues of one sort or
another. But unfortunately they won't need to cross over to
the other side of the Seine, unless one of them wants to do the
nightclubs.' He traced a street with his ballpoint, then shook
his head again and studied a different area. 'They'll need to
get off to a quick start to shake off the photographers. And
if you want to win the race, you go up the one-way streets,
the boulevards and, ideally, expressways! But that's precisely
how you give away the place where you want to end up; in
that case, you take a number of sharp bends and drive down
one or two alleys to throw your pursuers off the scent. And
then, when you're ahead of the game . . .' Red stared at the
map, drumming the ballpoint against the table. 'I bet you,

wherever their route begins or ends, we'll find one that starts off from a large and very busy traffic centre.'

Edward and Arthur gazed at Red in eager anticipation. Red was thinking aloud. 'For example, the Arc de Triomphe, the Obélisque, the Place de la Bastille, or else a massive traffic island, with fountains and flower-beds, or even a small block of flats.'

'Why?' asked Arthur.

'Quite simple. That's where I confuse my pursuers. When a vehicle negotiates a roundabout, you can assume that the driver won't do a complete circle but will turn off at some point. So you reduce your speed a little so that you can react and turn off fast, just at the right moment. But you know you're not going to turn off. You suddenly put your foot on the accelerator, and, if you're smart, drive two or three times round the roundabout, and find your pursuers right in front of you. Then you can turn off much faster than they can. They'll be furious and will have to control their speed, which has the effect of increasing distraction and reducing response time. And then if you have to thread your way through the other vehicles, which will obviously be the case, you simply get lost amongst them . . . That way, I can guarantee, nine chauffeurs out of ten would shake off any pursuers.'

'If I were chasing you, I'd simply stop and wait till I knew where you'd turn off,' Arthur reflected.

'Then you've lost the game!' Red grinned. 'The rabbit will be off before the huntsmen wake up and get into line. Besides, you've got to take their collective greediness into account. The more numerous they are, the more they get into each other's way. The rabbit has one clear advantage – he knows where he wants to go. The huntsmen wander around behind, confused. It takes quite a few guns to shoot a rabbit dead. If three or four of them decide to work together by radio, they might be able to set a trap.' Arthur jumped down from the table, a dubious expression on his face. 'Are you absolutely sure?'

Red ignored the question and buried his head in the road map. If one assumed that the car was parked somewhere just off the Avenue des Champs Elysées, the driver would never choose to go round the Arc de Triomphe, since it would take him direct to Dodi's apartment and also the Bois de Boulogne via Avenue Foch. Depending on which side of the Champs Elysées he was, he would make a detour via the Place de la Madeleine or along the right bank of the Seine. Red would have to find a suitable spot in that area. The rest would be up to Walter. He then realized that Arthur also had his motor cyclists' gear on. He looked up, his gazed fixed on Arthur, who had his back to him. He was not convinced that he was the right man for the job. He struck Red as being overzealous, which was always a bad omen. That meant either Edward, himself or George. Red waited until Edward looked in his direction; he signalled, behind Arthur's back, that he wanted to speak to Edward alone. Edward understood at once. He jumped from the table and walked up and down the shed. As he passed Arthur for the second time, he paused. 'Perhaps one of us should keep Walter company. Who knows how long the Mercedes will take to get here?'

'I need you, though, Edward,' Red butted in.

'Then maybe you should keep a lookout?' Edward asked Arthur, who nodded and ambled out of the shed.

Edward turned round to Red. 'What's the problem now?'

'We need a second man on the motorbike. Walter has to drive like mad and will only be able to keep his mind on the traffic. But I find this chap, Arthur, too arrogant and too enthusiastic. That sort of person is a big risk. We need a dependable type who does as he is told. No more and no less.'

'George?'

Red nodded. 'They both have roughly the same figure, so the leather suit should also fit him.'

'I'm not sure. Arthur's a good man. Maybe a little zealous, or fanatical perhaps. But George is the nervous type. I've always had my doubts whether it was right to put him on this job in the first place. He's too sympathetic to Diana and fails to understand the reason why we're taking action . . . have to take action.'

Red listened attentively. He let Edward carry on.

'I doubt George is your man. Why do you want to use him?'

Red was stroking his beard; he made no comment.

'This whole business is so dangerous and there are so many imponderables, that we have to eliminate any further risk,' Edward continued.

'Exactly!' Red stood up from his seat on the barrel and went over to Edward at the window. 'If I understand you correctly, you're not even sure that this man George will keep his mouth shut. Am I right?'

Edward gazed beyond Red, into empty space.

'Let's be frank with each other, Edward. I believe George is the type of person who has stamina, when it comes to the point.'

Red walked up close; his voice grew harder. 'You've *got* to put him on the bike! Put him in the hot seat so that he'll have a guilty conscience. He'll only keep quiet if he feels guilty himself – feels guilty because of his involvement in Diana's death. He will not go around saying that it wasn't really an accident; he'll have played an active role.' Red paused. 'Think about it!'

Edward moved off the window-ledge and went outside, deep in thought. Red sensed that he'd scored a bull's-eye by speaking his mind. He caught sight of Edward, as he walked over to the entrance gate and slowly walked back.

'You're right, Red. George will go with Walter.'

## 70

Arthur had sat down near Walter's motorbike, on a crumbling kerbstone. It was clear to him that Edward wanted to speak to Red in privacy; he felt he had been cold-shouldered. He looked around. Jean-Luc had really chosen the most godforsaken place! No one would wish to be seen dead here. On the site opposite stood a derelict old crane. The road beyond came to an end at a shoddily-built wall that blocked off the main road – the obvious reason why the site had been abandoned. On one side it had been more or less cut off from its surroundings; on the other the approach road was far too long. So time had taken its toll. Arthur grabbed a handful of pebbles from the side of the road and tried to hit the old factory signboard on the other side. It was rusty and illegible.

Walter had wandered up the road and had now turned back. He had taken off his leather jacket and slung it over his shoulders. 'Do you think it's going to rain today?' he called.

Arthur looked up into the clouds above. 'Hard to tell. This morning I'd have said it would, but I wouldn't bet on it.'

Walter sat down again on the bike saddle. 'I wish it was all over.'

'One can only hope that Red doesn't chicken out again at the last moment.' Arthur reached out and threw the last few pebbles at the board.

Walter put him right. 'Red has not chickened out. Time was too short. I haven't a clue what he was planning to do, but I don't think he was just being temperamental. Of course, he shouldn't have left us high and dry as he did . . .'

'Watch out, there's a car coming!' Arthur laboriously stood up and dusted the seat of his leather suit.

'Two!' Walter corrected him. It was not the Mercedes, but he recognized Jean-Luc's Citroën, followed by a white car of a different make. Walter got off his bike and waited till both vehicles had driven up to the entrance. Jean-Luc wound down the window. 'Has the Mercedes arrived yet?'

'No,' replied Walter. 'We wouldn't be standing here if it had.'

'How reliable is he – this fellow who was going to send it along?' asked Jean-Luc.

'I haven't a clue. We don't know him personally. He usually works for another department.' Walter had come up close to the Citroën. There was a whiff of tarragon and cheese from inside the car. 'You can leave a couple of pizzas right here,' he laughed, pointing to the passenger seat, which was piled high with pizza cartons. 'You might also hand over the numberplate for my bike.'

'It's on the rear seat of the Renault, with all the camera equipment. You'll see all the tools there as well. You ought to push your bike back into the compound to fix the numberplate. Somebody might turn up out here.'

Walter opened the boot of the Renault, took out the numberplate and the tool kit, then slammed the lid to. 'What's the traffic like in town?'

'Still very busy,' answered George.

'Then we can only hope and pray that the Mercedes arrives at some time or other.'

George gave a nod and followed Jean-Luc, who had now turned into the entrance.

Arthur offered Walter a pizza carton, from which a wonderful aroma escaped. 'Let's first relax and have something to eat. You can always attach the numberplate later. There's no urgency whilst we're still waiting for our crash vehicle.'

'Forget it!' Walter called out. 'Helmets on!' He pointed down the road. Two cars loomed into sight and slowly drove

up close to them. It suddenly occurred to Walter that Arthur
had not got his helmet with him. He grabbed hold of both pizza
cartons and shoved the numberplate and tool kit into Arthur's
hands. 'Take the bike and disappear. I'll handle this myself.'

Arthur stuffed the small tool kit inside his leather jacket,
clamped the numberplate under his arm and hurried off to
shove the BMW out of sight. Walter put on his helmet. 'Stay
near, just behind the wall. I may need you.' He then closed
the visor of his helmet.

By now, both cars were visible. The first was quite
recognizably a black Mercedes 280; the second, one of the
larger Renault models. The Renault halted just in front of
the entrance gate. The Mercedes crawled up to Walter and
stopped. The chauffeur, a thin man with light-grey hair and
a shiny black suit, got out. 'You are waiting for the car?'
he asked in a French dialect Walter did not recognize. He
nodded.

'How long do you need the car?' asked the chauffeur,
caressing the top edge of the open door. Walter wondered
what to say. How could he guess how long Red needed to
fix the vehicle? Also, he had no idea when Henry wanted
the car back.

The chauffeur noted his hesitation. He looked towards the
other driver and simply said, 'Give us a ring!' He turned and
walked briskly over to the Renault. Walter waited until it
had circled round and disappeared from view. He removed
his helmet and got inside the Mercedes. The interior had
been extremely well-maintained, although the car itself had
a few years under its belt. Walter moved off and drove it into
the shed.

Red put on his leather gloves and climbed into the driver's
seat. 'Lights!' he called out. The neon tubes flashed on. He
rotated the steering wheel, once to the left and once to the
right, and examined the dashboard. He opened the glove
compartment and glanced inside. He also opened the bonnet
and scrutinized the engine with interest.

Almost ten minutes passed by before he slowly drew himself upright, grinning at the onlookers triumphantly. 'Absolutely no problem! I never thought it would be so simple!' He winked at Edward. 'I just have to be patient, until the engine has cooled down a little.' He walked over to Walter. 'Did you wear gloves?' Walter shook his head. Red took a duster and a small bottle from his metal case. 'Did you just handle the steering wheel, or did you touch anything? Glove cabinet, radio?'

Again, Walter shook his head. Red poured a few drops out of the bottle and wiped the steering wheel, the gear lever and the door handles, inside and outside. 'Nobody is to come closer than two yards. Is that understood?' he ordered, in a surprisingly harsh tone of voice. He used the other side of the duster to give the car another wipe and got out. 'We can now eat our pizzas in peace. It'll be another half-hour before the engine has cooled down.' As he walked past Edward he whispered, 'Tell him!'

## 71

Edward beckoned to Arthur. He pulled him a few yards to one side and spoke to him quietly. 'Red thinks it's essential that Walter should not go into action on his own, but with a second person on the pillion. We have come to the conclusion that this second person should be George.'

Arthur was about to reply but Edward raised his hand. 'No questions, please! I'll tell you why when we're back in London; I'm sure you'll agree that we were right.'

Arthur screwed up his face and shook his head. 'If you say so. You're the boss. So have fun!'

'Please, Arthur! We can do with all the help we can get, but no quarrelling. I've made up my mind!'

Without a word, Arthur returned to the table where he had put his pizza. George joined him.

'Congratulations!' he said sarcastically.

'Why?' asked George innocently.

'You're hired!'

'What do you mean, hired?'

'We change clothes. You're going off with Walter.' Walter dug into his pizza and nodded in confirmation.

'Who says so?' demanded George.

Arthur pointed at Edward with his head. George threw his empty carton on the table and addressed Edward, who was standing in a small group, with Jean-Luc and Walter.

'So I'm to go on the bike. Are you joking?'

Edward gave Arthur a quick, meaningful glance. Arthur grinned shamelessly back at him. 'No, George, I'm not. Red and I are both convinced you're the ideal companion for Walter. But let me explain tomorrow, please; there's no time now.'

George stared at him silently. Edward fully realized that George had quickly worked out what that meant for him, personally. He just hoped George wouldn't quit now. He gently thumped him on the chest with his right hand. 'OK, George?'

There was no answer. George turned round and walked off towards the entrance.

Red had observed the scene. He got up from his seat on the barrel and followed George, giving Edward a curt sign to leave them both alone.

It was now cooler outside, probably because rain had fallen in the neighbourhood. Red had sidled up to George, who jumped with fright as he heard Red's voice. He turned round.

'Do you two have problems?' Red asked quietly.

At first George did not know what to say. Red was still a stranger to him, but on the other hand he was impartial.

'I've been told to go with Walter on his bike.'

'So?'

'What am I supposed to do?'

Red stuck both hands in his pockets and squared up to him. He addressed him in a warm, paternal manner. 'George, for me you're the most important man on the job tonight. I trust you and only you. Please don't disappoint me!'

George stuttered. 'Yes, but . . . yes, what . . . what am I to do?'

Red laid his hand on George's shoulder. 'I'll explain to Walter and you later. You'll just pretend to be part of the paparazzi and stay close to the Mercedes on your bike.'

'But,' George began in desperation, 'I won't see . . .'

Red's reaction was brief but firm. 'No!' he said. 'If you carry out your instructions properly, you won't witness the crash. That's what you wanted to hear, wasn't it?'

He left George standing at the entrance to the shed, without waiting for his response. As he passed Edward he gave him a reassuring glance and then buried himself in the road map.

Edward could not fail to observe George as he came back inside and immediately leant against the wall by the first window. With an impenetrable expression, he gazed into the falling darkness.

Arthur had now finished his pizza and collected his colleagues' empty cartons. He asked Edward, sarcastically, 'Where shall I put the rubbish, Boss? Or do I have a different job?'

Edward reacted with unexpected violence. 'Watch your step, Arthur! This is my final warning!'

'Oh,' replied Arthur curtly and went over to Walter. 'Could I have the key to the strongbox, please? I want to get changed.'

Walter took the key from his pocket and gave it to him. Jean-Luc gave him a second key. 'It would be best to put the rubbish in the Renault.'

Arthur took both keys and went out through the main door. 'Rather nervous, that chap,' Jean-Luc commented.

'More than that,' Edward retorted. 'But there's no time to discuss why.' He consulted his watch and saw that Red was still buried in the map.

'How do you know Red?' asked Jean-Luc, very quietly.

'Why? Do you know him too?'

Jean-Luc turned away and wandered over to the darker side of the room. Edward interpreted this as an invitation, left Walter and followed him.

'"Know" would be an overstatement,' continued Jean-Luc, 'but I've come across his name several times in the last six months. He works for other people, too.'

'We're aware of that,' Edward replied. 'Do you have any more on him?'

'Not much. He must have spent some time here in France earlier in the year. I've only heard that our secret service was very interested in him, but I don't know why. The fact is, however, that he suddenly vanished into thin air. Then the name Red suddenly cropped up again a few days ago. An Arab colleague, who does some arms dealing for his country here in Paris, asked me if I knew him. And that was that.'

'Red is very much in demand,' was Edward's reaction. 'We obtained his address from the CIA and checked him out.'

Jean-Luc stood still. 'Please don't get me wrong. We have no reservations at all. I was just surprised when he turned up with you, since I'd heard so much about him recently. Will he go back home once the job's over?'

'Earlier, if possible! I've already set the wheels in motion. When Red's done his bit, Arthur, rather than George, will drive him back in your car to the helicopter at Chavenay. It's equipped for night flying and will return him to London as soon as possible. He'll fly on to the USA immediately, by commercial airline.'

They wandered back to rejoin Walter, who was studying the map over Red's shoulder. Red had drawn a small red circle around the area of the Champs Elysées on the map. He traced the side-streets with the ballpoint pen, stopping at junctions, as if, mentally, he sat at the steering wheel.

Once or twice, he went through the motions of slamming on the brakes or accelerating fast. He picked up the red pencil again and drew another circle on the map. Suddenly, he tossed the pencil on to the table and shouted triumphantly, 'I've done it!' cautiously, he added, 'in theory.'

He grabbed the laptop, which lay next to the map, and dived inside his metal case. He opened the lid. A quick glance at the others convinced him that there was no risk that they could divulge its secrets. 'A magician never lets the others peep at his cards,' he said, noting their inquisitive stares. He took two diskettes and some electric cables from the case and shut the lid. 'Could somebody please roll the barrel over to the car?'

Walter volunteered. He removed the cloth from the barrel, tipped it over and rolled it up close to the car.

'Further forward, close to the engine compartment,' Red instructed them.

Walter rolled the barrel a few yards further and placed it upright. Red switched on his laptop and put it on top of the barrel. He then pulled out two diskettes, which he entered into the computer after the signal. He inserted the cables into the sockets at the back of the computer and vanished with the cable ends inside the engine compartment.

There were sounds of loud swearing from time to time. Suddenly, he emerged from the engine compartment and removed a small, heavy torch from his case. He bent down again, inside. A powerful ray of light shone, broken by strange shadows, on the shed floor under the Mercedes.

They could hear more groaning and cursing, but this time Red's efforts seemed to be rewarded. As he finally emerged he looked extremely pleased with himself. He sat inside the car and started up the engine. The picture of the laptop screen flickered.

Red jumped out and walked over to the long table. This time he took the case itself inside the car. He took out a few tools and dived into the engine compartment again. He finally switched off the engine and tested the brake and the gears. The wall of the shed reflected a sudden flash from the white rear lights. Only now did Edward notice that Arthur had returned and was standing against the section of the wall that was illuminated. He had changed back into his everyday clothes. Edward turned round towards Walter.

'Perhaps you should switch the number plates now.' Walter nodded. He went out of the shed and wheeled in the BMW. It was now very dark outside. Lying next to the leather suit Arthur had previously worn was the little tool kit. Walter got on with the job. He was in luck. The screw holes were placed at the same distance apart on both numberplates, so there was no need to bore new holes.

When he had finished, Walter went over to the window and handed George the leather suit. 'You've got to get dressed now. The strongbox is unlocked. You can put your trousers inside.'

George took the suit without a murmur and started to change. Walter left him alone. There was no point in trying to start a conversation.

Red had crawled under the Mercedes, his upper body beneath the car; his torch was placed under the engine, casting eerie shadows on to the shed roof. He emerged and glanced at his computer screen. Then he squeezed under the dashboard near the driver's seat, in the area of the pedals. Edward was impressed at the way he went about the job; he wondered how often Red must have practised these movements in his office workroom and then perfected them in his mind. Red tested the lock of the steering wheel to the right and to the left. He looked a little unhappy and, after studying the computer screen and entering some more data, disappeared again. Edward grabbed his mobile. Henry had made contact.

'Tell him he can start straightaway. The car's ready,' Red whispered. 'And ask him if he can also choose who's going to drive it.'

Edward must have received confirmation; he gave the thumbs up.

'Then he should see to it that the driver has a few drinks as soon as possible,' Red continued to whisper. 'No wine – strong stuff like vodka, whisky or cognac. Ask him, also, whether he can get hold of drugs like Prozac or Tiapridex. I don't know what the stuff's called in France. Give him to me!' Without waiting for an answer, Red grabbed the mobile from Edward's hands.

'Hello! Make sure the driver swallows three or four glasses of cognac, whisky, or whatever. Have you heard of Prozac? Or Fluoxetine? Perhaps that's what it's called in Europe. And what about Tiapridex? OK, mix them both in his alcohol without attracting his attention? Are you familiar with the dosage? Good. Can I rely on you?

He gave back the mobile to a very bewildered Edward and hurried over to the Mercedes.

'You can pick up the car now! Good, thanks!' Edward switched off the phone and gave a huge sigh of relief. 'Everything seems to be in order.' He felt a shudder run through his body. That phone call brought zero-hour one step irrevocably closer. Arthur and George came up to hear the news.

'Princess Diana and Dodi have changed their plans,' Edward informed them. 'The shopping expedition is over and they're now on their way to the Ritz, where, we are told, they will be dining tonight. They're expected any moment.'

'That must mean that Henry is also at the Ritz,' Arthur concluded.

'Why?' asked Edward.

'Otherwise Henry would have said, *we* will be arriving at the Ritz any minute,' Arthur replied.

Edward disagreed. 'Not necessarily. The statement implies that Henry's not with Diana and Dodi. He could have picked up the information from a third party. Whatever the case may be,' he said, looking again at his watch, 'we have still two or three hours. A good meal takes time.' He glanced in the direction of George, who returned his look.

'That's fine by me, Edward!'

## 72

Jean-Luc handed Edward a second street map that he had found in his Citroën. Edward in turn passed it on to Arthur. 'Jean-Luc will remind you of the way back to Chavenay, so that you can avoid unnecessary delay.'

Arthur nodded and went over to the long table to study the route with Jean-Luc, who handed him the keys to the Citroën.

'I'll take the Renault; it's more adaptable in the Paris traffic.'

Red had completed his work on the Mercedes; he was now running a few programs on his laptop. He obviously seemed thoroughly satisfied. A small, grey metal box stood near him, about the size of a TV remote control, with a large red button that he was pressing all the time.

Edward reflected on their next hour. If Red had finished, he would have to brief Walter and George. Edward himself had to inform the helicopter pilots at what time Red was due to leave, whilst Arthur would have to take Red to the airfield by the shortest route. Jean-Luc and he would . . .

At this thought, his heart began to race; his stomach ached. He had already decided that afternoon not to get in touch with London before the job was over. No, he wanted to get on with it and then announce, 'Mission accomplished!' Hopefully nothing could go wrong. He could not imagine what would happen if Red had miscalculated and the crash was not fatal, or was intercepted as an assassination attempt before he and his team, and Red in particular, had fled the country.

He felt his stomach turn acid. Tension was rising all round. Even Arthur was tense. Red, however was humming happily to himself, kneeling in front of his laptop. He then got up and leant over the engine compartment again. He resurfaced with the cable ends and shut the bonnet. He dived inside the car and groped around the pedals, fiddled with a panel, banged his fist several times and finally re-emerged, moaning and groaning. 'I've done it!' he shouted and pulled the plugs at the other end out of the computer. He shut down and shoved the various tools he had used back inside the metal case.

'You've still got my mobile,' Edward called. Red handed it to him; Edward then passed it to Arthur, whilst Red carefully picked up the small grey box and put it down by the street map.

'Please don't touch!' he commanded, then removed his gloves. 'Now listen, all of you! I don't need to tell you precisely what modifications I have made to the Mercedes. But I can assure you they will not be detected as manipulation, since they only affect the electronic control system. I have assumed, of course, that after the crash the car will be carefully examined, bit by bit. In fact, even if it was possible to check the electronic control system, a technical expert would say that the changes were due to factors other than human manipulation. This type of vehicle comes into contact with all sorts of electronic and electromagnetic apparatus – car phones, remote-controlled radio and radar – so electronic interference can never be excluded.' He turned to Edward. 'You realize what I am saying? Walter and George will play the role of two paparazzi. Now, do we know where our love-birds are at the moment?'

'At the Ritz!' Edward confirmed.

'Aha!' Red continued. 'Events are now moving in our favour. Fantastic! Walter and George should now shoot off to the Ritz.' He looked at Jean-Luc. 'We hope that our French colleague's hypothesis is correct and that Di and

Dodi will be spending the night elsewhere. In which case they will be picked up in this car at some time or other, provided that your undercover agent sees to it that this is the one!'

Edward nodded.

'Walter, you have now two jobs. If you pick up the street map, you'll see that I've marked two red circles. Familiarize yourself with the map and remember where the circles are.

'I'm making two basic assumptions. Firstly, that the chauffeur's driving ability is adversely affected by alcohol and a dose of Prozac, without it being obvious. Prozac exaggerates the purely external symptoms of a typical drunken man – starting with the glazed look and including the slurred speech. Secondly, the paparazzi, who will be hanging around the Ritz, will also join in the chase. So the chauffeur will not necessarily move off from the hotel at walking speed. He'll try to shake them off immediately. And you, Walter, follow them. Make sure you're always out front. Your helmet radio is linked to George's on the pillion. As soon as you approach one of the red circles, tell George, and you, George . . .' Red pointed to the small grey box behind him, 'just wait until Walter has got to within at least twenty yards from the Mercedes. When you're that close, then press for about three or four seconds on this red button here and lower the little trigger at the side. Tell Walter immediately when you've done it. And you, Walter, detach yourself from the crowd of paparazzi and quit the scene. Within two or three seconds the electronics of the Mercedes – according to the speed of the car – will be incapacitated after another fifty, or a hundred yards at the most. The car will accelerate out of control since the brake boosters and the automatic braking system will be paralysed.'

George was about to interrupt Red but was silenced by a wave of his hand. 'The red circles on the map are highly important. Experience tells me that, because

of the road network, they are the most likely areas for a
fatal crash. Unfortunately we don't have the time or the
opportunity to determine the precise location of the crash.
The responsibility for that now passes from myself to our
two motor-cyclists. But I think it should be clear what sort
of environment we ideally need – streets with fast-moving
traffic in the opposite lane, balustrades, high street lamps,
traffic islands. It's better to abort the action at the right
moment than to press the button too early. I have one
important request: Walter, please try not to involve too
many innocent people in the accident.'

There was a shocked silence in the shed as Red ended
his speech. No one dared to look anyone else in the eye.
Red had delivered the plan for a brutal murder like a recipe
for a fruit cake. A real killer, Edward reflected, incapable
even of uttering a single word. George stood between
Edward and Arthur, petrified. Even Arthur seemed to have
been affected by Red's briefing. Walter turned round in
silence, removed the street map from the table and folded
it slowly.

Jean-Luc was the first to break the silence. 'The Citroën
is ready for departure.'

'I think it is more important that our motor-cyclists set
off now,' Red considered. 'It doesn't matter if my helicopter
takes off five minutes earlier or later. What do you think?'
he asked Edward.

'You're right, Red. Walter and George should set off
first. Any questions?' Neither said a word, visibly shaken.
'Then off you go! Whatever happens, keep your helmets
on when you're on the job. Jean-Luc will give Walter the
photo equipment. As soon as you're at the Ritz, contact
me by mobile. I shall be with Jean-Luc somewhere, close
at hand. We'll be there if you need help. When the action's
over, whatever the result, we shall meet back here on the
forecourt.'

Walter went over to the motorbike without a word.

George followed him and helped him wheel the BMW out of the shed.

Jean-Luc turned to Arthur. 'I shall give you the photo equipment. It's inside the Renault. Perhaps you'd come with me.'

Edward was aware that Jean-Luc was not only very astute; he had a sixth sense for awkward situations. Jean-Luc obviously realized he should leave Edward alone with Red so that they could talk together without being disturbed.

Red looked very happy. 'Edward, we've done it! Success is guaranteed! Don't worry. Walter and George will work well together.' He turned round and looked towards the entrance of the shed. He stood right in front of Edward and repeated, triumphantly, 'It will succeed!'

'I recognized the car immediately. It belongs, or belonged, to someone called Musa, or something similar. I had to go over it earlier this year, probably some other business – a complete refit. We were stupid. The police found the car in our hideaway. They were searching for it because the owner had reported it as stolen. It might have gone seriously wrong. I had to break off. I shot back to the USA like a scalded cat. And you know what? A few weeks ago, I was sent the specification of a car and had to give my opinion whether it could fixed for a "nice accident". Do you get me? And what do you think? That was the specification of the Mercedes 280. Vehicle of fate, I'd call it!'

Edward was struggling for words. 'Then all the time . . .'

'For me it was just child's play, since I'd pulled the car to pieces before. Lucky for you, since I might not have had enough time otherwise. Congratulations! But after all those false starts we deserve a bit of luck, don't we?'

He gave Edward a friendly slap on the shoulder and held out his hand. 'We'll meet next week at my place, remember? You know, with that little black attaché case . . . Then I'll let you into all my secrets, in peace and quiet.'

'Give Lucy my best wishes,' Edward replied, expression-less, as Red walked out of the shed, grasping his metal case.

## 73

After a few moments Jean-Luc re-emerged from the darkness. He also looked quite happy. 'They've all gone; we can only wait and hope.'

Edward stood in the hall, motionless, staring at the Mercedes. He felt hollow inside. 'Come on, Edward, jump into my car and just relax a little. We'd better clear off.'

Jean-Luc took him by the arm and dragged him out of the shed. The white Renault was parked on the forecourt. Jean-Luc opened the door on the passenger side and pushed him gently on to the seat. 'I'll be right back.' Jean-Luc went to the boot, opened it and took out a pair of working gloves. He returned to the shed, got into the Mercedes and got it started. It slowly rolled through the front door. The headlight lit up Edward's features as he sat there in the Renault, still totally distracted. The Mercedes drove over the forecourt to the entrance gate, almost without a noise.

Jean-Luc parked beneath the metal signboard Arthur had been using for target practice with his pebbles. He turned off the lights and switched off the engine, leaving the ignition key inside. He then got out and walked through the darkness of the forecourt to the factory shed. He looked round. He took some time to wipe out the tracks of the Mercedes and the motorbike, raising clouds of dust. Then he cast a glance at the tables. They were empty. He walked over to the illuminated area of the shed where they had all been sitting, switched off the lights and climbed into the Renault with Edward.

In silence, he started the engine and drove the car into

the road, using only the parking lights. He turned to the right, away from Paris, and drove for about two hundred yards. He turned round, just in front of the wall, and halted. He switched off the parking lights and gazed down the road. Apart from the silhouette of the Mercedes and the eerie shadows of the wall and the surrounding buildings, nothing was to be seen on the unlit road.

'It wouldn't make much sense to enquire as to the reason for this assignment, would it?' Jean-Luc asked quietly. 'Or would you rather not talk about it now?'

Edward gently cleared his throat. He was still staring into space. He raised his right arm and propped himself up with his elbow on the small ledge of the passenger door. Then he leant his head to one side on his right hand.

'My head's about to burst. Not only with the job itself. I also worry how the others will cope after the crash, what Red is up to and – for some time now – why we are doing it at all? You're quite right. I've asked myself more than once, "Is it all necessary? Is there another solution?" I always felt I must speak to Diana just once and ask her, "Can't you see what you're walking into?"'

'Perhaps we French would also react the same way, I don't know. Thank God we're not in the same situation! Perhaps we would have found a different solution. We're more charitable towards beautiful women.' He added, in a lighter tone, 'You Brits take everything so seriously!'

Two headlights flickered uneasily at the other end of the street. The vehicle sped towards them, over the potholes, and came to a halt beside the Mercedes. A figure ran out in front of the headlights, turned the Mercedes and drove off. Suddenly, its red rear lights flashed; it was following the other car. The whole incident lasted no more than a couple of minutes. All was now dark and quiet.

Jean-Luc started his car and drove the first few yards slowly and without lights. But it was too dark to see properly, so he switched on the headlights and took the route towards Paris.

'Tell me, shouldn't you get in touch with the helicopter pilots now that Red's on his way back?'

In a flash, Edward was all there. He pulled out the pilot's note and passed it to Jean-Luc. 'Could you please tune into this frequency?'

Jean-Luc scanned the note and halted in the middle of the road. He switched on the transmitter and turned a couple of knobs. He then took the microphone and pressed the voice button. 'Metro two nine eight calling hotel alpha India zero zero one, please answer.'

The only response was a rustling noise from the loud-speaker.

'Maybe we should try another frequency,' Edward suggested.

Jean-Luc shook his head. 'Not so fast. They certainly won't be waiting next to the radio.' He pressed the button again. 'Metro two nine eight calling hotel alpha India four zero zero one.'

The pilot answered. Jean-Luc pushed the microphone into Edward's hand. 'Press the button when you speak.'

'Your guest is on his way,' Edward informed him. 'Is message understood?'

'Hotel alpha India four zero zero one. Message understood, over.'

## 74

George pressed himself against Walter's back and held on tight to the straps on his leather jacket. They had placed the small grey box in a black nylon bag they had found inside the strongbox; George then slung it over his back. The photo equipment had been packed into the holdall, carefully wrapped inside George's clothing to protect it from being jolted or damaged. They arrived at the centre of Paris around 10 p.m. Walter turned into the Rue Royale and stopped for a moment.

'Jump off for a minute. I'll strap the camera around my neck.'

Walter took the camera out of the case and slung it round his neck. He turned round to George.

'How do I look?' he asked.

'I'm wondering just how credible you'll be if you want to take photos with your helmet on.'

'I'm not worried about that at the moment. Anyway, first of all we should drive round the block and explore the situation.'

They both got on the bike and Walter drove off. They reached Place de Vendôme via the Rue de la Paix, which Walter had imagined to be much smaller from Jean-Luc's map. An imposing, well-illuminated pillar, the Colonne de la Grande Armée, loomed up at its centre into the night sky. The square, with its rows of street lamps, was surrounded by a beautiful old building on all sides. A number of brightly-lit jewellery shops were housed inside, all of them with famous names that Walter recognized. On the right-hand side, the

Ritz took up only a relatively modest amount of space within the row of buildings. It was less pretentious from outside than Walter had expected. Several paparazzi had already taken up positions in front of the entrance. Cars and motorbikes were parked in double rows, making access difficult for the hotel guests who arrived by limousine. A few casual onlookers had congregated amongst the photographers.

George had guessed correctly; none of the photographers wore a helmet. Walter drove slowly by the Ritz and some way further. He had formed the impression from Red's description that the going might have been a little easier. He drove across the square, circled round the column and back to the Rue de la Paix, where he turned off to the left, into the nearest street, and came to a halt.

'We shan't be able to spend all night waiting in front of the hotel,' he stated, taking off his helmet.

He took out his mobile from his jacket pocket and dialled Edward's number.

Edward came on immediately.

'We've reached our target. But it all looks different from what I had imagined. It's impossible for us to stick around so close for any length of time without looking suspicious. What should I do?'

Walter waited for a moment. 'Good. Check everything out and contact me later.'

He put the mobile back into his jacket pocket, then put on his helmet so that he could converse with George more easily. 'Edward will first put out feelers to see what's happening inside the Ritz. We don't even know if they're going to leave tonight. In the worst case we shall have to wait until tomorrow morning, when Princess Diana drives to the airport.'

'In broad daylight . . . ?' George was bewildered.

Walter shrugged his shoulders. 'Why not? It's hardly relevant.' He sprang on his bike. 'Come on, let's make a quick tour of the area; it won't do us any harm.'

They sped off along the Boulevard des Capucines in the direction of the Place de l'Opéra. At this time of day there was still an immense amount of traffic about. Walter headed back towards the Place de la Concorde down the Rue de Rivoli and then via the Place de la Madeleine, back to the Rue de la Paix. At this point he turned the corner, round the apartment block in which the Ritz was located, and finally ended up in the Rue Saint Honoré. He stopped and switched off the motor. The display of his mobile indicated that Edward had been trying to get in touch whilst he was on his round trip. He dialled Edward's number and had a few words with him.

'Dammit, Edward couldn't get through to Henry,' he explained to George. 'Stay here by the bike and I'll go across to the Ritz and see if I can squeeze any information out of the paparazzi.'

Walter shoved his helmet into George's hands and went off with his camera into a spacious, high marble passage leading to the Place Vendôme. He slunk slowly over to the Hotel, with a disinterested look on his face. He lit a cigarette. The paparazzi were all lurking in front of the hotel entrance. Someone passed round a bottle of champagne. Walter weaved his way through the onlookers and joined a group of three photographers who were chatting with each other, two of them obviously Italians and the third a Frenchman.

'What's new?' he asked casually in French, lighting a cigarette. 'Have they finished their meal?'

'No, they're still eating. Giuseppe has just got the menu from the kitchen staff,' the small Italian confirmed. 'They have just been served eggs with asparagus and mushrooms; Di's ordered fried sole and Dodi's having grilled halibut.'

'What are they drinking?'

'What Dodi normally drinks: Bollinger champagne!' replied the Frenchman, quick as a flash. 'Haven't you got his number yet?'

My God, Walter thought to himself, what on earth should I say? The Frenchman, however, carried on without waiting for an answer. 'All the Al Fayeds like their Bollinger. I'm not so keen on Di. I stick around the Ritz, the Bristol or the George V. That's my patch. Who do you specialize in?'

Walter's answer came like the shot out of a gun. 'Di!' He couldn't put a foot wrong now. He studied the three lions in the coat of arms on the floor of the hotel foyer.

'Were you over in Sardinia with her?' asked the taller Italian, who answered to the name of Giuseppe.

'No, I had a job in Scotland with her ex.' Walter did not know if he had hit the right note, but obviously no one's suspicions were aroused.

'I saw the pictures of him and the kids. Were there many there?'

'Colleagues?' asked Walter, 'No, not many; it was by invitation only, very formal indeed.'

Giuseppe glanced up at the hotel façade. 'Ricardo and I hired a boat at Olbia. But there wasn't much to be seen. I hope there's a chance of a shot tonight. I've tipped the waiter and given him my mobile number. He'll let me know as soon as he has cleared the table.'

'If that was Alain, you've backed the wrong horse,' the Frenchman laughed out loud. Alain takes everyone for a ride. He never phones; he cashes in on people who don't know him.'

'Just you wait,' replied Giuseppe. 'No one craps on me. If they do, they regret it afterwards.'

Immediately outside the swing-doors of the Ritz there was a sudden commotion. Walter was about to shoot across, but realized that his three companions did not budge. Ricardo explained. 'That was probably Belmondo's little blonde tart; she pops up here every so often. She should have learnt to give up her ambition of getting a film part; their affair is over. You should have seen her at Cannes! Pathetic. No one took a single shot of her.'

'Yes they did,' Giuseppe roared out loud, 'The tourists!'

A few flashlights exploded. Walter caught sight of a dainty blonde over Giuseppe's shoulder, as she got into a taxi. He could not quite see what she looked like.

'I should think that's all for today.' Walter looked around, a bored expression on his face, in the hope that he would pick up a few more bits of information from his three 'colleagues'. But they just shrugged their shoulders or pulled faces.

Almost simultaneously, Walter and Giuseppe trod out their cigarettes on the red carpet leading to the entrance of the Ritz.

'So long as it doesn't rain too hard . . .'

After his first few minutes among the paparazzi Walter felt more sure of himself. 'Do you know which suite they'll be staying in tonight?'

The Frenchman shifted his weight from one leg to the other and gave him an indulgent look.

'Boy! If I knew, I'd disguise myself as a chambermaid and hide under the bed. They are always supposed to sleep in the Imperial Suite. Romuald once succeeded in creeping in when they were due to spend the night there. A bad tip-off! Some tell lies to protect their guests, others do it for money, although they know nothing, just like Alain. You've got to find out for yourself.'

'Romuald? Who's Romuald?' asked Walter, taking a mental note of the name.

'You don't know Romuald? Romuald Rat from "Gamma"!' Giuseppe stood on tiptoe and looked round. 'I saw him only a few moments ago on the Champs Elysées with his driver, Stephane Darmon. Maybe they've gone off together for a meal.'

Walter would dearly have loved to ask who or what "Gamma" was, but refrained, so as not to draw attraction to himself. He turned round quickly, pretending that he had recognized another colleague and ambled over to a group

of bystanders a few yards away. He dived in amongst them
and crawled back to the hotel entrance on the other side,
teaming up with two paparazzi standing nearby.

'Have you seen Romuald?' he asked.

They both looked around amongst the crowd. 'He was
just here a moment ago,' answered the smaller of the two.

'My name's James, by the way. I'm standing in for Jack
today,' said Walter casually.

'I'm Serge. Which Jack do you mean?' replied Serge.

Walter turned round to the other man, who introduced
himself. 'Nicolas! I recall a chap by the name of Jack, a
skinny sort of person . . .'

'That's him,' confirmed Walter.

'I haven't seen him for a long time,' Nicolas reflected.
'What's he up to now?'

'With "Gamma",' Walter frivolously suggested.

'With "Gamma"? That can't be true!' replied Serge.

Damn, Walter cursed to himself, I stuck my neck out too
far! He was wondering how he could quickly climb out of
the hole he had dug for himself. By chance, his mobile
bleeped; it saved his skin. Walter answered without giving
away his name. Edward informed him that in the meantime
the Mercedes had been delivered to Henry and that Princess
Diana and Dodi did not intend to spend the night at the
Ritz. Walter thanked him and replaced the mobile in his
jacket pocket. 'Di and Dodi won't be staying at the Ritz
tonight,' he informed both paparazzi.

Serge grinned. 'That's probably one of those famous false
trails that cost us so much money. Where are they off to
afterwards?'

'I don't know yet,' answered Walter, furtively. 'As soon
as I've heard, you'll be the first to know.'

'You're new in the business, aren't you?' Nicolas asked.
Walter realized it was high time to move off elsewhere.

'No, why?' he replied casually. 'Have you never had a

hot tip from one of your colleagues before?' he retorted in an offended tone. He decided now to join George, who was waiting for him impatiently round the corner. Walter fought his way through a group of tourists and walked back along the front of the Ministry of Justice, close to the Ritz. It occurred to him that the photographers did not drive themselves but had their own drivers. He thought it was about time he passed the camera to George.

## 75

Shortly before 10 p.m. Lucy was woken by a banging noise. Red was standing next to the car, grinning through the window.

'Hand me the ignition key,' he shouted. 'I want to open the boot.'

Lucy took out the key from the ignition lock. She was about to get out but Red was standing so close that she could not open it. She wound down the window and passed him the key. He obviously wanted her to stay inside. There was no point in not taking a hint from Red; that would simply end in a quarrel, as had happened so often before.

As the boot slammed to, Lucy jumped out, embraced Red and kissed him. He could read her thoughts. Stroking her hair, he said, 'Not now, darling! I've got one little job to do. I have to sign something, then I'm all yours!'

He tossed his jacket on to the rear seat and took over Lucy's seat at the steering-wheel.

'Jump in. The sooner we leave, the more time we'll have together.'

That convinced her. She jumped in on the passenger side. Red put his foot on the accelerator and drove off towards Paris. The journey went smoothly, even through the area of the building sites near Saint-Nom. As they approached the motorway there was a signal from Red's mobile. He answered. After listening to the caller for a second or two, he gave an order. 'Delay action; not before midnight!' He broke off and threw the mobile on to the back seat.

He was happy. 'At last! We negotiated all day but there

were always some objections. Now they want to sign as soon as possible. Nothing will happen till midnight, though. We'll stop at a nice little bar I know at the Place de la Madeleine. I'll drop you there and then I'll drive off to sign the contract.'

He bent over and gave her a kiss, still at the wheel. 'Then, Lucy, a new life begins.'

She was leaning rather wearily against the window, observing Red's features, highlighted by the street lamps. 'I thought you had to do a second job before we could start a new life together.'

Red laughed. 'Why do you think I've been slaving away in the last few days? I was able to do both jobs at once. Quite an achievement, but well worth the effort.'

'Have you thought things over carefully?' Lucy asked. 'Won't it be boring, having me around all day long. Anyhow, I still haven't decided whether I'd join you if you moved to France.'

Red took a quick look at the road signs and turned sharply to the right. 'That doesn't worry me. When you've seen all the castles and farmyards for sale in the South of France, you won't want to live anywhere else.'

They were now driving along a boulevard in heavy traffic; he turned round into a parking space, right in front of Le Forum, a night bar.

'We're there. Let's get out.'

Red locked the car, then put his arm round Lucy. 'It's time for a kiss.' He looked really happy, Lucy thought. He was suddenly so attentive – completely different from his business manner. She would dearly have loved to know what the real reason was.

The walls of the bar were tiled and the lamps were dimmed; it was not very large but it had atmosphere. In a side-room, Red found two bar stools that had just been vacated. He threw his jacket over the second stool and excused himself. 'I'll be right back. Please order me a bourbon, with plenty of ice!' He kissed her lightly on the forehead and disappeared into the toilets.

Lucy did not notice at first. Only when a young man drew her attention to it did she realize that Red's mobile was bleeping inside his jacket pocket. Without thinking, she pulled it out and switched on. Before she could even utter a word, she heard an excited voice at the other end say, in broken English, 'Di and Dodi have finished their meal. What do we do now? Hello! Red?'

Quick as a flash, Lucy pressed the 'off' key and put the mobile back. Di and Dodi? Di and Dodi? What on earth did Red have to do with Princess Diana and Al Fayed? Her mind raced as she tried to work out what the message could mean. Suddenly, she glimpsed Red striding past the small tables back to the bar. He was surprised to find the counter empty. 'Haven't they brought you anything to drink yet?'

'You were too quick.' As she replied, she noticed she was trembling. She wondered whether Red had noticed. 'I didn't even have time to order.'

Red picked up his jacket and slung it deftly over his shoulder. 'Then I'll have something to drink later. Order yourself something nice and think of me!' He blew her a kiss, nearly colliding with another guest on the way out. 'Look after my wife!' he called to the barkeeper, who had just surfaced from behind the bar.

## 76

George was waiting outside Most, a boutique in the Rue Saint Honoré. He had propped up the bike and was staring absent-mindedly at the revolving red lights on top of two No Parking signs on the other side of the street. Walter laid his hand on George's shoulder and brought him back from his reverie.

'Why did you take so long? I've been waiting ages.'

'No need to panic! Edward just called me to say that Diana and Al Fayed won't be staying at the Ritz tonight. That means she's got to come out of this damned hotel sometime tonight.'

He did a few knee-bends next to his bike. 'Do you think Red has flown off yet?'

George looked at his watch. 'Probably. That depends, of course, on how successful Arthur was.' He yawned. 'Have you any idea what to do, other than just wait?'

'Nothing. But you must take the photo equipment. It's quite logical, in a way. One of us drives and concentrates on the roads; the other is the cameraman. None of those chaps over there knows which of us is the driver. For the time being I'll be the photographer, as my "colleagues" already know me.' He considered whether it was worth going back to the Ritz. No one knew how long the meal would drag on, or when they would finally break up.

'George, I've a funny feeling. Let's go back to the Ritz. We'll just wheel the bike a few yards through the passage to the Place Vendôme and park there so that we can get off to a flying start when things begin to hot up.'

It was clear that George was not wildly enthusiastic about this suggestion, but he nevertheless put on his helmet and helped Walter push the bike.

'Let's go that way,' said Walter, pointing to a spot at the end of the hotel drive. 'By the way, don't be surprised if somebody or other calls me "James". Think of a name for yourself, in case you're asked.'

'John,' came the reply. 'But why?'

'The paparazzi here call each other mainly by their first names, like a sort of Mafia, although they're all competing with one another.' Walter propped up the bike. 'It would be best if you stayed here. Firstly, I'll be able to find you, and secondly, there's little risk of anyone talking to you. If they speak to you, tell them you're James's driver.'

George still gave the impression that he had not come to terms with the job. Walter had no wish to know what was going on in his mind at that moment. His only concern was that he, himself, was in need of a little distraction. So he quickly told George he was off, without looking back.

He wandered back amongst the rows of onlookers, in search of the paparazzi he had spoken to earlier, and finally located Giuseppe close to the hotel entrance, playing with his camera.

'Problems?' he enquired, looking over Giuseppe's shoulder.

Giuseppe jumped and turned round. He looked most surly. 'Move!' he snarled and zoomed in on the hotel entrance. Did Giuseppe know more than he did? Had that waiter, Alain, tipped him off? Maybe they were ready to move on from the upstairs suite. What would happen if the door suddenly opened? He quickly suppressed the thought. Surely the Mercedes would first draw up, the bodyguards would force a passage through the crowd, and only then would they both step on to the stage – Princess Diana and Imameddin Al Fayed.

## 77

Jean-Luc had doggedly fought his way through the traffic in the city centre and was now driving past the Ritz. Edward looked out of the window. Walter and George, however, were nowhere to be seen.

'Is there always so much going on?' he asked.

'If there are VIPs at the Ritz, yes. And there's usually one or more staying here.' Jean-Luc was keeping his eyes open in all directions, impatiently drumming his fingers on the steering wheel. Suddenly, he put his foot on the accelerator and nipped into a parking place that had just been vacated by another car.

Edward worked out from the clock on the dashboard that Red was due to arrive at the helicopter any time now. He hoped that the transfer to Heathrow would work quickly and smoothly.

'Shall we stay inside the car?' Jean-Luc asked.

Edward thought for a moment. 'Yes. It could be that we have to give Walter a bit of assistance. Anyway, I have . . .'

He was interrupted by a call on the mobile. Henry announced that the Mercedes had arrived and that Di and Dodi's suite was only booked for the evening meal; they had to shorten the shopping trip because of continuous mobbing by the paparazzi.

Edward passed the news to Walter.

'Would you enjoy that sort of life?' Jean-Luc asked. 'Just imagine what it must be like. If you cough or stare at anyone, all the time you have to consider where you are, who's looking, and whether you're doing the right thing. Her ex has not known any other sort of existence since he was a child. That's why he's so screwed up. But she has spent half her life . . .'

'Jean-Luc, let's change the subject, please. I have to concentrate on the job; we can't afford to make a mistake. Not at this moment.' Why did this wretched fellow, Jean-Luc, have to bring that subject up now, of all times? He told himself to concentrate on the job in hand and to keep cool, in case sudden or perhaps extremely difficult decisions were called for.

Edward scrutinized the passers-by, silhouetted against shop-windows and the neon signs. He suddenly opened the door, jumped out of the car, propped both arms up against the car roof and stared at the opposite side of the street. He was short of breath.

Jean-Luc was taken quite by surprise. He got out and stared at Edward, wondering, as Red had, whether he had anything wrong with him. Edward groped around for his mobile inside his jacket pocket. 'I need some fresh air, Jean-Luc.'

Edward took a few steps in the direction of the Place Vendôme. They walked along in silence.

The Rue de la Paix, at this time of day, was still full of life. The warm, sultry weather over this final August weekend enticed the Parisians to stay out late rather than turn in for an early night. A thunderstorm would have brought welcome relief from the sultry atmosphere. For most people it was also the final weekend of the holidays, and they were eager to squeeze out the last few minutes of the day.

At the end of the Rue de la Paix, Edward stopped and gazed at the crowds of reporters, inquisitive locals and foreigners, all gathered outside the Ritz.

Amid the throng, he suddenly caught sight of a large, tall character in motor-cyclists' gear – it was Walter! Instinctively he ducked, so as not to be seen. He tugged at Jean-Luc's sleeve, ready to move away. Jean-Luc caught on immediately and followed him. Slowly, they made their way up the street, back to the car. Edward got in, leant back and wound down the window to let the air in. Jean-Luc followed his example. They sat there until the silence was broken by the bleeps from the mobile. Edward reached inside his jacket pocket. As he took it out, Jean-Luc noticed that Edward's hand was trembling. 'The window!' he whispered.

Edward wound up the window and answered the call. It was Henry. He gave a brief résumé of the latest situation.

'Can you find it?' Edward asked, then gave a nod. He switched off and slowly lowered the phone. In spite of the dark, Jean-Luc noticed that Edward's face was an ashen colour; beads of sweat had broken out on his forehead. 'We're on!' he whispered to Jean-Luc and dialled Walter's number.

## 78

By now, Walter had located Serge. He was standing with a
man called Christian Martinez, discussing a new Kodak film
which was particularly effective in difficult light conditions
and was about to come on to the market. Walter had
placed himself nearby, pretending to take an interest in
their conversation. It might well prove to be a useful topic
of conversation with other groups of paparazzi.

He was disturbed by a sudden hustle and bustle amongst
the photographers. Some news had been passed back from
the hotel entrance. At that moment his phone rang.

Edward informed him that there were signs inside the
hotel that the couple were about to depart. But Henry had
warned him not to have the car at the front entrance of
the hotel; the doctored Mercedes would be picking up Di
and Dodi at the rear exit.

Walter quickly switched off and thought for a minute.
Red had talked about the rabbit and the huntsmen. Should
he now follow the decoy vehicle like all the others? Serge
had run off to the hotel entrance, so Walter grabbed
Christian and whispered, 'I've just been given a reliable
tip. That car standing there, ready to move off, is just
a bluff. Di and Dodi will be leaving from the back of
the hotel.'

Christian gave him a puzzled look. 'Are you sure?'

'Absolutely!' Walter replied, forcing his way through the
crowd, back towards George and his bike.

George had sensed the disturbance amongst the reporters
and had tied his nylon bag to his chest. He passed Walter his

helmet as soon as he arrived. Walter put it on, jumped on
the bike and revved up. As soon as George had settled on
the rear seat, Walter turned the bike round and raced off at
high speed across the Place Vendôme. 'They're leaving from
the rear hotel exit,' he informed George through the helmet
link-up. 'You know what you've got to do. We keep our
helmets on as from now, whatever happens, OK?'

'OK!'

The rear exit of the Ritz was located in the Rue Cambon.
There were three rear doors in all, each of them guarded
by video-cameras. The staff entrance was equipped with an
automatic sliding door; the rear exit to the hotel lobby was
situated near the Hemingway bar; the third door opened
into the Club Ritz, with its own entrance. Which of these
doors would Princess Diana and Dodi use?

Walter noted with satisfaction that three motorbikes had
followed him; a fourth joined them a little later. Walter
drove past the cars parked to the left and halted in a
small gap between two cars. He pulled up his visor and
took out the street map. Red had really done a first-class
job. He had marked a number of red circles around
the Ritz in every direction, covering the centre of Paris
like a web.

'Hold on tight with one hand, whatever happens. We'll
be driving at a hell of a speed, whatever route we take. And
hold the transmitter like this, so that you can't accidentally
pull the trigger.'

'Don't worry!' George assured him. 'It's brilliantly con-
structed. Whatever the outside forces, there's no chance of
triggering it off accidentally because of the combination of
button and switches; they operate in sequence.'

Another light came on at one of the three rear doors.
Without dismounting, Walter walked his bike over to the
middle of the street to get a better view. Like the other
paparazzi, he kept the engine running.

Someone came out of one of the doors – presumably

the staff entrance – and shook his fist at the onlookers, then disappeared. It was now quiet once more.

Walter studied his map again. Once you understood Red's system, there was no need to memorize the position of the circles. They all indicated special street configurations, mainly junctions or side-roads, and also sections of boulevards with static obstacles, such as traffic lights, avenues lined with trees, and so on.

Red was quite a Francophile. One could guess he knew Paris well, or had, from memory at least, some recollection of the eighth arrondissement.

George had his eyes shut. His left hand gripped the leather straps on Walter's jacket; his right was placed deep inside the nylon bag in front of his chest, clasping the small grey box. He had spent the long wait working out his plan of action. His thighs were pressed tight against the seat. When Walter started the motor he would press his chest tight against the driver's back and wait for the command. He would close his ears and eyes to everything around. Some time or other he would wake up from this nightmare and hear about tonight's tragic event from the radio, television, or the newspapers, just like anyone else.

He shuddered each time he heard another motorbike draw up to move ahead of them or turn around, hoping that Walter would not notice his inner tension. He kept testing the fingers of his right hand to see if they still moved.

'Is everything OK?' came the message through the little loudspeaker inside his helmet.

'Yes,' George replied, expecting Walter to put his foot on the accelerator now. But nothing happened. Walter put the map back into his breast pocket and kept his eye on the exits.

In his mind, Walter was searching for gaps and holes so that he could be the first to catch up with the Mercedes, practising his start and going over the first ten or twenty yards. Everything else should happen of its own accord.

He had mentally rehearsed similar situations often enough in the past.

Some figures appeared again at the rear doors, this time three in number. They cast their eyes up and down the street, exchanged a few words, then vanished.

'I think things are about to happen!' whispered Walter; his mouth had gone dry. He had hardly got his words out when a man carrying a walkie-talkie ran across the street. At that moment a black Mercedes rolled up and screeched to a halt. Someone pulled a metal barrier out of a recess in a wall. The darkness of the street was suddenly illuminated by a battery of flashing light bulbs; the din grew louder and louder. In the bright light Walter caught a glimpse of Princess Diana and Al Fayed as they sprinted to the car and jumped inside, sheltered by their bodyguards.

The Mercedes then drove directly at Walter and George. There was another round of flashlights. The car raced past them both. Walter had a close-up view of Princess Diana. She held her hand up between her face and the glass to protect herself. The front passenger seat was occupied, evidently by a bodyguard, since Dodi was seated at the rear, next to Diana. They were travelling too fast for Walter to catch sight of him properly.

Walter raced off. He could feel George's body pressed tight against his back. He accelerated; in just seconds he had drawn up to within a few yards of the car. No. There was no red circle here, he remembered; the roads were too narrow and they were not travelling fast enough. The car drove across a road junction. Walter saw some frightened pedestrians leap to one side. In the corner of his eye he could see another motorbike drawing up alongside. It was obviously vital, not only to keep his eye on the Mercedes but also on the paparazzi.

The car in front was quite clearly the doctored Mercedes 280. Walter had noted the number: 688 LAV 75. It was going to work out just as Red had planned. Walter had

no idea of the direction he was going, nor how fast. He
could see no houses, no people, only the rear lights of the
Mercedes. Suddenly the brake lights came on in front; he
braked hard. There was a squealing of tires as they turned
into a right-hand bend. He felt George's body hard against
his back.

'Hold on tight!'

Walter now swerved to avoid some object or other,
he didn't know what. It suddenly appeared and then
disappeared. Another motorbike overtook him on the right.
The driver gave a hand-signal; Walter took no notice. Why
on earth hadn't he thought of shoving the photo gear into
the strongbox? Now it was just a bloody nuisance. The
brake lights flashed again; again he jammed on the brakes.
The traffic was now dense. Were they now in the Rue de
Rivoli or the Rue Royale. He accelerated; the other bike
fell back. On the left-hand side of the street there was a
sudden flash. Was that a radar trap or a paparazzo's camera?
Walter recognized the obelisk on the left. The Mercedes
shot ahead again. Could George already have pulled the
trigger by accident?

'George?'

'Yes, Walter?'

'Not long now!'

'I'm ready!' George's voice sounded shaky. The Mercedes
drove in a long curve down to the Seine. Which direction
would they take: right, left, straight on? Walter saw the
red circles in his mind's eye. If they drove straight ahead,
then they would cross over the bridge. George would then
have to press the button five or six seconds later. Walter
accelerated to get closer. But the Mercedes slowed down,
turned right, then switched from the outside to the middle
lane. Walter followed, but now lagged behind. They were
driving along the Seine; there should be a tunnel sooner
or later and then a long straight road. There were more
flashes. Walter glanced into the rear-view mirror. He saw

two motorbikes, followed by a car, possibly several. He
recalled that the next red circle was straight in front of
him. They were now in a brightly-lit tunnel.

'Watch out!' Walter opened the throttle. Not more than
twenty yards away, Red had said. He saw the person next
to Diana turn round and recognized him. It was Dodi. He
saw him glance quickly out of the window and give a
boyish laugh. Walter drew up in the right-hand lane. Only
five more yards. He cursed the photo gear.

George felt the red button with his finger. He sensed
the round top, a slight bump. He thought his finger was
shaking; he had suddenly lost his sense of touch. Did he
have the strength to press the button? He placed his middle
finger on the trigger switch, as he had practised for the last
half-hour. When would Walter give the go-ahead?

The end of the tunnel was now in sight. Walter tried
to get a little closer to the Mercedes. He had no time to
look at the speedometer, but felt sure he had not reached
maximum speed. He drove to the side of the car; Diana's
head was leaning against Dodi's shoulder, her blonde hair
now clearly visible. Fifteen yards! The end of the tunnel
loomed up.

'Now!' he shouted.

George pressed the little button with his index finger. It
did not react. He tried again, harder. Nothing happened.
What had gone wrong? Had he pressed it or not? He was
panic-stricken; his eyes were wide open. He saw two heads
ten yards in front of him. He recognized the blonde hair.

Walter spotted a chance to move to the right.

'What's up?' he shouted over the loudspeaker? 'What the
hell's happening?' He glanced into the right rear-mirror,
changed track and braked sharply. He was still going too fast
to turn off. Two, three, four motorbikes raced past, followed
by several cars. George saw the Mercedes draw away. His
middle finger felt the side of the transmitter. It was now
clear. The trigger switch was still in its original position!

Walter now tailed the Mercedes at moderate speed. The
seconds flashed by like hours. What had Red said? The car
would go out of control after one hundred yards maximum.
Nothing had happened yet. Another fifty, hundred yards.
No reaction at all! The next tunnel came into sight. Walter
suddenly saw a small white car moving on to the road from
the right. The Mercedes moved over immediately to the left
lane, but the white car did not seem to take any notice. It
also drove over to the left. Walter held his breath. Why had
there been no reaction? The Mercedes accelerated; it was
now drawing very close to the white car. Walter thought
they had both bumped each other for a fraction of a second.
They both dived into the tunnel at the same moment. Walter
held back a little; there was a chance to turn off to the right
just before the tunnel.

'What's up?' asked George.

'Have you pulled the trigger?'

There was no reply. Walter turned round.

'I said, have you pulled the trigger?'

'No,' George stammered.

Walter looked ahead again. What had happened? What
was wrong with George? He saw three paparazzi brake
furiously. One skidded and was only just able to stop on
the motorway surface. The front motor-cyclist halted his
bike at the edge of the motorway and ran into the tunnel.
The others followed. One of the motor-cyclists came out
of the tunnel and called out to someone above. A small
crowd was gathering along the parapet. Cars ground to a
halt. The tunnel seemed to be completely blocked. People
were clambering down through the shrubbery. Flashlights
lit up the tunnel. Walter could hear shouting, even through
his helmet. He drew up so as to get a glimpse inside the
tunnel. The tragic scene came slowly into view.

'What happened?' asked George.

'I think we've done it! I'll draw up a little closer,' Walter
replied. By now a number of people had run on to the scene

inside the tunnel. The unmistakable signs of wreckage could
be seen. It could only be the Mercedes. There was no sign
of the small white car.

'It wasn't me, Walter! I didn't pull the trigger!' yelled
George. He pulled the grey box from the nylon bag and
held it to Walter's face. Walter grabbed the transmitter and
stuffed it in his jacket pocket.

'Are you mad?' he shouted back. 'It worked, and that's
that! No one's going to blame you. You acted under orders.
You ought to be thankful it's all over.'

He pulled his mobile out of his trouser pocket, pushed
up his visor and dialled Edward. At first he couldn't get his
words out; he cleared his throat and tried again.

'There's been an accident in a tunnel under the Seine.'

There was no reaction. He felt George over-balance and
pulled him up at the rear with his free hand. 'Don't be so
wet, man! Hold on tight to the straps of my jacket, both
sides. We've got to make a move. Do you hear me? We've
got to get away from here!'

He felt George's hands grip on to his jacket. He got
into gear and carefully released the clutch. Slowly and
ponderously, the BMW moved off. Walter took a last look
inside the tunnel. More and more people had collected at
the scene of the crash. The rear door of the car was open.
Someone was kneeling on the tarmac nearby. Walter then
raced off and turned into the Rue Goujon.

## 79

Jean-Luc started his car as soon as Edward had put the phone down, turned into the Rue de la Paix and slowly drove off towards Place Vendôme. The paparazzi who had stayed behind at the entrance were now loitering near a car which they thought belonged to Di and Dodi and was now driving across the Place Vendôme.

'We should halt over there by the road junction,' Jean-Luc suggested. 'Then we'll be able to see which direction the genuine car takes and simply tail them.'

'Fine. I don't know my way around here.' Edward tried to control his trembling body and wavering voice. He disengaged his stiff fingers from the mobile. Why was time dragging? What was happening behind the scene at the Ritz?

Jean-Luc halted in the second row, leaving his motor running. He adjusted his rear-view mirror to get a better view of the street behind. He scrutinized the area between the three junctions in his field of vision, backwards and forwards. A motorbike drew up from behind. One of the paparazzi had noticed that the car at the front entrance was a decoy. He drove round the Place Vendôme and turned off to the left, into the next street.

The rider had attracted Edward's attention. At high speed it would be difficult to tell one from the other. He would probably be able to identify Walter and George by their helmets. Nervously, he glanced at the clock on the dashboard, wondering whether he should give Walter another ring and find out the latest news from the rear of the hotel? He decided against it; he might well be distracted by the phone call and lose valuable time.

Another motorbike came up from behind.

'Over there!' Jean-Luc suddenly shouted and put his foot on the accelerator. The Renault raced off. Edward saw a dark car shoot by in a cross-street a few yards away, pursued by several motorbikes. As Jean-Luc reached the next junction, they saw two motor-cyclists just turning the corner.

'They're going to the Place de la Concorde,' Jean-Luc confirmed. Edward grasped the door-handle as Jean-Luc cornered sharply without braking.

'We shouldn't get too close,' Edward said. 'We know where they're going.'

'We'll lose them anyway, once they're under the Seine. The boulevards and the quays are well-designed, so the Mercedes should make good progress.'

Jean-Luc was not far wrong. As they hit the Seine motorway at the Place de la Concorde, there was not a Mercedes or motor-cyclist to be seen. He drove to the right side of the road and halted.

'We'll wait here until we hear from your colleagues. It shouldn't be long.'

Edward nodded. 'I hope not!' He tried to regulate his breathing. His pulse was racing; beads of sweat covered his brow. He pulled out his handkerchief and wiped his face.

Another motor cyclist shot past, turning right in a westerly direction.

'Aha! Someone else has just realized he's been fooled. It seems they're making their way to the Bois de Boulogne.' Jean-Luc quickly considered whether there would be any point in following him, on a hunch, but decided against it.

There was a ring on Edward's mobile. Jean-Luc overheard something about a tunnel. He accelerated, turned right and drove down the Cours Albert Premier on the parallel upper street, along which the Mercedes and its pursuers had driven some moments earlier. There was nothing to be seen inside the first tunnel. After about a mile, they reached the second tunnel, at the Pont de l'Alma. A number of vehicles blocked the entrance, people were running around in excitement, flashlight cameras were on the scene. Jean-Luc decided to halt.

'Please wait for me here.' Edward got out and walked towards the tunnel. His eyes fell on the shattered Mercedes. A few paparazzi were taking photos. Inquisitive onlookers lingered around the scene, some of them in tears. Somebody tried to pull Edward back; he shook them off and pushed on.

'I'm a doctor!' he said, first in English, then in French. He ran to the Mercedes. It had evidently somersaulted against a support-pillar and slewed across the road at high speed. The whole of the front body was crushed.

One of the rear doors was open. Edward could see Diana. She was still alive! Her lips were visibly moving. Her eyes had opened. One of the photographers was kneeling on the ground, holding her arm. Her body was strangely dislocated, probably because it had been squashed between front and rear seats. Close to her lay a lifeless blood-stained hand, presumably Dodi's. Edward could not see the driver, but he recognized another man lying on the passenger seat, his body also contorted. He was bleeding, his head slumped motionless against the cross-beam of the car.

There was no trace of blood on Diana's jacket, her blouse or her slacks. Edward asked himself whether it had all been in vain. Dodi was probably dead – but was his death the end of it all?

The distant siren of an ambulance sounded closer and closer every second. Edward rapidly turned round and ran back through the tunnel. Two police vehicles drove inside with the ambulance; one of them halted sideways on, blocking the entrance. Two policemen jumped out and started to seal off the road and force back the spectators.

Several more ambulances raced to the scene.

Jean-Luc was still waiting, parked above the tunnel on the Cours Albert Premier; he had switched on the engine by the time Edward collapsed into the Renault.

'Back to the factory, quick!' Edward gasped.

Jean-Luc glanced at the clock; it had just turned half past midnight. He switched on the radio, eager to find out when the news would be broadcast. 'How does it look?' he asked excitedly.

Edward could no longer control himself, physically or mentally. Tears poured down his face, unrestrained. He managed to speak. 'She's still alive! I can't tell about the others. The Mercedes must have hit a pillar and crashed into the wall. It's a complete write-off. But Diana's still alive! There's no doubt about that. I saw her speak!'

'So it's been in vain?'

'I hope not!'

## 80

Walter lost his way three times driving back to the factory and had to stop to get on to the right road. He would much rather have dozed off in one of the road-side ditches and gone to sleep. He was a nervous wreck; fatigue had built up over the last twenty-four hours and had left him shattered. He had a strange sensation that it was not over by a long way. And he had to admit to himself that he would never be able to erase those images inside the tunnel from his memory.

He had already turned off the receiver inside his helmet, since George, who was in an even worse state, was sobbing all the time. George had raised his visor, which amplified the noise of the rushing wind in Walter's earphones.

At last they arrived at the factory, expecting Arthur to be waiting for them, as arranged. He was nowhere in sight. The forecourt was dark and deserted. It appeared that Edward and Jean-Luc were late.

'We were all supposed to meet up back here, weren't we?' asked Walter. There was no reply from George. Walter propped up the bike and took off George's helmet. 'It's all over. Pull yourself together. We've done it!' He laid his hand on George's shoulder; George brushed it away angrily.

'Leave me alone! I didn't kill Diana; I didn't pull the trigger!' he shouted.

'Calm down, old chap!' Walter cautioned him. 'Do you want the whole world to hear you? Stop this nonsense! Of course you pulled the trigger. I saw the car accelerate. It was about to collide with another vehicle. Couldn't you see?'

George fell on the ground in a heap, stammering, 'I . . . it wasn't me . . . believe me, it wasn't . . . I didn't kill her! Not me!'

Walter let George carry on talking. He understood his reaction. In fact, this had basically been Edward's aim when he decided that George, rather than Arthur, should go with him on the bike. He questioned his own feelings. Did he, himself, have a guilty conscience? He was not really sure; he was only thankful that the job had gone smoothly. The sound of an engine in the distance could now be heard; seconds later, a round ball of light shone on the opposite side of the street. That was either Arthur or Edward. A car turned into the drive and slowly came to a halt nearby.

It was Jean-Luc and Edward who emerged. Edward saw George slumped on the ground and asked, anxiously, 'What's up?'

'Leave him alone; George is utterly exhausted. He thinks he didn't pull the trigger!'

'I didn't!' George screamed.

Edward pulled Walter to one side, hinting to Jean-Luc that he should not leave George on his own.

They walked off into the darkness.

'How did it go?' Edward asked him.

'In fact, it all went according to plan. Of course, I realized George was very nervous to begin with. But when we moved into action, everything seemed to be under control. I gave him the order to pull the trigger and behind my back I could feel that he was holding the little box tightly in his hand. If he says he didn't pull the trigger, it's his defence mechanism. Obviously, he could see inside the tunnel and witnessed . . .'

Edward interrupted him. 'And how did it go, exactly?'

'We drove up very close, just under twenty yards to one side. Then I gave George the order and he pressed the trigger. Then we slowed down. In fact it took much longer than Red had said. The Mercedes drove a good three or four hundred yards further and nearly collided with a small white car that suddenly came on the scene.'

'What make?' asked Edward.

'I haven't a clue. A small white Peugeot 204 or a Fiat Uno. It suddenly popped up from the right and tried to move into their lane. I almost thought it was trying to ram the Mercedes. Then they both shot into the tunnel and things began to happen very quickly. The paparazzi were on the scene in no time. They stopped at the entrance of the tunnel and ran inside with their cameras loaded. Were you there as well?'

'Yes, it looked simply awful, but Princess Diana is still alive!'

'She's alive?' Walter shouted.

'Don't make such a noise! You said it took longer for the car to accelerate than you thought? Perhaps George didn't pull the trigger, after all.'

Walter was caught again. 'Nonsense! Why shouldn't he have pulled the trigger? Anyway, the crash worked out just as Red told us it would.'

Edward paused and looked over towards George and Jean-Luc, who could clearly be picked out in the glare of the headlights. 'I have to be absolutely sure whether George pulled the trigger or not. Maybe we can find that out by looking at the box or its inside. Where's Arthur, incidentally?'

Walter shrugged his shoulders. 'I was wondering, too. He hasn't arrived yet.'

'That's strange!' murmured Edward. The radio was not switched on but it was tuned into the same frequency that he and Jean-Luc had used to contact the helicopter pilots at least three hours ago. Edward grabbed the microphone. 'Metro two nine eight calling hotel alpha India four zero zero one.' He released the voice button.

The pilot responded instantaneously, as though he was expecting the call.

'How's your flight and what's your location?' Edward called.

The answer came after some rustling. 'Flight OK, but we're still waiting for our guest to turn up. We've been try-ing to reach you for over two hours. What should we do?'

Edward's brain was working feverishly. Why hadn't Red yet arrived at the helicopter site? What could have happened? Had Arthur had an accident?

'Metro two nine eight, is my message understood? Con-firm please,' blabbered the little loudspeaker. Edward pressed the voice button.

'We've got a problem over here and we're trying to solve it. Over.'

Jean-Luc and Walter had overheard everything through the open door of the Renault.

'What does that mean?' asked Walter. 'Red should have arrived in London by now.'

Edward jumped out of the car. 'I haven't a clue.' He thumped his fist on the roof of the car.

'Can we contact the Citroën by radio?'

Jean-Luc shook his head. 'No. The Citroën's radio would have to be switched on.'

'Then we should drive over to the helicopter right now – and maybe get the hell out of France if we have to. The Learjet will have to fly back on its own tomorrow morning. But where can Red and Arthur be?'

'Hasn't Arthur got his mobile on him?'

Edward slapped his brow. He pulled his phone from his pocket, input a number, but got no answer. 'As things stand,' he told them, 'we'd better join the pilots.'

Walter ran across to George, who was still sitting on the ground, staring ahead apathetically. He pulled him to his feet, assisted by Jean-Luc. Together, they dragged him over to the car and bundled him into the back seat. Edward tried Arthur again. 'How long will it take us to get to the helicopter?' he asked.

Jean-Luc started the engine. 'Less than twenty minutes at this hour of the morning.'

Edward looked at the clock. It was just before half past one. He beckoned to Walter, who had already mounted his motorbike. 'Change of instruction!' he called. 'You go back to the scene of the accident. Take another look, but don't get too close. We'll stay in contact.'

## 81

As Jean-Luc drove off in his Renault towards the west, Walter returned to the centre of Paris. Shortly before two o'clock, he arrived at the Avenue du Président Wilson, where he parked his bike, close to the Palais de Tokyo. He covered the rest of the journey on foot, having been told that the tunnel had been blocked off. Blue and yellow warning and danger lights flashed continuously. Spectators were packed tight against the police cordons. It was not really possible to get near enough to the tunnel to get a good view inside. Walter shoved through the crowd and weaved his way to the entrance.

There was an ambulance standing nearby, with doctors and medical staff on hand; one of the car's passengers was obviously receiving medical attention. As Walter leant over the barrier to get a better view, a firm hand grabbed hold of him. He stood up, now rather alarmed. A gendarme stood there. He asked him, in a very unfriendly tone, 'What do you think the police barrier is here for? You're not one of those photographers, by any chance?'

Walter cursed silently to himself. He had still got his leather gear on.

'Photographers?' he asked in astonishment. 'What sort of a photographer?'

The gendarme ordered him to move on.

'But what's happened? Has there been an accident?'

There was no reply. A young man behind him joined in the conversation. 'There's been a bad accident. Probably fatal. Princess Diana was inside – you know, Prince Charles's ex-wife.'

'Are you sure?' asked Walter.

'She's not dead,' another man interjected. 'I just heard a reporter dictate a message. The driver is supposed to be dead, and probably her lover as well. Diana's undergoing emergency treatment, over there, inside that vehicle, so the reporter said.'

'And what about the other car?' asked Walter.

'What other car?'

Walter shrugged his shoulders. 'That was just a guess. Normally there are always two cars involved in a crash.'

'No, it drove too fast inside the tunnel. A taxi driver who witnessed the accident told the reporter it was doing at least one hundred and twenty-five miles an hour.'

Walter pulled out of the crowd. He walked slowly over to the bridge to see if he could get a better view from the other side. There were very few people on top of the tunnel, since it was impossible to view the scene of action from that spot. The only sign of life at this level was the traffic, which had been specially diverted.

He was unable to cross the street, as he had hoped, so as to get a glimpse inside from that angle, but noticed just in time that it had been blocked by the police from that point as well, so he decided to return to the exit of the tunnel. Two policemen and a medical orderly came out. Their gestures could only be interpreted as a request to lift the barrier and open up a path. He could see that a vehicle was now making its way out of the tunnel and noticed that the doors of the ambulance were shut. He then shoved through the crowd and raced over to his motorbike.

He hung back some distance behind the convoy; it was moving at snail's pace. He would dearly have loved to know who was inside the vehicle. It might well have been Princess Diana, if Edward's own conclusions and the information from the man at the tunnel were correct. The journey lasted about ten minutes, wound

its way over a bridge in an easterly direction along
the Seine. Walter worked out the street sign for the
Gare d'Austerlitz. A few yards further on, the journey came to a halt outside a large clinic, the name of
which, as Edward read above the entrance, was La Pitié
Salpétrière.

No sooner had the convoy entered the compound than
the first motorbikes and taxis moved up from behind. About
a hundred people had gathered round the hospital building,
in record time. It must have been Princess Diana inside
the ambulance. Walter turned off the engine and mingled
amongst the crowd. He spied Giuseppe, thankful he had
kept his helmet on. It was unlikely that the photographer
would recognize him. Walter, however, stuck close to him
in the hope of picking up some bits of information from
him here and there.

Giuseppe was talking to a man of about forty. Walter
raised his visor to hear their conversation more clearly.
Giuseppe called the other man 'Patron', who was speaking
into two mobiles simultaneously. The patron was buying
and selling photos. Giuseppe seemed to disagree with
him on the question of pricing. 'You won't get better
photos from anyone else. They've all had to hand in their
cameras. Some of them were even taken into custody,
believe you me!'

'If you don't agree, then I'll buy from Nicolas,' answered
the patron.

'You can forget Nicolas! He didn't even have a flash on
him. You can't sell his photos. Besides, he was too late on
the scene.'

The patron was about to leave and shoved Giuseppe to
one side. The photographer grabbed him by the sleeve. 'If
you don't want them, I'll sell them to 'Gamma'. Romuald
also arrived too late on the scene and tried to give assistance
before he started to take any photos. The police barrier, you
understand.'

The patron cut loose and disappeared into the crowd. Giuseppe cursed to himself and looked around. Walter instinctively ducked and quickly turned away. He couldn't run the risk that Giuseppe would recognize him.

## 82

Edward and George had fallen asleep on the back seat, out of sheer exhaustion. The car suddenly braked hard and woke them up.

'What's up?' shouted George. Jean-Luc reversed a few yards down a dark, empty street. He had glimpsed the Citroën in a country lane as he drove past.

Arthur was sitting at the driver's seat, his hands bound to the steering wheel with sticking tape, his head lying on the wheel, and his mouth also taped. Jean-Luc ripped open the car doors. He carefully removed the sticking tape.

'Thank God!' Arthur groaned. 'I thought I'd have to spend the night here.'

'What happened?' asked Edward.

'That bastard Red is a con-man. I always told you he was. We were gently driving along the road to Chavenay when he suddenly asked me to stop since he felt ill. I turned into this lane and he bashed me on the head. When I came to, he'd vanished without trace and I realized he'd tied me up and gagged me.'

'What time was that?' Edwards asked him.

'I calculated that we'd be at the helicopter by about ten.'

'Did Red say anything whilst you were driving?'

Arthur said no. 'We hardly said a word to each other during the journey.'

Edward looked around the car and opened the boot. The metal case and the laptop had been taken.

What had happened to Red? However hard he racked

his brains he couldn't think of an answer. Where could he have gone? What was he playing at? Had he played a double-game after all? He had once mentioned that he'd seen the Mercedes twice before – once earlier in the year, and just now. Had someone else also given him the same assignment? The question of Princess Diana's death now had to be verified immediately. Edward did not hesitate for a split second; he rang Walter, who passed on the message that Diana had since been taken to a hospital. So Red had not fulfilled his part of the contract.

From inside the car Edward could hear that the helicopter pilot was trying to contact him. He leapt in, grabbed the microphone and pressed the answer button.

'A white Fiat has just driven up,' the pilot announced. 'Our guest has just been brought here by car. Should we take off now? Please advise!'

Edward did not waste a second. 'Take one guest on board only and take off straightaway. But stay on this wavelength. I'll get back to you. Over.'

He leant back in the seat. Getting to the bottom of the Red mystery was like trying to put pieces of a jigsaw together. Red had been recommended by the CIA. He was a free agent. He had been most anxious to know if Edward was an IRA agent. Red was a maverick who was only interested in money.

Had somebody offered him more money? At the time of his second visit, Edward recalled, the Indian had said something about two men with rings and gold bracelets visiting Red a few days earlier.

Maybe they had also given him an assignment. Who had commissioned Red earlier this year to take the Mercedes 280 apart; according to Red, it did not belong to the Al Fayed car fleet or to the Ritz Hotel. Where was the key to all these questions?

Edward's mind was racing. And what about this mysterious white Fiat that Walter had seen? Was it the same vehicle that had brought Red to the helicopter. Was Red not, in fact, a free agent, after all? Questions, questions, questions . . .

'Jean-Luc gave me a brief run-down. What's the next step?' Arthur stood by the car, bleary-eyed. He pointed at George, who was staring at them both like a madman.

'George!' asked Edward, 'Are you feeling better?'

'No, Edward.' He looked totally exhausted.

'Do you know where we can all grab a few hours' sleep?' Edward asked Jean-Luc. 'I just can't face the idea of driving back to the plane right now.'

The reply came without a moment's hesitation. 'You can take some sleep at my sister's. Her house is not far from the road into Paris.'

'At this time of night?'

Jean-Luc smiled. 'She owns a nightclub in Nanterre; this is her busiest time. I've often taken people there at a moment's notice. So long as you don't all want a private bathroom, there should be no problem.'

'Good, then let's drive to your sister's. George and Arthur can sleep there. I must now try and contact Walter.'

Edward gazed at Arthur sceptically. 'Are you fit to drive?'

Arthur gave a tired nod. 'I'll be alright.'

'No,' Edward decided. 'Jean-Luc will take the wheel and I'll follow behind in the Renault. You help me get George into the big car.'

Jean-Luc got in and Arthur made himself comfortable next to George on the back seat.

Edward flashed his lights to signal the all-clear; they then drove off towards Nanterre, Edward, in a daze, following behind. What would happen to George when they found out back in London that he had given up on the job? His career would be at an end. Edward asked himself if London need ever get to hear about the incident. In any case, Red bore the whole responsibility for success or failure of the assignment.

The question of Red was still unsolved. What would he

do now? Would he let himself be taken to Heathrow, or would he go to ground in London? The man he had come to like during the last few weeks had suddenly turned into a security risk. Red had been dealing them marked cards.

Edward stared into the flashing rear lights of the car in front like a startled rabbit. Arthur and George disappeared into the club entrance. Jean-Luc came up in the Renault. 'Do you know your way back to the centre of Paris? And where the hospital is?'

'I'll find it,' he replied. 'I'll also find my way back. Just leave the neon lights on above the door.'

He accelerated, leaving Jean-Luc standing by the roadside. Rear lights! Red rear lights! The first story Red had told him was about those stupid rear lights fixed to the wooden board; he couldn't shake it out of his head ... 'One of the commanders at that meeting had obviously got out of control ...' Red had said. 'He had become a security risk.'

Red had then decided to eliminate that person. Was Edward not forced, now, to eliminate Red? Could he afford to let him stay alive? The closer he came to the centre of Paris, the clearer it became that he had basically no other option left. This was not an emotional reaction, nor was it due to being over-tired, but because of his overall responsibility for all his team members and the good name of his country. He, and only he, assumed full responsibility.

Edward reached for the transmitter; it was switched on. The pilot answered. Edward could hear his words clearly, despite the background noise.

'There's been an incident,' Edward informed the pilot. 'Your guest must on no account set foot in England again. This is an order, do you understand? Please repeat message.'

The pilot repeated the order. It was absolutely clear.

'Please confirm when you have carried out my instructions. Over.' Edward sank back, utterly exhausted.

## 83

Walter could hardly keep his eyes open; he had been fighting off sleep for almost one hour. He had done a few knee-bends every now and again in order to get his circulation going. A number of reporters and spectators were still hovering around the clinic. Ambulances rushed by from time to time, bringing in the sick or wounded.

Did we make an error, Walter wondered? Was George right when he said that he never pulled the trigger? It was altogether credible. They could only be thankful; they were lucky that the accident had happened, after all. Perhaps Red had fixed the vehicle so that it would crash under any circumstances. Walter racked his brains but could not find the answer.

Suddenly, he saw Edward standing nearby; he almost hugged him for joy.

'What's new?' asked Edward testily. He was also at the end of his tether.

'Nothing. We're all waiting for news,' Walter assured him. They wandered silently along the Boulevard de l'Hôpital. 'How's George?'

'Jean-Luc took us all to his sister's place to rest. Both George and Arthur are there.'

'Did Arthur find his way back to the helicopter alright?' Walter enquired. Edward then quickly told him what had happened. As he mentioned the Fiat car that delivered Red to the helicopter, Walter suddenly came to life.

'Do you realize something?' he asked excitedly. Edward nodded.

'It can't be a coincidence then? asked Walter.

'I don't think so. But what about the driver?' Edward looked over to the main building of the hospital. 'Do you know where we can get a cup of tea or coffee?'

Walter shook his head. Edward was reflecting whether or not to take Walter into his confidence. Walter could almost read his thoughts. 'Have you ever considered what damage this man Red might do? He's a con-man, I'm convinced.'

Edward stood still and looked Walter straight in the eye. Walter sensed how difficult it must have been for him to talk. 'Walter, I had to make sure Red never returns to England again.'

Loud voices and shouts could now be heard by the hospital entrance. Edward and Walter took no notice at first, since they were far too engrossed with each other. Not until they were elbowed and shoved to one side did Walter realize that something must have happened. He saw people throw themselves, sobbing, into each others' arms and reporters yelling frantically into their mobile phones.

'Edward, what's happened? Look at those people over there!'

He looked round. Indeed, something had happened. They ran over to the main hospital entrance. After a few yards they stood stock still. A woman had lit a cigarette lighter and held it aloft, weeping. She wailed in a tearful voice: 'Diana is dead! My God, she's dead!'

# 84

The pilot turned round towards Red, from the cockpit, and saw that he was fast asleep. He carefully removed the plug from his earphones, placed it inside his breast pocket and gave a sign to his co-pilot. Then he got up from his seat and took down a small fire-extinguisher that was attached to the wall at the side of the cabin. He took a couple of steps nearer the passenger. He had practised this action often enough during his basic self-defence training. Holding the fire-extinguisher well away from himself, he gave it all he'd got. Red opened his eyes for a split second, stared at the pilot and slumped into a heap.

The pilot clicked the fire-extinguisher back into its holder and grabbed hold of Red's heavy metal case. He took hold of the rope they had used to secure Walter's motorbike and tied one end to the case. He wound the other end round Red's ankles and knotted it tight. Then he opened the helicopter's sliding door. A strong wind blew into his face. He took a firm hold on a pair of nets that served as luggage-holders and with his right foot shoved Red up to the edge of the open door. With a firm kick he sent the case flying over the open door-ledge; the lifeless body was dragged from its seat. The pilot unfastened the belts hanging from the roof and despatched Red into the darkness of the night.

## 85

Having left Red at the helicopter site, Lucy looked for a hotel in the neighbourhood of the Bois de Boulogne. She listened to the radio as she was doing her toilet in the bathroom the next morning and heard the news that Princess Diana and Dodi had been killed in a fatal accident in Paris. There was no news about any further casualties.

She dialled Red's mobile phone number but got no reply. After breakfast, she paid the bill and climbed into her rented car. She could now examine the damage to the Fiat in broad daylight. Apart from the damaged rear light, there were two small black scratches above the mudguard. Was the damage really caused by squeezing in between two cars in a parking lot, as Red had maintained? Red wanted to pay compensation of nine thousand francs to Bastian for the vehicle he had hired. Maybe he was scared that the car might have been seen somewhere, in which case the cash offer was hush money.

Lucy got into the car and returned to the village where Bastian's workshop was. Several times she took the wrong road and it was already midday when she finally arrived. It was pouring with rain. The gate to the courtyard was wide open, but Bastian was nowhere to be found. She rang at the doorbell. A young girl answered, still in her dressing-gown; she looked as though she had just got out of bed.

'May I speak to Monsieur Bastian, please?' Lucy enquired.

'He's in church now, and then he'll be going to Victor's afterwards,' came the reply.

Lucy had noticed the sign, Victor, over the door of a bar

on her way in. She thanked the girl and got into the car
again. She was about to drive back on to the road when
she caught sight of Bastian on his way back, holding a
bottle in his hand. Lucy waited until he reached the gate
and got out.

'Monsieur Bastian, I'm returning your car. Unfortunately,
there was a little accident at the hotel car park.' She pointed
at the rear light and both scratches.

Bastian swore, furiously, refusing to listen to any expla-
nations. Lucy finally pulled the nine thousand francs from
her purse. Bastian was rooted to the spot. He stared at the
notes, pulled the cork from the bottle and gave a strong gulp.
He took the money from Lucy's hand and simply said, 'It's
settled, we're quits!'

Lucy took her things out of the car, making sure that
nothing was left behind. Bastian, meanwhile, was rummaging
around inside his wallet for Mrs Broomfield's passport. He
swapped it for the car keys that Lucy was holding out. She
then turned round quickly, hurried to the nearest phone
box and called a taxi.

## 86

Sir David entered the room with a very contented expression on his face. This time, he walked into the room without a file in his hands, wearing a dark, double-breasted suit; with his white hair and silver tie, he cut a most elegant figure. He beamed at Edward, Walter and Arthur with an almost paternal smile.

'Gentlemen, in the name of the United Kingdom, may I thank you for your efforts and your decisive action. This meeting marks the conclusion of the assignment.' He adjusted his tie. 'I have just returned from Paris, from where we have flown Princess Diana's body over to this country. The investigations of the French police are now, of course, in full swing. A Press statement from Madame Monteil, Commandant of the Brigade Criminelle, included a comment to the effect that they will carry out the most extensive enquiries.'

Sir David's face now took on a more serious expression. 'I assume that those enquiries will not reveal any additional information. Both the British and the French Press have been most reticent as regards possible rumours or other reports of a speculative nature, thank God! I should like you, gentlemen, to study the statements by the Cairo newspaper *Al-Ahram* and the reports of the Mena agency. So far as we can gather from our own sources of information, the Arabic weekly newspaper *Al-Jadeedah* will carry an article on the same lines. Prince Charles, as he mentioned to me in the aeroplane, is very angry about the speculations circulating in the Arab Press. My opposite number in Paris has categorically assured me that the French secret service will not be reacting to such accusations and neither, of course, shall we.' Sir David cleared his throat and paused. 'We now come to the most pressing item before us today. The Spencer family will be arranging the funeral and Buckingham Palace will advise on the timing, insofar as it is to be involved in the formalities. We have advised the Palace to distance itself from the tragic event but to fly the Union Jack at half-mast. I rather think, I must admit, that Her Majesty may have some reservations in this regard.'

Sir David noticed that Edward had put up his hand and gave him permission to speak, with a wave of the hand.

'Will Prince Charles participate in the funeral service?'

'Yes. That is to say, provided that the Queen gives him leave. William and Harry will certainly be present. If Prince Charles does not obtain Her Majesty's assent, the children will be accompanied by Princess Diana's sisters. This is the state of the discussions so far.'

'Then we should continue the PR campaign with Prince Charles,' Edward continued. 'A single Press engagement on the River Dee won't have much effect.'

Sir David nodded in agreement and put on his glasses. 'These various issues and considerations have taken us on to a totally different subject. I should like, however, to bring the main topic to a close. As you will be aware, George is absent from our discussions today. Before I left for Paris he asked me in confidence whether he might take some leave immediately. I accepted his request, of course. Are there any further questions, please?' Sir David gave a sort of bow from the chair. 'Then the meeting is formally concluded. Edward, I should like you to stay behind for a few minutes.'

Arthur and Walter looked at each other, stood up together and left the room. After they had closed the door behind them, Sir David looked at Edward with a twinkle in his eye. 'Are you sure that this fellow Red was playing a double game?'

Edward was aware that he could not honestly answer such a direct question. He had asked himself the same question many times in the last twenty-four hours and had always reached the same conclusion. 'I am unable to prove it at this moment, Sir. It was clear to me in Paris that the damage Red might have done to our country by playing that sort of game, could not be ignored. No matter who he took his orders from or what the results might have been. I had no other choice.'

Sir David made a gesture of disagreement. He interrupted him. 'Edward, let me assure you that I do not reproach you in any way. We are all behind you. I can't imagine what Red could have been up to if he was also involved with the Arabs in this affair. Your decision was absolutely right and correct. Only . . .' Sir David paused, 'it is vital that we discover who his driver, and possible accomplice, was. We have been requested to find out the facts and I am now passing on that request. Try to do as much of the work as possible yourself.'

'Yes, I shall. But we still have a little problem.'

Sir David looked surprised.

'We owe Red half a million pounds. According to our agreement, I was due to hand them over to him in the USA next week, at the latest. Now, nobody yet knows what has become of him. Both pilots are top-rate servicemen; they are our own chaps and they're thoroughly reliable. But there is always the chance that somebody will notice that he has disappeared. I think I should, therefore, fly to the USA, as agreed . . . It is sure to attract the immediate suspicion of any accomplice if, suddenly, the money doesn't arrive.'

He's right, Sir David reflected. We should carry on as if Red had returned to London according to schedule and then flew on to the States.

'But what if he already made contact with his partner here in London? They will soon find out that Red failed to show up by helicopter, as we arranged.'

Edward drew himself up. 'In that case, Red is his own best advocate. We separated in Paris and he failed to turn up at the helicopter pad as planned. We had to assume from his solo turn at Cannes that he changed his mind, for reasons best known to himself, and flew back to London by ordinary scheduled airline. Since he didn't contact me when he was over here, I flew over to the States and brought his money and his clothing with me . . .'

Sir David stood up and smiled at Edward. 'I agree. Please inform Walter, Arthur and both pilots immediately. And please get in touch with me when you have anything to report.'

## 87

Night was falling as Edward made his way up the narrow path to his mother's house. It suddenly occurred to him that all the downstairs lights were on. His mother was a thrifty person, who usually made do with a standard lamp. What was the reason for her festive mood?

Edward parked his car in front of the house. He saw a black Mercedes with a London numberplate. Red! It had to be Red's hire-car. Edward wondered whether to phone his mother from inside his car. What was Red's little game? He would surely not take his revenge in front of Edward's own mother. That was most unlikely.

As soon as he stepped inside, his mother came up. 'Thank goodness you're back, at last. You've got a visitor. A most delightful young lady . . .'

Edward threw her a surprised glance. But before he could say a word his mother took him by the arm. 'I am disappointed you never told me about her . . .' she prattled on happily.

'Mother, perhaps you could tell me who our visitor is,' he whispered, holding his mother back as she tried to drag him into the living room.

'Ann Webster. Who else?' she laughed.

'Ann Webster? I don't know anyone by the name of Ann Webster, Mother!'

'But that's impossible! She told me you were colleagues; she's known you for a long time.'

'But what does she look like?' he asked.

'Slim, very slim, with a blonde mop of hair,' was his

mother's description. She raised her eyebrows and added, significantly, 'and a very good figure!'

Lucy, Edward guessed immediately. It had to be Lucy. Here in London, looking for Red. His brain was spinning. How on earth did she find out where he lived? He was trying to think, nervously. She had charmed her way in here, posing as one of his colleagues. There was no point in not making her feel welcome. But he had to hide her in his own flat, as a matter of urgency. Perhaps he was now closer to unmasking Red than he ever thought was possible.

He conjured up a smile. 'Ann Webster,' he exclaimed, 'of course! I can only recall her maiden name. The penny's just dropped. I remember her well!' He led his mother into the living room. Lucy was sitting on the couch in an elegant grey suit and a tight black rollneck, a red handkerchief in her breast pocket. Her legs, in black tights and high heels, were crossed over casually. With a dazzling smile, she held out her arms to Edward.

'Edward, let me give you a hug! How are you?'

'Lovely to see you again! I had no idea who to expect, but from Mother's description it couldn't be anyone else!'

Lucy gave him a knowing look.

'Should we go upstairs to my room?' he asked. 'Then we can talk over old times without being disturbed. Political talk bores Mother to tears.'

Lucy jumped up. 'Great! I'd just love to see how you hang out over here! I had a ball, talking to your wonderful mother!' Lucy was a born actress. She picked up her handbag, waved at her bewildered hostess and disappeared with Edward.

She followed him up the stairs. Edward opened the door to his sitting room and stood aside for her. She sat down in an armchair and rested her head on the back. What was coming next?

Without even pausing for breath, he went straight on to the offensive. 'What are you doing here? What's all this nonsense? Where's Red?'

The smile had vanished from Lucy's face. Frowning, she replied, 'OK then, let's be formal.' She opened her handbag, pulled out a small ID card and held it out. 'My real name's Ann Webster. I work for the CIA, under the cover name of Lucy. I was planted on Red at least twelve years ago and have been working as his shadow ever since. We have had him under surveillance ever since two of my colleagues lost their life because of some assignment the Iraqis gave him. The CIA had to find out what he did and who he worked for.'

The news took Edward's breath away; he dropped into a chair. Ann, still standing up, looked down at him from above. 'To spare you any further questions, I was already divorced at the time. Red and I had a relationship, which was fun, but in my case business came first, of course.'

Lucy, a CIA agent!

And Red, the complete pro, hadn't suspected or noticed anything over all these years! Ann Webster anticipated the question. 'Red didn't meet me by chance, as he always thought. I gave the barkeeper at Roy's bar a couple of dollars to spike Red's drink; I just happened to be standing opposite as he tried to get into his car. Oh, and by the way, the Indian's real name is Billy. He's been working for me right from the start, so I knew at any time who visited Red and for how long Red would be away from home. There was never any need for me to go with him, nor for him to tell me where he was going. Billy also told me that you'd brought a small attaché case with you on your second visit.' Ann glanced around the room. 'Would you pour me a drink, please? Do you have any whisky, or a cognac maybe?'

'You can have either,' Edward replied.

'Then I'd rather have a cognac.'

Edward filled a cognac glass and helped himself to one as well. 'Why don't you sit down? Where's Red then?' he asked, trying to probe.

'Actually, I was going to ask you the same question.' She sounded genuine enough.

Edward was embarrassed. 'How did you know where to find me?'

Ann laughed. 'That was easy. I arrived in London four days after Red, as I usually did when he went away on longer jobs. He never liked being separated from me for any length of time, which, of course, suited me fine. He checked me into the Dorchester. Whilst he was away at meetings with his so-called business partners, it was basically impossible for me to get in touch with my organization. I just kept my eyes and ears open all the time. So I spied on you both when you met in Hyde Park. I recognized you and then realized that your visit was linked with some assignment for Red; I had worked out who his so-called business partners in London were. But a few days before he left he had a few other visitors; neither the CIA nor I had any idea who had ultimately called him to London. Then it all became clear. Whilst you were trying to stop him tailing you on the way to the office and to your home, you didn't notice that I was on your tracks. The CIA has to know urgently who's giving Red his jobs and why.'

'How much do you know about the scope of our job?'

'We knew nothing. I was told who you were and who the other two visitors were, but we had no details about the background to the assignment. I was asked to find out precisely what Red was hired to do. Until last Saturday evening, I hadn't the slightest clue what he was up to. It wasn't until I was in Paris that I worked out what it might be all about. My guess was confirmed only the next morning, when I heard the news.'

'Was it you who drove the white car then?' Edward asked in astonishment.

'No. At any rate, not at the time of the accident.' Ann Webster now told Edward that Red had asked her to join him in Paris, hire the car and finally wait for him that evening near Chavenay. Then she told him how she had listened in on the phone call in the bar. 'What I did was mad, but I was certain something would happen that night. I just had no idea what. When I picked up the mobile, there was no longer any doubt in my mind; it had to be an attempt on the life of Dodi or Princess Diana. I was trembling all over when Red left the bar. The barman took pity on me and brought me a glass of champagne. I asked him where VIPs like Di and Dodi stayed when they were in Paris and he told me the Ritz. I asked for the phone book and the cordless phone from the bar. I finally found the number of the Ritz. I expect you can guess what happened next!'

Ann sipped some cognac, stood up and paced up and down the room. 'First, the switchboard answered. I tried my French but my vocabulary was not good enough. Then I spoke in English. You try getting through to the important son of an even more important hotel owner! Somehow or other I was switched through; I said I was speaking on behalf of Bill Clinton and wished to speak to Princess Diana. I remembered that Di and the Clintons had recently met. Then another man came on the line; I told him it was a matter of life and death. That seemed to work, but it took at least three or four minutes before Dodi came to the phone. I can't be sure whether it was really him or not. I told him I was a CIA agent and said we had learnt about an assassination attempt. I advised him to leave the hotel as soon as possible. He just said "Yes" and hung up.'

Ann looked at Edward sadly. 'I don't know whether my phone call mightn't have put the whole thing in motion. Anyway, unfortunately I didn't prevent the murder.'

'No,' Edward repeated. 'You didn't bring it off and you didn't stop it happening. Thanks to us, Red had lured Diana and Dodi into a trap, but . . .' He stopped and stood up. 'I am convinced that at the end of the day we British do not have them on our conscience. We wanted Princess Diana out of the way, that's true. But there are a number of facts that argue against our responsibility . . . So Red came back after the incident?'

'Yes, he drank a glass of bourbon. He seemed to be in a bad mood and just told me that there had been some last-minute problems with the contract, so he had to fly back to London that night. I had to drop him by the helicopter, which was waiting for him. When I offered to fly with him, he simply told me to return the hire car. In the parking space in front of the bar he noticed a few little scratches and a broken rear light. He started to swear and told me to compensate the owner; I should give him the remainder of the nine thousand francs I had exchanged for the trip.'

'You then took him to the helicopter?'

'Yes. He was very silent on the journey. There were no tender gestures, no declarations of love, nothing about our dreams of a life together. When I suggested I should stay behind in Paris till his London job was over and then join him to look for something in the South of France, he became rather unpleasant. I was told to fly back to the States the next day and take my things from the Dorchester with me.'

Edward sat down again in the chair opposite. He had only seen her in jeans before; she looked even more attractive in her elegant suit. He had to find out if she knew, or suspected, what had happened to Red. 'And why did you come back to London and not fly directly to the States?'

Ann revolved the cognac glass in her hand and stared at her drink. 'When we said goodbye something very strange happened. He took his metal case and laptop from the car boot without any sense of embarrassment. For years and years he had always cleverly kept them out of my sight. He just dumped them next to me, as if he expected me to ask him what was inside the case.'

Ann took another sip. 'I never did. Maybe that was a mistake. He kissed me tenderly but without passion, just like you would kiss your own child. Then he said, in a rather

threatening sort of voice, "Never go near my mobile again!"
I went hot and cold all over; I didn't know what to say. He
picked up his case and dragged it over to the helicopter.
That was all. I drove straight back to Paris; I didn't even
wait for the helicopter to start. I just drove around, turning
that last sentence over and over in my mind. So he must
have found out that I had overheard a conversation on his
mobile. I wonder if he knew *everything*?'

Ann paused and made a gesture, as if to chase away an
unpleasant memory. 'I then phoned Red from a hotel. He
came on the line quickly, but I couldn't understand a word
he said because of the din inside the helicopter. I only said,
"I love you!" I don't know if he heard me. I didn't sleep a
wink all night. I tried to reach him again in the morning.
He must have landed by then, but there was no reply.'

There was a long silence. Edward wondered how far Ann
could assist him in his search for any of Red's other partners.
After all, she knew much more about his secret life than he
had previously assumed. 'We have an undercover agent on
old Al Fayed's staff. He helped us trace Diana and Dodi's
movements. The whole exercise would have been impossible
without him.'

'Was Red aware of this?' Ann asked.

'Yes. He was also aware of his code name; he couldn't help
overhearing our phone conversations.' Edward felt that he
had to lay the bait now, if he was to solicit any information
from her. She had in fact told him about her phone call to
Dodi, which she need not have done. Perhaps, it suddenly
dawned on him, his contact man and Red's were one and
the same person. He quickly rejected the idea, as he recalled
Ann's comment that the caller had spoken bad English. That
didn't apply to Henry.

'Did Red ever phone his contact people in your presence?'

Ann thought for a minute. 'Occasionally; yourself, for
example, but he was always very brief.'

'Did the name Henry ever crop up?' Edward probed.

'Henry? No, he never mentioned that name in my presence. Why do you ask?'

Edward leant forward, looking intently into her eyes, scrutinizing them for any reaction.

'Henry is our undercover agent.'

Her eyes were blank. She stared back at him; her reaction gave nothing away.

'The name means nothing to me. I'm also quite sure Red never mentioned the name.'

She appeared to be speaking the truth. He had to find another way of identifying the people behind this affair.

Ann suddenly leapt to her feet. 'What did you say your agent's name was?' she asked excitedly.

'Henry, why?'

'Just how stupid and arrogant you Brits can be!' she cried out, laughing hysterically. Edward pointed at the door and made a sign not to make so much noise.

'Yes, just how observant you lot are! You can't see something even when it's staring you in the face!'

Edward gazed at her, stupefied. What, in heaven's name, had they overlooked?

'Tell me what your agent's called again!' she demanded.

'Henry!' he repeated, now rather irritated.

'OK. Then how do you pronounce his name in French?'

'Henri? Yes, Henri!'

'Yes, Henri,' she imitated him. 'And that doesn't strike a bell with you?'

Edward stared back at her in amazement. 'No, why?'

Ann placed her glass on the little table next to her chair and sat down. 'Henri Paul, born at Lorient, 1956, baccalaureate, military service with the air force, parachutist, latterly DST and DGSE. Do I need to continue, or is there a bug in your computer? Henri Paul, the driver of the Mercedes, deceased 31 August 1997, presumably around half past midnight.'

Edward was dumbfounded. Was Henri Paul one and the

same person as their undercover agent, Henry? It was true that the man was close to Al Fayed and would have been able to select the vehicles and their drivers. He was Deputy Security Officer of the Ritz Hotel and a friend of Dodi's. He had all the contacts. He was widely trusted.

'But why should he drive himself to his own death?' Edward asked.

'Did he, in fact? Or did he wish to prevent something from happening?' Ann retorted. 'He served several masters. An employee of the Al Fayed's but your man at the same time, perhaps even a French or Arab mercenary. Who knows? He's dead now!'

'But Red's instructions were to get the driver drunk and drug him. Why should Henri go through all that, if he knew what was planned?'

'Well, suppose he wished to protect Dodi and Princess Diana and help prevent the accident?' Ann stood up again and walked round the chair. She clasped the back of the chair with both hands and stared at the wall opposite. 'Edward, short of a miracle we shall never know the truth. Either this Henri has nothing to do with your Henry. Or else he intended to protect his own master and his master's lover, and took the wheel himself because he was convinced that only he could stop the accident. Perhaps it was he who advised Trevor Rees-Jones to fasten his seat belt. Have you ever met a security officer who fastened himself in whilst he was on duty? He took the alcohol and the drugs, knowing their potential effect, simply to avoid suspicion if anything went wrong. But Red spoiled it all for him with the Fiat.'

Ann had worked herself up into a rage, but she realized this was all speculation. Perhaps Henri Paul was the poor devil whom the other Henry consigned to his fate.

'It's all over,' she sighed. 'The crash can't ever be undone. I haven't the remotest idea who sent Red the helicopter. If he's not got in touch by now, I assume he must have been killed!'

To bring the matter to a close Edward quickly interjected. 'What did you do the following morning?'

'I handed back the Fiat Uno and flew to London the same evening, as I still hadn't managed to contact Red. Nothing had been touched at our suite at the Dorchester. The porter assured me that Mr Rosenzweig had not returned.'

Edward saw that there were tears in Ann's eyes. 'You were in love with him, weren't you?' He studied her face intently, but recognized no real signs of emotion. She shrugged her shoulders.

'I don't know. Maybe it was just another job. Maybe it was love. After twelve years, I shall miss him . . .'

'What did you do then?' Edward continued slowly.

'I then checked out of the Dorchester, which is far too expensive, into the Churchill Inter-Continental, which is more in line with my daily allowance. I'm now standing by for instructions from Washington. Till then, I stay here in London. And you?'

'My task is to find out who Red's partner was and who drove the white Fiat Uno,' he replied. Ann looked at Edward expectantly.

'Who gave you your instructions?' she asked. Her feelings towards Red had suddenly vanished. Ann Webster, the professional CIA investigator, had sprung back into action.

'My boss,' he replied evasively. 'I can pass on one part of the answer: it was you who drove the Fiat to the helicopter. Red may have driven it into the tunnel, but that's just speculation. Who gave him his orders? Were they really Arabs? Or arms dealers? After all, Princess Diana had been extremely committed to the campaign against land mines recently, a highly-sensitive issue that had every arms dealer worried, from Washington to Peking.'

Ann crossed her legs. Her skirt, Edward noticed, moved a few inches higher. He looked away in embarrassment.

'Would you kindly arrange a confidential meeting between your superior and myself?' she pleaded.

'What possible reason could I have for arranging such a meeting?' he replied in astonishment. Her answer took him completely by surprise.

'Because you want to sleep with me, for instance!'

## 88

The evening, after Princess Diana's funeral, Edward was summoned to Sir David's office. Sir David was visibly agitated. He came straight to the point. 'I have to speak to you, as a matter of urgency.'

'Yes, Sir?'

'How far have you got with your enquiries concerning the driver and other partners?'

Edward knew that in the meantime Ann had had a conversation with Sir David, to which he had not been invited. He had no idea whether Ann had told him that she had driven the Fiat. He paused for a moment or two, but Sir David continued.

'I assume you have not had much opportunity to make any investigations so far, because of the funeral and the security arrangements.'

Edward replied promptly but sadly. 'Yes,' he said.

'As you know, I had an extremely interesting and informative meeting with the CIA . . .'

Aha, Ann Webster, thought Edward to himself. He let Sir David carry on.

'. . . We both came to the conclusion that it would be sensible, not to say essential, to terminate all further enquiries immediately, in the interests of a number of countries. Our mission is now completed; there are plenty of other jobs we should be getting on with.'

'Yes, Sir!'

'Good. Then I must thank you for all your efforts and now consider the matter closed.' Sir David gave Edward a friendly nod and left the room.

POCKET
B O O K S

# THE SURGEON'S DAUGHTER

## CAMPBELL ARMSTRONG
## writing as Thomas Weldon

Driving through fierce storms at the request of her father,
Andrea Malle makes it all the way to his lonely cabin, only
to find Dennis Malle lying murdered in the snow.

Who could possibly want Dennis Malle dead? And how to
find them?

Andrea soon becomes the target of the same assassins but
she is determined to go all the way to the bottom of the
mystery. But she keeps hearing the words that will haunt
her forever: 'You really don't have a clue about your
precious Daddy, do you?'

**Published in paperback September 1999
0 671 01586 9
£5.99**

SIMON &
SCHUSTER

*Coming soon from Clive Cussler*

## SERPENT

**With Paul Kemprecos**

*SERPENT* is the first novel in a new series, THE NUMA
FILES (National Underwater Marine Association),
featuring Kurt Austin, head of the NUMA Special
Assignments team.

The discovery of an artifact by an archaeologist at
a Moroccan dig leads to the massacre of her entire
excavation group. Escaping, the woman is rescued by Kurt
Austin and his three member NUMA team who are then
attacked by the same assassins. Following the clues revealed
by the artifact, the men uncover a sinister plot, the key to
which lies in the hulking wreck of the *Andrea Doria* which
sank 50 years before.

**Price £10.99**
**ISBN 0 684 86080 5**
**Published September 1999**